Father McGargles

Norman Morrow

Father McGargles

Author: Norman Morrow
Publisher: Norman Morrow
Cover Design: Marika Kraukle
Cover Art: Durham Ranger Salmon Fly – Courtesy of Michael Maggs
e-confession by Simon Everett

Acknowledgements:

My grateful thanks for their help and encouragement to:

Sebnem Sanders
C. McDonald
Angelika Rust
Max China
JJ Kendrick
Morven James
DJ Meyers
Darius Stransky
Brian Barry
Padraig Byrne
Maynooth Writers Group
McGargles Brewers, Rye River Brewery, Kilcock Co. Kildare

To my family.

Success is not a measure of the result, but of the journey.

Chapter 1.

To savour the delights of an artery-clogging breakfast fry-up, one must do the job properly. After dispatching a few crumbs and stray grease from his lips with a swift wipe from his sleeve, James Brennan lit his first cigarette of the day. A concerto of belches, farts and spluttering coughs confirmed him ready to face the monotonous duties that were the daily life of a parish priest.

As he took the last pull of the cigarette, he glanced at the horrendous yellow clock on the mantelpiece. Absence of religious or gothic overtones saved it from being thrown in the bin. Above it hung a picture of the Sacred Heart, to its right a wooden cross. Behind him, the gaggle of Popes, all lined up in gold frames, glared down on his back.

He contemplated a quick gin before donning his frock and making his way to the church. However this was Lent, so he fought the demons that suggested a large glass would make the saying of Mass and the hearing of confessions more endurable.

'Bacon and cabbage this evening,' shouted his housekeeper Maggie, as he made towards the front door.

Jesus, Mary and Joseph! If Christ had to eat Bacon and Cabbage five days a week, he would have nailed himself to the cross. 'Thank you, Maggie. That's something I look forward to. I'm off to say Mass.'

James had only reached the front gate when he remembered he'd left his fags on the hallstand. On his way back, through the dining room window, he saw Maggie, and from the looks of things, she stood pouring herself a glass of gin with one hand and had her mobile held to her ear with her other.

He growled, and eased open the door. At the mention of his name, he stopped and listened to Maggie's agitated chattering. 'Bloody priest, what curse is on me that I have to cook bacon and cabbage five days a week?'

To stifle a burst of laughter, James clamped his mouth with his hand as he made his way out and down the path again.

It was a short walk from the priest's house to the Church. With each passing year, it seemed to get longer, each lethargic step a battle. This morning, he spotted Emily Jane, as she shuffled up to the main gate. He strolled past the side entrance and caught up with her. Twice in the past six months, he'd given her the last rites. Each time she'd walked towards the light, she'd given it a two-fingered salute and returned. "God had his hands out, beckoning me to come," she'd claimed. "But I could see my daughter's hands open and eager to accept her inheritance. I winked at the Almighty. Eternity could wait a while, as could the extension my daughter planned for her house."

Like many actresses and dancers, she exuded an infectious zest for living. He enjoyed her company, for she lit up the world with her wit, determination and, above all, her contempt for pomp or ceremony.

'Good morning, Emily, you look like shite! Have you been smoking the cannabis again?'

Emily lifted her walking stick and struck his knee, gentle enough so that there would be no long-term damage, and hard enough that he grimaced.

'Brennan, that's for thinking you had the right to send me on my way to meet your boss before I was ready. A few more dances are left in these withered legs. The cannabis keeps the pain at bay. You mind your own business.'

'You arty-farty types are all the same. One law for you and one l... Ouch!'

'And priests don't think themselves a law unto themselves?'

With Emily's walking stick poised to strike for the third time, he declined to answer. 'Come! Let us waltz.'

The offer of a dance could not be refused. With a tender hand, he aided her up the steps and into the church. They stopped inside and Emily blessed herself with holy water. Her laughter echoed off the cold walls after she cupped her hand and splashed James.

'Brennan, when was the last time you showered? Dry yourself and get into character. You're playing a priest today, are you not?'

She understood him like no other person he'd ever met. His spirit lifted by this remarkable woman, he marched up to the altar.

Looking down over his ever decreasing and decrepit audience, his shoulders sagged. Every day, the same wrinkled faces of the faithful sat and prayed. His duty worn thin through ritual and boredom, had long since lost its meaning, Desiring only to be finished, he folded his arms and stared at the two elderly ladies, who stood lighting candles at the back of the church, urging them to take their seats. He raised his eyes, and not for the first time, counted the wooden crossbeams that were running the length of the church, realising that soon, his years as a priest would exceed their number.

The door clanged, shaking him from his near slumber. A man lurched up the aisle, glanced around and slid onto the nearest pew. Watching the newcomer peer out between his cap and the upturned lapels of his overcoat, James smirked, amused at this miserable attempt at being inconspicuous. The two ladies, now kneeling in front of the candle stand, glanced in the stranger's direction, gave him the evil eye and then continued their little ceremony. The man bowed his head as though the pretence of silent prayer would make him invisible. As the two women waddled to the front pew, James wondered if the fellow was lost.

One of the ladies stumbled as she stepped into a pew, causing a commotion. This stirred him to action. He nodded at the two altar boys. On cue, they genuflected before taking their positions on stage.

'In the name of the Father, and of the Son, and the Holy Spirit.'

All through the Mass, he glanced at the stranger, noting his bowed head and occasional furtive glances at others, apparently unsure of when to sit or stand. During a reading from the Old Testament, the newcomer had a fit of sneezing. Instinctively he raised a hand to his nose, revealing his mobile phone. When he realised James looked in his direction, he panicked and dropped it.

James stopped midsentence, growled as the phone clattered on the floor, glared at the stranger and then continued. From the Liturgy to the Eucharist, he inwardly groaned at the monotony of this daily ritual. He raced through the concluding rites, dismissed the Mass goers, and in order to avoid idle chat, he bounded towards the confessional.

Sealed from prying eyes, the good Father read through texts on his phone, paying particular attention to those from his army of horse racing tipsters. At the sound of approaching footsteps, he switched off the phone. The door of the confessional opened and closed, announcing the arrival of a penitent.

James waited a moment and then coughed. He scratched his bearded chin as he waited for a response.

'Ahem!'

'Bless me, Father, for I have sinned. It's been a while since my last confession'.

'Has it, my son, how long?'

'Err ..., twenty-four years, Father.'

Twenty-four years. O Lord, this is a real sinner. 'You must have a lot to confess,' he said, glancing at his watch. *I'll miss getting to the bookies.* In his well-practised confessional voice he continued, 'Christ forgives the most ardent sinner. Open your heart and tell me of your multitude of sins.'

'No multitude, Father, just one. Jealousy.'

'What are you jealous of?'

'Jimmy Egan, Father.'

A grin stole over James's face. Jimmy Egan lived in a mansion outside the village. Wealthy, despicably handsome and captain of the local golf club, these were the recipes for envy. Jimmy sat at the head of every committee, was everyone's best friend, and had a wife so beautiful that Miss World would seem like an old sea hag in her company.

'Say three Hail Marys and have no more thoughts about Jimmy's wife.'

'No! It's the fishing, Father. I get to the river twice a week, but Jimmy goes every day.'

James almost fell off his stool in shock. In thirty-seven years of being a priest, he'd never been faced with such a confession.

'Envy, my son, is one of the Seven Deadly sins. Jealousy is a close relative. Say one Our Father when you get home. Now wait outside until I rid myself of this frock. In the name of the Father, and of Son, and the Holy Spirit. Amen.'

James appeared from behind the church, dressed in his civilian clothes. Wearing a tattered jumper over a pair of baggy jeans, it did not seem possible that this dishevelled looking man had earlier been perched on his high altar, delivering the word of God to the faithful.

But for the cap, tilted sideways above his mop of mousy hair, the stranger from the confessional would have melded into the greyness of the church. Hands deep in his pockets, he shuffled his feet as James strode in his direction.

'Ah, my jealous sinner remains concealed beneath his cap. Would you have a name?' said James.

'I'm Liam O'Brien. You may remember my devout mother, Lorenza.'

Confident hazel eyes, also intent on probing, were set above high cheek-bones. In his early thirties, broad shoulders filled his winter coat, and his firm handshake contradicted his earlier furtive behaviour.

'Lorenza O'Brien, of course I do. Of Italian extraction if my memory is honest. The resemblance is there, in your eyes, though sadly not in your devotions. I'm curious. Do you usually use your mobile phone at Mass?'

'I was talking to Google.'

'What?'

'I asked Google how to make a confession.'

'Add a second Our Father to your penance, and if you don't know the words to Our Lord's Prayer, you can ask Google.'

Liam grinned. 'I'll do that, Father.'

'Good man. Are ya busy on Friday morning?'

'I might be. Why do you ask?'

4

'I haven't discussed fishing in years and your confession leaves me more than a little curious. Can you meet me after Mass on Friday morning for a pint and a quick chat about your jealousy?'

'Grand, as long as it's about fishing and not religion.'

'Is there a difference?' said James.

Chapter 2.

Situated some forty miles from Dublin, the rural village of
Castlebridge nestled between a motorway and the river Shereen. With
little land available for development, it had for the most part,
remained unmolested by the Celtic Tiger. Unremarkable, forgettable,
few cars that daily zipped up and down the motorway had cause to
take the Castlebridge exit. A treasure in some respects, it remained a
quaint reminder of times past and a way of life where the mundane
can lead to happenings with unusual consequences. Such is the way of
many similar villages, where the disappearance of a randy dog would
invite more discussion than a general election.

Sean Lavelle, proprietor of Lavelle's pub, stood in the lane outside
the back gate, leaned on his sweeping brush and muttered
obscenities. As James approached, Sean set to work and raised his
voice. 'Do I look like a muck sweeper, a cleaner-upper, or am I just
soft in the head. Cleaning the chip shop's rubbish from this lane is
giving me lumbago.'

'All three, in no particular order,' said James, walking through the
mound of rubbish gathered by Sean, scattering most of it. Striding
through the rear entrance to the pub, he pointed to the disarray in the
backyard. 'A pig that grunts at other's rubbish should clean his own
backyard first. Stop fussing like an old sow and pull me a pint.'

In his wake, he heard Sean slam the gate, a bottle break, and a
plethora of curses followed him all the way to the bar.

Middle-aged, rough at the edges and balding in the middle, Sean
appeared of average height when standing on the raised floor behind
the counter. In building the floor, his deceased father, challenged by a
similar stature, had halted the flow of midget jokes previously cursing
generations of Lavelle's. Well almost, there is always one mischievous
dissenter, and he now sat waiting for his pint, ready to parry any
thrust from Sean's limited vocabulary. Silence followed the pint onto
the counter and continued when James stuck his thumb in the creamy
head, and sucked it.

'Sean, if one waits long enough, miracles happen. That is one of
your better pints.' His whispered taunt purpled Sean's face. On the

cusp of an expected explosion, he cushioned the blow. 'Mind, this is still the best pub in town. Is there a smidgen of gossip worth reporting to me?'

'No. Nobody tells me anything. Knowing you would weasel it out of me, they keep their gobs shut.'

'My fault? By the way, one of the fishing lads came to Mass this morning. Liam O'Brien, do you know him?'

'Lorenza's youngest lad, he is a decent skin but quieter than a moth. Is he sick or something? He's too young to be paying your wages.'

'Ask him yourself on Friday. He is joining me here to discuss everything and anything piscatorial.'

'Pisca...?'

'Piscatorial is fishing. Do you know anything beyond pulling flat pints?'

Frowning, Sean leaned across the counter. 'Fishing? I thought the Bishop slammed the door shut on all fishing activity.'

James sunk his pint and grinned at Sean. 'True, but partaking and talking about fishing are worlds apart. Besides, his Eminence is now harassing God and everyone who passed through the pearly gates. Liam has given me an itch and an itch must be what?'

'Scratched. I smell a storm coming,' said Sean.

'No, no storm, S...S...Sean. It's me, Pups,' said a familiar voice from the front bar.

James swivelled on his stool. He saw Evan 'Pups' O'Leary leering around the corner that led to out front. Pups doffed his cap and muttered. 'Good morning,' as James grabbed him by the collar, and whisked him toward the back door.

If Pups had a tail, it would have wagged. Rubbing his hands to take the chill away, he hopped around the yard, and avoided too close a contact with the priest. An only child, innocence had followed him from the crib and likely to the grave. That is not to say he played the fool willingly. Pups' misfortunes stemmed from a stammer and his inability to separate dreams from reality, friend from foe. Preoccupied with the training of greyhounds, this passion consumed him and amused others. Relying on his homespun methods, he produced happy hounds, but their pedigree and ability on the track was hardly likely to be the stuff of legend.

James glared at Pup's. 'What are you doing here?'

Pups shuffled his feet, stuck his hands in his pockets, and stammered, 'J...J...James, sorry to intrude on yer, yer drinking. I need a few quid for the d... do...'

'Spit it out for fecks sake.'

'Sorry, Fa... Father, a few quid for the dog.'

7

'Afflicted by a terrible hangover on the day I buried your poor mother, I made a fatal mistake. When you offered me half a share in a hound, I should've told you to shove it up your arse. Do you see 'BANK' written on my forehead?'

'No! I see a wise investor that will qua...quadruple his money.'

'All right, stop squawking and give me one good reason to open my wallet again.'

Pups, at the mention of the wallet, ceased stuttering and pointed to his dishevelled head. 'Pupsy has a plan.'

'Pupsy always has a plan. Out with it, ya fool.'

'Castlebridge Lad is the fastest hound that I ever bred, but he has one small problem ...'

'Yeah, his bloody trainer!'

'He still refuses to pass the other dogs. For the past week I made him chase Old Ned around the field.'

'And?'

'Old Ned keeled over onto his back, raised his paws, and the poor divil died. I swear Castlebridge Lad looked like he was about to race past him.'

'Jesus! A one legged, blind poodle could have beaten Old Ned. I've heard enough.'

'Wa...wait, Father. I'm getting Old Ned stuffed and mounted onto a skateboard.'

James's mouth opened, incredulity hampered his speech and mirth tempered his reply. 'For Sale. Dead hound on wheels. One careful owner. Low mileage.'

Pups rubbed his ear, grinned widely, and raised his hands in submission.

'Funny idea, but Pupsy has a better one. I'm having a frame welded to a skateboard so that I can tow it around with my bicycle.'

Unable to take much more, James sat on an empty keg.

'Just so I'm reading this correctly. You are going to cycle around the parish, towing a dead greyhound on a skateboard with a For Sale sign on its back.'

'Apart from the sign, that is exactly what I'll do. I only need two hundred.'

'Here's three hundred, the extra is in case you need an undertakers licence. Let me know when you are ready to go. As God is my witness, I would pay double to see a dead mutt on a skateboard, chase a gobshite on a bicycle.'

'Ya...ya w...won't regret it.' Pups snatched the loot and hugged James.

James's pledge to a dying mother tested the depth of his wallet and the limits of his patience. In keeping Pups out of harm's way, his affection for the lad took him into the realms of parenthood. Still laughing after Pups had left by the back gate, he sauntered toward the bookies, wondering as he went. *What prompted Liam to make that confession?*

Chapter 3.

At the end of Mass on Friday, James announced that confessions were cancelled. Excited at the prospect of meeting Liam, he discarded his uniform, raced outside and whistled when he spotted Liam sitting on the boundary wall.

'It's a cold one, Liam. C'mon let's find a high stool.'

Leaving the church by a side gate, Liam followed him down the narrow lane. The priest walked even faster than he said Mass. Though he appeared fit, Liam struggled to keep abreast. James stopped outside Lavelle's rusty gate, paused for a moment, glanced around and then banged on it three times. He winked at Liam.

'This is the tradesman's entrance for us workmen. A man of the cloth can't be seen going in the front door, especially this time of the morning.'

A few minutes later, someone knocked twice on the far side and the gate opened just wide enough for them to enter. Sean nodded at the priest and winked at Liam.

'The coast is clear, no busybodies around this morning.'

They led Liam through a yard littered with crates of empty bottles and kegs. The lingering stench of stale beer would deter all but professional drinkers. A black and white cat eyed them from a window ledge. James grabbed an empty tin off the top of a rubbish bin and hurled it towards her. Eyes narrowed, she watched the spiralling tin with a contemptuous gaze. When it struck the wall to her left, she leapt onto the roof of the shed beneath, and darted over the sidewall to relative safety.

'Liam, cats are sneaky creatures. Sorry for dragging you in this way.'

Liam blurted, 'That's a terrible cruel thing to do. Did you ever hit the poor cat?'

'Don't be daft. I always aim a little to the left. That cat would be as fat as a fool if it didn't get some exercise.' He grabbed a second can, took aim, and it struck the windowsill dead centre.

In through a small kitchen, the priest led Liam to the dim backroom. He gestured to Liam to sit on one of the stools, while he settled on the other and toyed with his cigarette lighter. Liam removed his cap, the offending item that had brought him to James's notice some days earlier. The ravages of life had yet to etch his forehead, lighten his hair or blemish his youthful face.

'The usual?' Sean arranged two beer mats on the counter.

'Saying Mass is thirsty work. Two pints and two whiskeys. No make that two and two large ones.'

When two large whiskeys arrived, Liam raised his hands.

'Not for me, Father, it's far too early. I'm not a drinker as such.'

'Nonsense, confessions require a loose tongue and that's the best tongue loosener in the parish. So, you fish a bit?'

'I do. I have been addicted to fly fishing for years. Did you ever try it?'

James scratched his beard, laughed and turned to Sean, as he arrived with two creamy pints of Guinness.

'Liam would like to know if I ever caught a trout. Show him the picture. *Sláinte!*'

Sean placed a black and white framed photograph on the counter. Fingers fumbling, eyes riveted to the image, Liam whistled as he read the inscription. 'Shereen Anglers June Competition 1973, Winner: Father James Brennan, One Trout. 5lbs-11oz.' Arms folded, James smirked, as did Sean.

'Father, that's a decent trout,' said Liam.

'James Brennan, they christened me. So, as long as we are in Lavelle's pub, James will do. Now, tell me about your jealousy.'

'Father, sorry, I mean, James, I'll get straight to the point. Every year, Egan wins most of the monthly competitions. Until recently, I couldn't get to the river often enough. More through embarrassment than anything, I neglected to tell my wife that I was put on a three day week at work, and that meant two extra days on the river.'

'Did you hear that? Deceiving his wife to go fishing, it's disgraceful. Keep going! Another two pints, barman, and open the skylight so I can have a smoke.'

Built like a Sumo wrestler, Sean folded his arms and stared at James. 'No! The feckin Garda will have me up before Judge Chambers. If I lost my licence, where would you drink then? No other publican in the village would tolerate your stubbornness. Apart from that, you are killing yourself.'

Taking a cigarette in one hand, the lighter in the other, James addressed Sean.

'Judge Chambers smokes in his office and I in mine. When the Archbishop in Dublin decreed that all screened confessional boxes were to be removed ...'

'Save your bloody homilies for Mass. Anything longer than two sentences in a pub can start a row,' said Sean.

Liam waved away the suffocating smoke, gulped back the whiskey, and continued, 'The two days practising made all the difference. Going into the final competition, I'd accumulated the same number of points as Egan. For five weeks, I searched the river. Thursday two weeks ago, under the branches of the willow below the bottom fence of Casey's field, I discovered a trout as big as the one in the picture.'

'I bet that blood coursed through your veins faster than Guinness from a tap when you spied the enormous trout under Casey's willow,' said James. 'Now that I think on it, you were unbelievably fortunate to find one there. Sorry for interrupting, please continue.'

Sean leaned over the counter so as not to miss a word. 'Go on, Liam, don't leave any detail out.' He nodded and winked at James, who now sat on the edge of his stool.

'I replayed my plan to capture that trout over and over in my head. I was certain she would be mine, but that bastard, Jimmy Egan thwarted me. He ...,' Liam shook with rage, sunk the remainder of his drink, and banged his glass on the counter.

The plume of smoke hung like a halo over James's head. A cigarette dangled from the corner of his mouth, ash dropping all over his beard and onto the flagstone floor. 'Jesus! Liam, don't stop. What did Jimmy Egan do?'

'Grinning like a politician does after getting elected; he accosted me in the supermarket. "Liam," he said, "I brought the young fella fishing and he caught the finest wild trout that ever came out of the river, 6lbs 6oz." Where, I asked? "At the willow in Casey's field, on a worm," he replied. On a bloody worm! He caught my trout on a feckin worm.'

'The bastard,' said James.

'The bloody thieving bastard,' roared Sean.

Liam seemed surprised, almost embarrassed at their reaction. 'That's it, folks. Now that I've spat it out, I wonder why it annoyed me so much. It all seems rather childish. Forget I ever mentioned it.'

Still leaning on the counter, Sean shook his head, mumbling, 'The thieving bastard, the thieving lowlife bastard. Did you know, his wife, Emma, was my girlfriend until he stole her heart?'

Seemingly amazed at this, Liam gasped. 'You went out with Emma? In your dreams you did!'

'I feckin did, for eleven months, three days and nine hours to be precise,' said Sean, his sullen face suggested tears were not far away.

'When she had laser eye surgery, beauty lost interest in the beast,' said Liam.

'Feck off! The miserable spectacle in front of your eyes may belie that I was a handsome youth. While you suckled your poor mother's breast, I was the most sought after stud in the parish. Ask anyone. We were in love and that's a fact. We would be married if that cur hadn't turned up at my twenty-first in his father's Ferrari,' said Sean, banging his fist on the counter.

'Chased you away would be more like the truth,' said Liam, 'She obviously prefers thoroughbreds. I'm thirty one, so for me to be suckling, that would make you at least an old looking forty-nine.'

'Egan is a thoroughbred, thieving bollox. Take my advice; stay clear of him. I'm a mature looking forty-something year old, and will remain so for many years to come. When your own hair thins and your belly bulges, we will compare pecs.'

'No contest. I work out every day.' Liam stood, and posed as would a bodybuilder.

'So did I, so did I,' Sean shook his head, dried some glasses and turned to James for support.

Eyes closed, deep in contemplation, after an age, James blessed himself, downed a whiskey and spoke from the gospel of James P. Brennan. 'Vengeance is a dangerous pursuit. Christ was fond of fishermen, so I'm sure he will see fit to forgive us. To take another man's trout, even doing so unwittingly, is an unforgiveable and unwritten sin. The Eighth Deadly Sin is ignorance, and Jimmy Egan must be punished.'

Sean nodded. 'You're right, Father, hang the bastard. No, hanging is too good, let's cut off his manhood and feed it to the cat out back. He will be of no further use to Emma after that.'

'No! I'm not looking for revenge,' pleaded Liam. 'We all know that he is a decent skin, and few with his wealth are like that. I just needed to tell someone my tale of woe and feel the better for the telling of it. No reprisal!'

Placing a firm hand on Liam's shoulder, James spoke. 'You're wrong, Liam. Men like him are born lucky, not their fault. No matter what they touch, it turns to gold. Sure, he's one of the good ones, but men that are so blessed, sometimes need a gentle reminder that others are not so fortunate. You worked hard for that trout. It was yours and yours alone for the catching. No, we will have retribution and when I have it all figured out, I'll let you know the plan.'

'Good! Father, please don't be thinking for too long,' said Sean, rubbing his hands.

'Have I ever let you down?'

Sean scratched his belly, buying time to think, and about to reply, James interrupted him. 'Liam, you mentioned work. What do you actually do?'

'I'm a website designer, but work has been scarce due to the recession.'

'That might be advantageous. Website design is a very useful skill. Stuck in front of an impersonal computer all day explains your quiet disposition.'

Obviously aware of his personality, Liam responded with a tentative grin. 'Were you in my boots, you would appreciate silence. My wife does the talking for me and at me, and then complains that she is talking to the proverbial wall. This wall chooses to speak when something is worth saying.'

With a nose leading his rotund face, Sean sniffed the air as though something mysterious pervaded his senses. Turning his head towards Liam, he sniffed with more intensity. 'The silent ones are deadly.'

Ignoring the childish nonsense, Liam turned toward James, 'James, do you fish at all these days?'

As he pondered on this question, James's shoulders sagged.

'No, I haven't cast a line in years. It's a long story,' he said, as he glanced at his watch. 'What the hell. The horses will still be running tomorrow. Sean, fill another two pints, toss me a packet of cigarettes and pour a drink for yourself.'

Sean emptied the ashtray and wiped the counter. 'Father long-tale is winding up for a sermon. I know the signs. Liam, settle back, put on your seatbelt and try not to yawn.'

On hearing shouts, Sean grunted, and tended to the needs of customers in the front bar. On his return, James lit a cigarette and composed himself.

'As sure as Christ was born the Son of God, I was born to be a fisherman, as was my father and grandfather before me. That trout in the picture was caught using my father's rod, the fly a tying of my grandfather's. I never kicked a football as a young lad. I fished, I tied flies, and at every opportunity, I studied my river.

'Aged seventeen, I hunted a trout as fine as that one in the photograph. For weeks, I studied it as you did. Like you, I had my plan but disaster struck. When I arrived home late one evening, a visitor stood by the fire in the kitchen, warming his behind. It was our local priest, Father Hickey. My father turned to me, "James, it's decided. You're to become a Sky Pilot." I stood there with a grin on my spotty face, thinking I would be flying aeroplanes.'

Liam glanced at Sean, both seemed puzzled.

'What the feck is a Sky Pilot?' said Sean.

'That's what I asked him, without the profanity, as confused as you are now. His answer was as unexpected as it was devastating. "Son, a Sky Pilot is a priest. Your mother has your bag packed. Tomorrow you travel to the seminary in Maynooth. I'll miss you, Son". I cursed the Popes that tricked mothers into believing that they would go straight to heaven if they offered up one of their sons to be a priest. Damn them all to hell.'

'The bastards. More thieves, the world is full of them,' said Sean as he swatted a fly with a tea towel.

'To answer your question, ever since they sacrificed me to the priesthood, I have thought about that trout. Last thing at night, every night for the past forty-three years, I've hooked and landed that trout. Catch and release, three hundred and sixty five times a year. Work it out later, and don't forget the leap years.'

Sean used his fingers as an abacus, but gave up when he reached a thumb. 'At a rough guess, that would be close to the number of pints you drink a year.'

'Thankfully ...'

'Sorry to interrupt, your Holiness, tis almost the witching hour,' said Sean, pointing to the digital clock on the back wall. 'A cold morning, but it's dry. I say bang on time. You?'

Liam followed James's gaze to the clock. Twenty-seven minutes past ten, not a noteworthy time in anyone's book.

Brennan coughed, winked at a puzzled Liam and placed a twenty Euro note on the counter. 'Late by about six minutes but late nonetheless.

Sean dug out a crisp, fifty Euro note hidden in the depths of his wallet, placed it alongside the twenty, and also winked at Liam. 'Father, will you match my fifty?'

Brennan winked at Liam, grabbed his twenty and replaced it with a fifty.

'Stop winking at me. What the hell is going on?' said Liam.

'A bet on a bet,' said Sean.

Brennan clapped. 'Well put, barman. Liam, keep your eye on the clock.'

Cloaked in silence and cigarette smoke, they stared at the illuminated display, watching the seconds roll onwards. At ten-thirty Sean roared, 'C'mon ya fucker.' A minute later, he groaned and watched his hard earned money fly off the counter and into Brennan's pocket.

At ten thirty-five, the front door opened and an old man hobbled into the back bar. Wearing royal-blue paisley pyjamas and matching slippers, only his long winter coat suggested he wasn't entirely mad. Without so much as a 'hello', he leaned his walking stick against the counter, took a stethoscope from his pocket, and stood wheezing in front of the priest. Brennan stood, lifted his jumper and noticing the puzzlement on Liam's face, he smirked. The old man held it against Brennan's chest and listened.

The stethoscope disappeared back into the pocket, five Euros dropped into Sean's waiting hand, and in return, two glasses of whiskey were placed on the counter. Brennan grabbed a glass, the old man reached for his; both said *Sláinte* before they downed their tipples, and the old man left.

15

Sean poured a large brandy and handed it to Liam. 'Drink that, me lad. You look as though you are about to collapse.'

Liam downed the brandy. 'I am. That's the weirdest thing I've ever seen.'

Raucous laughter filled the room.

'A bet on a bet, young man,' said James. 'Nine years ago I had a bad chest infection and went to old Doc Higgins, the man who just left. He warned me that if I didn't quit the fags, I'd be dead before he retired. We placed a bet. For the past seven years, every Friday, he walks in that door at half-ten, checks that I'm still alive and pays up.'

Liam looked from to the other. 'The pair of you are half mad.'

'You're half right. Sean is a nutter. Where was I? Thankfully this parish had a river. As the older priest loved an occasional trout for supper, he supported my piscatorial wandering, procured top quality fly tying materials from the hunting lads, and even made an appearance at an occasional hare coursing event. I covered for him; he covered for me. When he died, I became the elder priest.'

'Ya sure did. Head honcho, top gun, and a right pain in the arse,' said Sean,

'My behaviour offended the pious soul of his young replacement, making life difficult, but every man has a weakness. When I discovered his taste in magazines, I laid down the law and spent even more time on the river than before. Just to be certain that there would be no issues, once or twice a year, I bought a few magazines, and gave them to him as a gentle reminder of who was the boss.'

'Would they be car or football magazines?' Sean guffawed. 'I remember that priest, a spotty little wanker. I hear he is a Bishop now.'

James laughed. 'I only glanced at the covers. You could be right. Some girls were lying on the bonnet of a car.'

Liam sipped his pint and gaped at James, clearly gobsmacked at the conversation and Brennan's unpriestly behaviour.

'All the club competitions were held on a Sunday, the busiest day of the week in my trade. I had to convince the bishop that I would get more sinners in the door if the twelve o'clock Mass was switched to ten o'clock. A crate of single malt scotch secured his blessing.'

'Father Brennan and bishops, chalk and smelly-cheese,' muttered Sean.

'The bloody nuns scuppered my passion.'

Sean leaned over the counter and eyeballed James. 'What passion would that be, Father?'

'Feck off! Sister Margaret spotted me during one of the competitions, waddled to the palace and reported me to the bishop. His eminence threw the proverbial Bible at me and banned me from fishing. Undeterred, I just had to be more careful. My God, this talking is thirsty work.'

After refuelling the father's glass, Sean poured one for himself, yawned and winked at Liam. 'Riveting, Father. Have a drop of that and out with the rest of the history lesson.'

'When I caught that trout in the photo, my good luck ran dry. Michael Egan, Jimmy the bastard Egan's bastard father, sent the picture to the newspaper, and the bishop threatened to send me to Dublin if I ever fished again. I would prefer an eternity in hell rather than live in Dublin. To this day, I have not wet a line.'

'Me too! The only good thing about Dublin is the road out of it.' said Liam. 'It seems we all have just cause. Jimmy will have to pay his dues.' Raising his glass, he waited for the others to do the same. 'Revenge it is!'

'Amen to that. Safe in the knowledge God is on my side, the sins of the father shall be added to those of the son. We will meet here this time next week, and as sure as Jesus died on the cross and Jimmy Egan stole Liam's trout, I will have a plan ready.'

Chapter 4.

For the first time in many years, James walked straight past the bookies without so much as a thought of the horses. His mind raced as he considered the dilemma of putting his plan together. The outline was in place, but the delivery of the vengeance required careful consideration, planning and a clear mind. 'No more drink until this is over,' he uttered aloud, passing the second pub in Castlebridge on his journey home.

He opened the front door. 'Maggie!' As he strode towards the kitchen, he almost bumped into her. Flustered by his early return, she struggled to tie the strings of her apron.

'Yes, Father, you're back early, I haven't started dinner yet.'

'Thank God. I'll get straight to the point.'

Surprised by the shocked expression on her face, he decided not to mention the gin, and spoke in a gentler tone.

'My dear Maggie, I could not face another bacon and cabbage dinner. I have a craving for a good Indian curry. Can you manage something as exotic as that? No more bacon and cabbage, not this week, not next, not ever!'

'What? Mary Kavanagh, your old housekeeper, told me that was all you ate?'

James laughed. 'Well, I'll be damned. That was the only dinner the witch could cook.'

'Holy ..., sorry, Father. Every day, I cook all sorts of exotic dishes for my own family. Indian food is my speciality. Lamb Tikka Masala, would that be a good start?'

'I'd swear the smell of bacon and cabbage has infiltrated the floorboards, the bed linen and the walls. Even a squeeze of lemon no longer rids the gin of the taste of cabbage. Let's shake hands on it, Maggie. Please cook something new at least once a week. There will be a few Euros extra in your pay packet. '

They shook hands and both went their separate ways, each delighted at the outcome.

My God! No more pig.

He raced upstairs, and stood before the door of the back room, which he hadn't opened in years. Taking the sole key from his pocket, he inserted it into the lock. Despite feeling anxious, his resolve to end the years of regret won through, and he opened the door. It was as though Pope John Paul II and Madonna still topped the charts. Everything was as he'd left it all those years ago. The silent room held so many memories that he felt an overwhelming desire to cry.

In the corner, several rods leaned against the wall, caked in dust. Beside them, his ash landing net, that he'd handcrafted while a novice at Maynooth. At their feet, his olive canvas fishing bag, with a spool of nylon peeping out. Along one wall, a line of office cabinets held his enormous collection of feathers and fur, each labelled. He smiled as he rubbed the grime of one of the labels, "Hare, winter pelts", procured by his predecessor at the coursing meets no doubt.

Turning crisply, he gazed at the centre of operations, his fly tying table. On one side, a wooden rack held row upon row of glittering tinsels and wires. Its twin, on the other side, held the silks, threads and flosses. Centre stage stood his vice, clamped to the table, an unfinished fly held in its jaws and a bobbin of yellow silk hanging beneath. He edged around the table, and sat on the chair. Reaching forward, he touched the bobbin, mesmerised as it swung and spiralled.

Lifting a hare's mask, he pulled some dark fur from the ear, a pinch from the cheek, and a little lower down, another of a different shade. Laying them on the table, he blended them into different shaded mixes. He spun the bobbin clockwise, and opened the silk with the needle, still stuck in the cork from a 1963 Chardonnay, and held the loop open with the index finger and the thumb of his left hand. Guided by memory, he inserted a tiny amount of dubbing from each little pile, and then closed the silk loop.

Now came the tricky bit! Needing a gentle touch, he spun the bobbin anti-clockwise, each twist tightening the silk and forming a perfect rope of variegated hare's fur. Despite his clumsy fingers, he wound the rope up the hook shank towards the eye, stroking the fur with each twist, stopping just short of the eye. This was a remarkable display of craftsmanship, considering he'd not tied a fly for many years. Taking a pinch of guard hair, he twisted it onto the silk, and wound it behind the eye. Without thinking, he executed a perfect whip finish by hand, and released the completed fly from the vice.

He ambled to the window, drew open the dusty curtains and held the fly up. Dazzled by the light, he squinted as he gazed at his creation through a haze of sparkling dust.

James P Brennan, your grandfather would be proud of that fly.

* * *

For the next few evenings, he sat at the table after dinner, sipping water. On Thursday, he dozed off, and waking well after midnight he scribbled in his notebook. Most of the best ideas came just before the onset of sleep. At nine PM on Friday night, when the clock chimed, he closed the book with a thud. 'That's it! Vengeance is most satisfying when served in small doses.'

On the Sunday, he gave the sermon of his life on the parable of the Loaves and the Fishes. Told with the religious fervour of a Baptist minister, most of the parishioners were convinced that he must have given up the drink.

'A fine Sunday dinner, Maggie, best I have had in years! Had I known that Thai curries were so tasty, I would have asked the bishop for a transfer to Thailand years ago. Well done and thanks,' said James as she started to clear away the dishes.

'You are very welcome, Father. Would you like a taste of Mexico tomorrow perhaps?'

As was his custom on a Sunday afternoon, he lay on the couch watching football. His monthly investment in a TV Sports subscription usually made a significant return for the parish coffers. Betting on soccer matches wasn't sanctioned, nor condoned, by either the bishop or Rome. Having placed fifty Euros on a draw, a nice return would be realised if Lady Luck shone down on him.

At half time the score was one-all and a very pleased old priest took unfair advantage of his position. 'Our Father who art in heaven, I don't mind if United score eleven. Holy Mary full of grace, please ensure that Liverpool draw this race. Amen.' Confident that his prayer would be answered, he lifted his phone and dialled a number that he'd not called for many years.

'Hugh, it has been a while since we had a chat.'

'Jesus! Father, J.P., I thought you had drowned, I haven't seen you near the river in years, not since you foul-hooked that huge trout.'

'Foul-hooked my arse,' said James. 'Fair and square, on my grandfather's fly, as you well know. Didn't you help me land it? Have you succumbed to senility?'

'My good long suffering wife says I have, the sons wish I had, so they could rob all my money. No, the memory is as good as ever. The eyesight is a bit knackered, even with the glasses I struggle to see anything small. That was a great trout JP, as wild as you.'

'I have an itch to go fishing next season. Can you get me back into the club? How has the river been all these years? Is she still producing those fine yellow-bellied trout that would test the skill of any fly fisher?'

'I'll ask the secretary to send you the form. Sadly, the river is not as you remember it. When Jimmy Egan's father, Michael, wormed his way onto the committee, he convinced the members that she should be stocked. As you well know, if he fished every day of the season, he could not catch anything, and the rest of the committee were equally skilled.'

'Hugh, some of them could not tie their laces, never mind a fishing knot.'

'A few of us protested the madness. The year after you left, the stocking began, and has continued every year since. Five times a year they put in thousands of the docile creatures, all between one and two pounds weight. I only fish once or twice a year now! Sure, what's the point? There is no challenge.' Hugh sighed. 'I have given up all hope that the river could ever again produce fine wild trout.

'Good God! Hugh, that's the daftest thing I have ever heard. I understand that Jimmy Egan wins most of the competitions with big wild trout. There must be a few wild ones left?'

'Jimmy, he wins a good few but... I suppose they are wild fish, I guess they must be. All the stocked fish have the top tip of their tails cut off and most are Rainbows. The big browns that he weighs in have perfect fins, and are much heavier than anything that's stocked, but...'

James smelled a rat. 'Is that so, Hugh, stocked trout? Who looks after the stocking?'

'Jimmy does, and he even pays for the trout himself. At the back of his house, he installed a fish tank; large enough to hold hundreds. Every few weeks he puts them in the river.'

More than curious, James jumped to his feet and paced around the room. 'It's nice to know that the son is a skilled angler and a generous man as well! I must have a day on the river with him. Next season, Hugh, we will wet a line together. I will talk to you soon, my friend.'

After hanging up the phone, he laughed out loud. You did not need to be a Sherlock Holmes to figure out that Egan cheated. This new information would make his plans even easier to implement.

He glanced at the television. Annoyed that the score was 2-1 to United he pleaded with the Almighty. 'Father, why have you forsaken me in my hour of need?'

The referee pointed to the spot, awarding a penalty to Liverpool in injury time. Up stepped Gerrard. Goaaaal!

'Thank you Lord. That's two hundred Euros for the parish.'

Chapter 5.

Sean leaned on the counter. Two glasses of whiskey already filled, he awaited his expected customers. When James and Liam had settled onto their stools, he aired his anxiety. 'I thought ye'd never get here. Will it be the usual? Two and two large?'

'Indeed not, do you not realise it's Lent? Of course you don't, you haven't been at Mass in twenty years. Two Ballygowan please, the real stuff, not the ones you refill from the tap.'

'As you wish, your Holiness.'

The servant of God reached down into the bowels of his long black overcoat and felt around until he located his hip flask. He struggled to free it from the tentacles of loose threads, manoeuvred it up through the hole in the lining and poured the two whiskeys into it.

'Sean, dump the rest of that gut rot down the sink before I call the customs man, and tell him about that bootleg whiskey. The drop in this flask is evidence.'

Composure somehow maintained; Sean valiantly struck a decisive blow.

'So the rumours are true?'

'Rumours, what bloody rumours would they be?' James snapped.

Liam remained silent.

An unexpected and rare result achieved, Sean smirked. 'Rumours that you're off the drink. If you don't mind me saying so, isn't it a bit premature to be talking about Lent? This is October! I'll get those two glasses of girlie water for you.'

Holy St. Patrick! 'It's that gut rot whiskey he's been feeding me. Liam, it has withered my senses, and I'm afraid to consider the damage it has done to my insides.'

Sean opened two bottles of water, and laughed when James apologised for his sober behaviour.

James placed his notebook on the counter. 'It's all in here.' He tapped it twice. 'The Grand Plan to sort out Egan.'

All three stared at it as though it was the Holy Grail.

When James revealed his conversation with Hugh, Liam shook with rage.

22

'I don't believe he's been cheating. How could anyone stoop so low as to buy trout to win a fishing competition?'

Sean's false teeth rattled, and almost fell into the sink. 'The cheating, thieving, lying bastard. Father, show us the plan!' Not one to miss a chance to turn a coin, he added, 'Do you want a real drink, Liam? You look like you need one.'

'No alcohol until this is all over,' said James as he dropped three fifty euro notes onto the counter. 'Take this as compensation for lost business, you penny-grabbing, philistine publican.'

'Right you be, Father,' said a grateful Sean. He stuffed the notes deep into his pocket, another three prisoners secured away.

With that, James revealed his plan, every detail and every nuance, nothing left to chance. Liam shook with laughter, and Sean knocked a bottle onto the floor as he danced behind the counter.

'That's a master plan. The bastard is done for sure. His wife will realise that she married a toad,' said Sean.

Pleased that they seemed happy with his scheme, James laid down the law. 'Liam, you start work on the website. It needs to be operational by the first of March. I'll look after the merchandise, and as soon as is possible, Jimmy Egan will become my best friend, capisce? If this plan is to succeed, I have to know our enemy inside out, and if he differs at all from my perceptions of his character, I will adjust the plan to compensate. Sean, I need that case of Scotch by Thursday. One final thing, lads, don't utter a word about this to another living soul. Is that agreed?'

'Agreed,' said Sean and Liam.

After Liam had left, James reached into his pocket. Taking out a sealed envelope, he handed it to Sean. 'Hide this behind the till. Keep it safe please.'

Chapter 6.

Late Tuesday evening James attended the parish paperwork, a task that he neglected until the bishop got on his case. It would be panic stations for several hours, while he sorted it all out. Baptismal certs were an episcopal pain in the arse. If he'd his way, he would insist that his parishioners did a compulsory course on birth control, as they seemed to breed like rabbits.

When the doorbell rang, he was surprised to have a late caller, but he welcomed the distraction from the mess of papers strewn all over the floor. On his doorstep stood a drunken Sean Lavelle, carrying a case of Scotch under his left arm and a half empty bottle of Paddy in his right hand.

'Hello, James, I'm a wee bit pished,' said Sean, handing over the case of Scotch, he pushed past into the hall.

'I would never have guessed!' He considered reminding him of their pact of not drinking, but decided that there was no point. Sean was beyond admonishment.

With little dignity, Sean collapsed onto a chair and attempted to twist the lid off the bottle of Paddy.

'Feck! This is tighter than a ducks arse.' He tried gripping the cap with his false teeth, but that also proved unsuccessful.

Fearful that Sean would injure himself, James reached for a glass. Lifting the bottle, his sober hands opened it and he poured a small drop. Topped up with a copious amount of water, no further damage would be done. He'd never seen him so agitated or so drunk.

'Who's looking after the pub?'

Tears rolling down his cheek, Sean looked up. 'James, Father, forgive this lonely old man. I've no one else to talk to. I threw them all out of the pub, and told them it was closed until further notice.'

'Why?'

'The loneliness is killing me. All the worse recently, at the thought of that bastard Egan being with my lovely Emma. She should be Emma Lavelle, not Emma bloody Egan. I know people laugh at me, call me Scrooge and claim that I still have my communion money. It wasn't always that way. The day he stole her, my heart turned to granite. You know what it's like! The loneliness, when you lie alone in your bed with nothing for comfort except the cobwebs on the ceiling. Is it any wonder we seek comfort at the bottom of a glass?'

'It's a terrible thing! If you let it take hold, it will destroy you.'

'You're right there, James, it's worse than the gout. I thought of ending it all by taking a coward's way out.'

When James did not respond in a timely fashion, the tears were replaced by a cheesy grin.

'I have a flight booked for the Philippines. When I get back, I'll march up your aisle with a new bride. It's all arranged,' he said, pulling a photograph from his packet and handing it to James.

'Christ almighty! Sean, she's a looker. Is she half your age?'

'Fifteen years younger. That's not too much, is it?'

'Sean, like you, God works in mysterious ways. If the unfortunate girl is happy, and you're happy, then neither God nor I will stand in your way. Every man, even a Scrooge like yourself, is entitled to a little bit of happiness.'

'I've earned me share, that's for sure.'

'Promise me that when you get there, you make sure that both you and the young lady are coming together for the right reasons. Loneliness and poverty cloud one's judgement. Love is not a matter to be trifled with. No matter the width of your wallet, or the depth of your despair, she is your equal. Always remember that.'

Sean stood, wobbled for a moment, and stuck out his hand. 'Father, if her heart has a corner for this old fool, will you say the Mass?'

'I will! Sean, if you're half the man you claim to be, I'll baptise the young Lavelles when they arrive. There is one condition, though. No more drinking! You'll need to stay sober if you intend on keeping the young lady happy.'

James raised a glass of water. 'To the bride and groom. May they live long and prosper.'

Sean took the photo back and stared at the picture through his bloodshot eyes. 'Mr and Missus Lavelle! That will shut the bastards up, won't it?'

'It will!' For a fleeting moment, James felt very jealous. Was it the sin of lust or envy that sought to test him? Whichever, he let it pass, glad that Sean was seeking a new and more fruitful life.

'Goodnight, Sean, safe home and good man for remembering the case of Scotch. I'll visit Jimmy Egan tomorrow night. It will put it to good use.'

'I'll be back before Christmas,' said Sean as he attempted to dance a drunken jig down to the gate.

As was his habit when confused or deep in contemplation, James scratched his beard. When he returned to his paperwork, he giggled like a schoolgirl on her first date.

God almighty! Sean Lavelle is marrying a young one, who would have guessed it possible?

Chapter 7.

Jimmy Egan's wife Emma organised the Zumba dancing. Every Wednesday night, she enjoyed several hours on the dance floor of the parish hall. That would give him all the time he needed to weasel his way into Jimmy Egan's life.

The electric wrought iron gates opened. James stopped inside, lit a cigarette and drove up the long winding avenue. The front of the mansion, lit up like a small town, provided ample parking for a dozen cars. He grinned, as he parked his old Renault Clio between a Ferrari and a black SUV. Even though he placed little value on such things, he felt uneasy. Pillars guarded an equally imposing front door. It all seemed more suitable for the Pope's retreat at Castelgandolfo than the home of an engineer. He waited on the doorstep for a few minutes, tossed his cigarette butt into some flowers and rang the doorbell.

An expensive designer shirt over a pair of immaculate slacks confirmed that the man standing before him lived in a different world than he. Jimmy seemed a little taken aback at the sight of a priest, but his success in life had not been achieved by being hostile.

'Father Brennan, you're most welcome to my humble home. Please come in out of the cold. Let me take your coat, there's a nice fire burning in the living room.'

'Thank you, Jimmy, the winter is about its business. Here is a small bottle to take the chill away.'

He followed his host into the living room and stood in front of the enormous fireplace.

Jimmy glanced at the label. '1992 Laphroaig 11-year-old. That's a fine whiskey. I have a bottle that you might like to try, a twenty-two-year-old Brora. Will I pour you a dram?'

'I will indeed enjoy the pleasure of such a generous offer. If the Lord himself took up brewing, he could not brew a finer malt than that. At least five years must have passed since a Brora passed my lips. My appreciation of it, you'll not find wanting. God bless your hospitality.'

James hummed with unfeigned pleasure. The malt warmed his palate, taking him on an incredible journey as it aroused his taste buds. 'Glorious, this nectar is glorious.'

The ice broken, Jimmy beamed with apparent delight. 'It saddens me that so few understand the joy of fine whiskey, and to share with a fellow connoisseur is too rare an event. The pleasure is mine. Any man that shares my passion for the finest of whiskeys is always welcome here.'

'I had no idea we shared more than one passion. I'll get to the point of my visit, tis the fly fishing. I did a bit as a lad and would love to do it again before St Peter calls me on my way. When asked, a few people all pointed me in the direction of your door. Jimmy Egan's your man, Father! Ask Jimmy Egan, there is nothing about the fly fishing that Jimmy Egan doesn't know. So here I am, Jimmy, can you help this old man fulfil his dream?' He cast his fly with great skill and guile, certain that soon he would see the rings of the rise.

James smirked when Jimmy feigned astonishment that he would be held in such high esteem.

'Sure I know a bit about the art, but calling me an expert is overgenerous praise.'

Drifting downstream, he tracked the fly. Then with a flick of his tail, he propelled to the surface, and with flaring gills he sucked it in. 'Father, I would be delighted to show you the river, and teach you how to fly fish. If luck is with us, we can have a dram or two after.'

'That's great news. Now don't worry, I'm not a beginner, just a little rusty. At my age, it wouldn't be safe for me to be alone wandering around the river. I won't be too much of a hindrance. I used to tie my own flies when my eyesight was a bit better than it is now. Do you tie flies?' *Reel him in.* He downed the last few warming drops of whiskey.

Jimmy poured them another glass of malt. 'I love fly tying, and not a day passes without tying at least a half dozen. Take your glass and follow me. I have a small room dedicated to the fishing.'

'You have a room dedicated to your hobby! That's the mark of an artisan. I'm a bit behind the times and would be thrilled to see how you young fellas go about your business; lead on.'

Nothing could have prepared the padre for what he was about to see. Shocked, he almost blessed himself unwittingly. Jimmy's fishing room was in the basement. More accurately, Jimmy's fishing room *was* the basement, the same size as the entire ground floor of the house. Two and a half thousand square foot of space dedicated to his hobby. Mahogany cases, filled with rods, lined the back wall and each series of cases labelled. Nearest the door, a long line of mahogany bookcases almost full. Row upon row of every book on trout fishing ever written, many first editions long since out of print.

He gasped as he followed Jimmy, unable to grasp how one individual could have collected so much stuff, or why one would do so. Jimmy switched on some more lights, and the entire east wing area lit up, revealing an enormous desk with three leather swivel chairs placed along its length.

'This is where I dress a few flies, Father, take a seat.'

James sat on one of the luxurious chairs. Jimmy pointed to a small row of coloured buttons on the desk. 'The command centre!' He pressed the red button, and grinned as his prowess as an engineer was revealed in all its glory.

Utterly speechless, James watched, as a series of spotlights dropped from a hidden cavity in the ceiling. In unison a pedestal vice rose up from another similar hidey-hole from the desk. As the vice locked into place, a series of mahogany racks lifted from their chambers, revealing drawers containing every fly tying material known to man. All would be within easy enough reach of the tier. The finale, a pyramid shaped copper vessel, rose beside the vice and the sides collapsed outwards, revealing Jimmy's handmade fly tying tools.

'This is the fly tying factory, and this is the pinnacle of my engineering,' he said, as he pushed another button.

James could hear a motor humming. After a minute or so, he looked at Jimmy and wondered what was happening. What appeared next was extraordinary indeed. An enclosed clear boxed plastic pipe, some thirty foot long, three feet wide, rose up from the centre of the room. Jimmy pressed another button. Water came rushing from one end of the pipe and flowed out the other.

'The Lab. I can control the rate of flow; this is where I test the flies. What do you think?'

'Jimmy, I think I need another drink, preferably a large one.'

James could not take it all in. He knew that many fly fishermen were hoarders, but this was genius bordering on insanity. He looked at Jimmy as he poured another Scotch and came very close to uttering those immortal words. *Shaken not stirred! Brennan, James Brennan.*

'This is an incredible feat of engineering, a credit to your skills. What sort of flies do you have? They must be good, I'll wager.'

He led James to a mahogany cabinet that stretched from floor to ceiling. Opening the door, he revealed a series of drawers labelled with gold plates. Jimmy pulled out one of the drawers, marked *Large Dark Olives*. It contained at least five hundred flies. Wets, Dries, Emergers and Nymphs, some modern, many of them ancient designs, and each one tied to perfection.

'I did an entomology course in England. When I came back from it, for each significant hatch, I set myself the task of identifying the most used patterns of the last two hundred years. Then I tied the prototypes. Finally, I tested them in the Lab in varying flows and

29

wrote my results up in a database.' Jimmy grinned, more than proud of his ingenuity.

'How... Jimmy, how do you know which fly to use?'

'Good question. Let me go back a step. For many years after my father first took me fishing, I caught very few trout. I bought every trout fishing book and magazine that I could get my hands on. I studied them all. With each book, I followed the recommendations, buying the recommended rods, reels and lines, but nothing changed. I spent thousands.'

'I bet you did. Every angler has been robbed more than once,' said James. *Quite soon, I'll lighten your wallet...*

'One evening, after another blank day on the river, I sat down with a bottle of malt, and I contemplated my lack of success. It took an hour or two, but eventually I solved my dilemma. The secret to catching trout is an engineering problem. After that eureka moment, I applied my skills as an engineer. What you see before you is a thorough scientific and engineering approach. Do you follow me?'

'Indeed I do! An engineering problem, solved by a genius engineer.' James struggled to hold back the sarcasm that tickled the tip of his tongue.

Jimmy took out his iPhone and loaded an app that he'd developed.

'This, Father, is how I choose my flies. I enter the water temperature, the time of day, the time of year and the water height. With a Bluetooth device of my own design, I measure the light intensity and enter that as well. The app chooses the flies. I fish them.'

'So that's how you win most of the competitions, Jimmy. I knew you must have some special skills. That's pure genius, if you don't mind me saying so.' *A nutcase; he should be locked up!*

'The seal of the confession, Father, consider everything I have shown and told you this evening, as being told in confession. All this is between me, you, and God. Please do no mention this to anyone.'

He waited for James to nod in agreement before continuing. 'The engineering approach, I thought it to be fool-proof. But a loophole existed in the theory, a factor that I could have never foreseen. Like many a great discovery, comparable to those even of the great Isaac Newton, mine arrived by chance. You see, trout simply cannot resist bees.'

Once again he paused.

'Three years ago I found the secret. For some reason that day, I caught very few trout. We had stocked the river a few days earlier. Perhaps the trout were a bit off colour. A bee attacked me! Did that ever happen to you?'

'A bee, no, I don't believe bees ever assaulted me while fishing. Once or twice, I have been attacked by a terrible thirst, but a bee, never. How did you escape from the bee attack?' James almost bursting out laughing, but somehow managed to maintain his poker face.

'I slapped the bee off my face, and it fell on the river. Would you believe me if I said the bee floated no more than ten yards downstream, before being engulfed by an enormous trout? This unusual occurrence amazed me. Bees were not mentioned in the entomology course and barely get a mention in the annals of fly fishing history,' said Jimmy, pointing to his fishing library. 'I knew this warranted investigation. I packed up, went home, and then sat at my vice to design my Bee Flies.'

He fetched some drawers from a cabinet and laid them open on the mahogany table. Row upon row of bees, all carefully graded for size, practically a perfect swarm. He lifted one and offered it to James.

Enthralled, with much aplomb, he carefully examined the bee. It seemed to be constructed from orange deer hair; the black markings made with a marker. Then he surveyed the contents of the rest of the drawers. He almost choked as he had his own eureka moment. Farmed trout were fed on pellets. These were trout pellet imitations. *The stupid bollox is imitating trout pellets.*

'They look so real, Jimmy, I'm afraid to touch them in case I get stung.'

'I only fish them in the competitions. It would be cheating to use them all the time, wouldn't you agree?'

'Indeed it would be cheating. I'm so glad I paid you a visit. Will you take me fishing next March? I would love a few days on the river with you to see those bees in action.'

'Father Brennan, I look forward to it, and I will tie up a few bees for you. It will be our little secret.' He pointed at his nose, confirming the oath of secrecy that surrounded the bees.

'Not a word,' said James, winking at Jimmy.

* * *

James twisted and turned in his bed that night. He woke regularly and burst out laughing. What he'd seen in Jimmy's house was beyond compare, almost a theme for a bad science fiction movie. The first of March could not come soon enough. *Buzz, buzz.*

31

Chapter 8.

Ever since his fishing tackle business had closed, Martin Jackson had struggled to pass the time. There's only so much reading, or so much TV that one can do in one day. He could not get his head around the reality TV shows watched by his wife and took to walking the dog several times a day, to escape their less than real reality.

Martin grabbed the dog leash and whistled for Blackie when a repeat episode of 'Celebrity Mud Wrestling' appeared on the screen. Taking a slice of bread from the kitchen, he walked to the pond on the edge of the village and tied the leash to his favourite bench. He sat, broke up the bread into little pieces and fed the mallard ducks. Each bird had a unique personality. Naming the more interesting ones was a challenge that he enjoyed. His favourite was a young drake, MP, named after a famous Olympic swimmer.

MP was the cleverest duck in the parish. He'd learned that Martin often threw the bread beyond the ducks closest to him. MP would wait behind the flock in anticipation.

Martin fed the closest ducks first. He smiled when MP got frustrated and swam from side to side. Then he threw one over those closest, and all hell broke loose. In a haze of flapping wings, the flock turned. MP had built up a head of steam and stretching his short neck for the finishing line, he secured his meal.

'Feeding my Sunday dinner again? Martin, that one there would be nice with orange sauce and a nice bottle of French wine,' said James, slapping Martin on the back.

'Father, you're like the devil himself. The way you sneak up on people is creepy. Touch my ducks and you'll be saying Mass at your own funeral.'

'Don't fret. I expect to eat Chicken Chow Mein this Sunday. I have a small job for you. Do you still have your contacts in the fishing supply game?' he said, handing Martin a list of his requirements.

After taking his reading glasses from his pocket, Martin studied the list and nodded, as he contemplated each item. 'You could open a shop with all that equipment. What are you up to? Okay, I know, I should know better than to ask. When do you need it?'

Reaching into his pocket, James took out and handed Martin a bulky envelope, 'There's a thousand Euros in there. Let me know if you need more. Is a month long enough to get it?'

'Two weeks, Father. I will have it all within two weeks.'

'Good man. Not a word to anyone, or else MP will be sitting in orange sauce on my dinner table,' said the wily priest. He left Martin on the bench, surveying the list.

Martin kept his word. Two weeks later, James helped carry in the purchases from Martin's van and secreted them away in his fly tying room. They had a cup of tea and a chat about the weather, politics and of course how MP got faster by the day. When Martin left, he opened the various parcels and checked each item against the list. Everything that he'd ordered had arrived.

For the next three weeks, all through Christmas, every spare moment was spent in the fly tying room, or in the shed at the bottom of his garden. When he'd completed his mission, he gave Liam a call, and invited him over that evening. Everything had been placed on the floor in the sitting room. Content that preparations were running smoothly, he opened a bottle of wine. He'd not had a drink in weeks, so he convinced himself that a small celebration was allowable. Stage one of 'Operation Vengeance' neared completion. He hoped that Liam was on schedule with his end of the bargain.

Liam arrived later than expected, so a second bottle had to be uncorked. While the merry priest poured two glasses of the finest that Chile had to offer, Liam set up his laptop on the kitchen table.

'Well, Liam, how is progress on the website, are we on schedule?' James glanced at the screen.

'I borrowed ideas from other sites and I have a viable website ready. Would you like to see it?' he asked as he placed the mouse over an icon. James nodded in anticipation. With a click, their new website appeared on the screen. 'The Pope's Angling Emporium – Purveyor of Angling Products for the expert fly angler'

'Brilliant! She is ready to have the blanks filled in. Follow me.' He led Liam into the sitting room, revealing the treasure trove that he'd accumulated.

As he surveyed the items laid out on the floor, Liam whistled. 'James Brennan, you should've been a con-artist, those being essential skills for a seller of fishing tackle.'

Looking rather smug, James read from his prepared list. 'The Pope's Dry Fly Rods; The Pope's French Nymph Rods; The Pope's Czech Nymph Rods,' all were magnificent examples of the craft of rod building.

The Pope's Trout Net and French Leaders lay in a tidy bundle beside the rods. The Pope's Secret Nymphs, Secret Dry's, Secret Czech

Nymphs, Secret Spiders and Secret French Nymphs all tied to perfection.

Taking a deep breath he paused. 'The Pope's Secret Guide to Piscatorial Heaven. I have a lot of typing to do.'

Taking a large sip of wine, he waited for Liam's reaction.

He convulsed, unable to speak in a coherent manner, but eventually he asked. 'What quality are the fly rods?'

'Let's just say, my one, and the first one we'll sell Jimmy, will be of excellent quality, but we will not have enough stock to fulfil the lifetime warranty on the rest. *Caveat Emptor*, let the buyer beware.'

Every single item, except the flies and lines, were matt black, and all had the Pope's logo. The simple hand-painted Celtic cross in gold looked stunning and very satirical. Even James had been surprised at how well the kit looked.

Liam took out his camera and took a photo of each item that would go into The Pope's catalogue. When finished, he peeped into The Pope's Secret Nymphs box. Envy, one of the seven deadly, showed on Liam's face

Returning to the kitchen, they sat and discussed pricing. James reckoned that cost price multiplied by twenty was right for the items they'd bought. For the rest they plucked a silly figure from the air.

'James, where is Sean? His regular drinkers will be hard shifted from their new stools if he does not return soon.'

'I suppose I can tell you. Sean and his Filipino bride will be back the first week in March.'

'Bride? You're joking?'

'I jest not. They got married in Rome just before Christmas and have been on a lengthy honeymoon ever since. Now back to more pressing matters. You finish building the website, I'll get the fish tank installed at the back of Sean's pub, and that will be everything completed. Roll on the first of March.'

'To the first of March, *Caveat Emptor*,' said James.

Raising their glasses, they toasted what they knew would be the most interesting trout season ever.

Chapter 9.

The fish tanks were central to the conspiracy for revenge. Frankie Joyce, a plumber and welder by trade and a good friend of James's, was the ideal man for making the tanks.

Frankie, a Galway man lived in Kildare for twenty years. He still considered himself an emigrant, no less an emigrant than his friends that left for America and Australia. Castlebridge, nestled hidden away, just off the main Dublin-Galway road, and a mere stepping stone on his route back home. The five year plan had rolled into six, then seven and twenty years on, he still dreamed that one day, he would again look out on the dry stone walls of Connemara.

Sandwiched between American football on one side of the Atlantic and Cricket, Soccer, and Rugby in Britain, Irelands brightest, rebellious minds formed the Gaelic Athletic Association to promote Gaelic field-sports. Gaelic football, Hurling and Camogie, games played by amateurs with the fervour and passion of professionals.

Frankie's involvement with the GAA had started at six, when he was big enough to hold a hurley. Now his love for this amateur sporting organisation consumed him. He was a hurling man first, a GAA man second and a family man when time permitted. Lisa, his long suffering wife, knew his back better than his front. For her to spend time with Frankie, often meant standing on the side of a GAA pitch, in the lashings of rain. That she wasn't alone in this regard was scant consolation.

James strolled up to the back pitch, swinging his umbrella and whistling a favourite tune. Like many priests, it was considered to be his duty to be a patron of the GAA. His patronage had been reluctant at first, but Frankie had turned him into a lover of hurling. Weekly involvement in 'the clash of the ash', with the under-elevens, distracted him from less favoured religious duties.

Frankie stood on the side-line. Wearing a club tracksuit, he cut a fine figure. Gathered round, some of his warriors in their club jerseys listened to his battle song, while others cut the tops off clumps of grass with scything swings of their hurley stick.

35

'Right, lads, see your mothers on the side-line? Do you think for a minute that they enjoy watching ye get thrashed? Listen up. Ye have what it takes, and all that's needed is a bit of luck.'

One of the kids plucked the sleeve of Frankie's jumper. Like all coaches, he hated any interruption while he made his pre-match speech. 'What in the name of God is up with you? What are ye gawking at, Morrison?'

Rory Morrison, the smallest lad on the team, pointed his trembling finger at the Moorhouse players. All saw the fear in his eyes, visible through the mesh shield of his helmet.

'Three of them are bigger than you, Frankie.'

Frankie glanced across, honing in on the largest kid, clearly shocked at what he saw. 'Don't worry about their size. It shows that they're afraid of your skills. Hickey, you take the puck outs and keep the *sliothar* away from those three skyscrapers. Keep it tight lads. When you strike the *sliothar*, strike hard, and mark tight.' Phil Cassidy sniggered, his timing on and off the pitch was appalling.

'What does mark tight mean, Cassidy?'

Cassidy was to hurling what Beethoven was to golf. In three years, he'd not hit a *sliothar* in anger during a match. He looked up with his usual distant grin.

'Be close enough to rub the snot of their nose, Frankie.'

Frankie nodded. 'The snot of their nose, lads, that's how close ye have to be. If I see any of you standing up, having a chat, or picking daisies, there will be fifty press-ups for everyone after the match. Men, ye know what ye have to do. Are we going to win?'

A few tentatively replied, 'Yes, Frankie.'

Four times he asked the question, until finally, a great roar lifted to the heavens, 'YESSSSSSS FRANKIE!'

They ran with gusto onto the pitch, wielding their hurleys with the bravery of the legendary *Cú Chulainn*. The closer they got to the opposition players, the slower they ran. The last spark of bravery having deserted them, with bowed heads, they walked the last few yards to their positions.

'Father, would you look at them, beaten and the match hasn't even started. Did you see the referee? It's Heffernan, the bollox that robbed us last season. Look at his skinny white legs. An albino heron, if such a thing could exist.'

James nodded. 'I see that the black eye you gave him last year has healed. Did you talk to him?'

Frankie grinned. 'I did! I apologised, telling him that I had just found out that Lisa was having an affair, and that he was unlucky to be in the wrong place, at the wrong time. I then told him that it was all a mistake. For good measure, I sent Lisa over to charm the pants off him. She opened the top two buttons of her blouse and did that thing she does with her eyes. He watched her every step back to the side-line.'

James glanced at Heffernan and was appalled that he unashamedly stared at Lisa. 'Are we that desperate for a win?'

'Desperate? I was desperate two years ago. I would shag a goat if it meant getting a win.'

The referee threw in the *sliothar* and the match began. Within minutes the Castlebridge parents, who huddled together on one side-line, were in full flow.

'Pull on it lads! Drive it long! Feck it lads, ye know it's a free for striking the kneecap of another player.'

Frankie marched up and down the side-line, issuing orders, holding his head each time they conceded a score. The referee had given them a dozen soft frees, even a penalty for no apparent reason, but it mattered little, as by half-time they were losing by seven goals to nil.

One by one the desolate warriors, with heads hung low, made for the comfort of the side-line. They needed to rest their bruised and battered bodies.

While Frankie attended the walking wounded, James took control. 'Well done lads! It's only half-time. We're not beaten yet! Ye have the wind and the hill in the second half. I'm going to make a small change.' He pointed to the twins. 'Too many goals conceded. I want the two of you between the posts in the second half. Hickey, you'll have to mark two players. Now get out there and knock lumps out of them.'

After the match, James walked over to Frankie and helped him pack away the spare hurleys and water bottles.

'I may find you that goat. Worse they're getting. Still, it's the best game in the world.'

Frankie stood looking over the hallowed sod. 'It's the best game, the fastest, when it's played right. Oh, it matters little. They're Kildare lads and hurling isn't in their blood. Still, we battle on.'

When James outlined his requirements for the fish tanks, Frankie took from his pocket the scrap of paper that he used for keeping the score. He carefully noted the dimensions on the blank side, the side he'd reserved for the Castlebridge scores.

'I need them in two weeks, any problem?'

Frankie stuffed the paper into his bag. 'I'll have them ready. Away match next week against Na Gaels, the last friendly match before the league starts. Will you go?'

'I will, and we might even win. Not a word to anyone about the fish tanks. Put them in Lavelle's back yard when you have them made.'

James returned to his car, his duty done and another part of the plan progressed. Operation Vengeance would commence in earnest when the trout season opened on the first of March. A return to his passion and a trout for a trout.

Chapter 10.

Pups had encountered various problems in the engineering department, none insurmountable, but each tested his genius and the patience of the best welder in the parish. Eager to witness field-testing of the mutt on a skateboard, James had phoned Emily the previous evening. He invited her to attend what he claimed would be the best comedy show in town.

When a lady dressed for a night at the Oscars opened the front door, James stifled a surprised grin. Emily had removed the moth balls from her finest evening dress, assuming the invitation was for the theatre. Her pearl necklace, a lover's gift from bygone days, danced above the sequins of her revealing cleavage.

She curtsied as best her creaking limbs allowed. 'Jamie boy, my gallant knight has brought his carriage to take me to the ball. I would've expected you to dress for the occasion.'

'Madame, you are a delight to my eyes, the date of my dreams. My wardrobe, alas it has fallen on hard times; an unpaid tailor's bill renders me bereft of suitable armour.'

With lips that were seldom pursed, he kissed Emily's proffered hand. Grimaced smiles accompanied each painful step as she hobbled to his rust bucket.

'My kingdom for a horse,' she exclaimed, 'My Lord would have me ride bareback on a mule.'

'Fair Maiden, though it's many years since you were one, this mule delights in carrying such beauty. Let's be off, afore cutthroats and vagabonds espy our departure.'

Her eyelids flicking demurely, she clutched his hand and stared deep into his eyes. 'Jamie boy, you are a rogue.'

'Emily, in your company, no man could be anything else. Oh, how I wish I had trod the boards with you, looking out on a captivated audience, one spellbound by our words and artistry. Perhaps, the name of James P Brennan would have lit the neon signs on Broadway.'

'Don't be an arse. You already play to your audience at Mass, though some would argue that your lines are stale.'

Ribaldry accompanied them out of the village, but when he ignored the turn-off for the motorway, she hollered. 'Whoa Mule, Dublin is the other way.

Hands clenched the steering wheel, eyes focused on the road ahead; he ignored her questions until he drove up a narrow country lane, and pulled into the yard at the back of Pup's cottage. 'This, my fair lady is the theatre of your dreams.'

'Of my nightmares,' said Emily, gawking at the mounds of litter that stretched all the way to the shed at the end of the back garden, listening to the yelping from inside the cottage. 'I should have bloody known you were an impostor, a charlatan and a goddamn liar.'

James grinned, 'Never! I promised you the best comedy show on earth and will deliver on same. Wait here till I find Pups.'

James went into the cottage and returned moments later with Castlebridge Lad on a leash, and carrying a stool. Pups pushed his invention out the back door. Emily, mouth wide open, stared out the window of the car. Eyes shifting from Pups to the bicycle and then Old Ned, mounted on the skateboard, she burst out laughing. James walked to the edge of the road where he placed the stool, returned to the car and helped Emily climb out.

'Madame, your shrieks have sent the rabbits to ground and the show has not yet started. You of course know my trusted jester, Pups.'

'Hello, Evan. Are you well?'

Pups removed his cap, as he always did in the company of ladies. He wiped his hand on his trousers before offering it to Emily. 'Emily Jane, I'm very well and pleased that you are here.'

'Right! Emily, your seat awaits thy bonny arse. Off up the road with you, Pups,' said James, linking Emily's arm and walking her to the stool. When Pups and the hounds were out of sight, he offered Emily his hip flask and explained everything. She near fell off the stool and required several sips from the flask to calm her incessant laughing. James lit a cigarette, Emily a joint, both allergic to the fresh, country air. They listened for any sound of the bicycle, skateboard or hound.

'Jesus! He must be gone to Dublin,' whispered James, patience not being one of his few virtues.

The tinkling of a bell and the yelping of the hound grew louder as Pups approached. Round the bend they came, on the home straight now, the rider pedalled as fast as he could and close behind, the hound gave chase. Cap pointing backwards, goggles underneath, Pup's head hung low over the handlebars. He screamed, 'C'mon Lad, you can do it.'

'Fecking Nora, the hound has legs, look at him go,' said the incredulous priest. Clapping wildly, James roared encouragement, and Emily beat her walking stick on the tarmac. The bike flew past the cottage, and in its wake, Castlebridge Lad, panting like a mad thing; spurned on by the shouting, he lunged forward and tried to mount Old Ned.

'Oh dear,' Emily said, between bouts of giggles. 'What now, Jamie Boy?'

'Well, my dear, at least Pups has proven that the Lad is fast. The trouble will be finding a race suitable for a gay hound with a tendency towards Necrophilia.

Pups cycled back into the yard, hopped of the bike, first patted Old Ned, then hugged Castlebridge Lad, who thankfully no longer found Ned attractive.

'I told ya the Lad is a wise investment. He's ready to race, isn't he, Father?'

James winked at Emily and turned to Pups. 'Evan Pups O'Leary, you are without doubt, the cleverest greyhound trainer in the country. Of course we will race him. Please dig a deep hole, and bury Old Ned before he gets any more buggered than he already is.'

Chapter 11.

March the first, nine o'clock, the start of the fishing season. There was just a hint of mist and a pleasant freshness to the air, a freshness which every angler knew to hold infinite promise for a good day on the river. James whistled cheerfully as he closed the boot and opened the front door of the car. Old Clio, rattled and spluttered into life at the third turn of the key. Having waited years for this day, ready to continue the journey that had been cruelly halted by the Bishop, he broke several laws as he sped to the river.

Months earlier, he'd made a decision. The top of Casey's second field would be the venue; here his love affair with fly fishing would begin again. Pleasantly surprised that his was the first car there, he blessed himself, giving thanks to the Almighty in appreciation of his good fortune.

Brass ferrules glinted in the early morning light as he made up his grandfather's sixty years old cane rod. Deeply ingrained in its every scratch were happy memories of an old man and that young boy, a passion passed on and shared. As always, in reaching back, sweetness turned sour, succumbing to wistful thoughts that his lineage would die with him, he fought back the tears.

'Excuse me, what are you doing parking that old bucket of rust there?'

Startled, James turned around to see a frail old man with a walking stick in hand, wobbling down the road and pausing occasionally to wave the stick at him. It was old Casey the farmer, a ninety-seven year old, contrary but loveable rogue.

'Mick, I pay my road tax, which is more than you ever did. How are you, my old cantankerous friend?'

Once again Mick waved his walking stick. 'Old friend? You've not called in to see me in fifteen years. Some friend you are.' He was old, but his nimble mind made short work of the daily crossword and any that presumed to test his wit.

'Mick, the Church hasn't moved either. Are you waiting to die before you go to Mass again? Without the fishing, it was too painful to be close to the river, that's why I didn't call.'

42

'It's time you hung up your cross and let some young priest take over. At least half of your audience are down in the graveyard. If there was a God, He would have taken you back long ago.'

'When I stand over your grave, I'll throw toilet water on your cheap, second-hand coffin. How's the fishing?'

Everyone knew that Mick Casey's season started in February, a month before it was legal. Mick laughed as loud as his lungs would allow.

'Not much use James, they're not on the fly yet. As you well know, a worm is rarely ignored. I have missed your company and it's good to see your hairy face along the river. Will you be a regular, Your Holiness?'

Shaking his hand, James told him he would call for a mug of tea before he went home. He crossed over a stile and walked briskly towards the river.

Standing on the brow of a hill, he gazed at the river and inhaled the vista of his favourite trout pool. The river's character had changed during the intervening years and he struggled to map it all out. Using familiar reference points, he soon realised that most of the changes were cosmetic. The old sycamore that had stood majestically on the far bank was now a small stump. He wondered about the lie beneath its branches, a lie that had always held a good trout. Had it also gone when the tree had succumbed to a winter storm?

Such dilemmas and unanswered questions have tested the minds of anglers since the beginning of time. Heaven, Earth and Water, three domains whose mysteries James had laboured to understand. None held him more entranced than the Water. The creatures within its dominion never ceased to amaze him. According to the gospel of James Brennan, there is a glaring omission in the Old Testament. 'On the eighth day, God created Brown Trout. Seeing that His work was good, God went fishing, never completed His work and left Man to his own devices. Amen.'

It felt good to be pulling his fly line up through the guides, tying on a leader and a tippet and remembering forgotten knots. Watching the flow of the stream, he looked for any signs of a feeding trout. These seemingly minor events, when added together, formed a passion that had consumed anglers for thousands of years.

Even though he knew what flies he would attach to the leader, he sat, lit a cigarette and quietly observed. As sure as a devout Catholic should say their prayers twice a day and thrice on Sundays, a good angler should take time to observe and time to allow their hunter instincts to come to the fore.

He opened his fly box and selected two. Carefully wetting the nylon before slowly tightening the knots, he tested each of them. Finally he opened his little canister of Fullers Earth and degreased the entire leader and tippet.

Am I ready to go hunting?

He was more than ready and gasped as sheer delight sought to overwhelm him. Crouching low, he slid down to the river's edge and made his first cast in fifteen years. Like the prodigal son, Father James P Brennan had come home.

He made one cast after another, feeling the flex of the rod, watching the fly line unfurl. Soon he felt a rhythm develop. Only then did he start to fan out his casts, and the flies landed where he intended them to go.

Right, James P, you're ready to hunt.

He positioned himself at the tail of the pool. On his side, shallows ran right up to the neck some one hundred yards ahead; on the far side deeper, faster water. He probed the shallows with accurate casts.

Wading carefully out into the stream, he searched the edge of the faster current, watching the point where the nylon entered the water. Just ahead, he knew there was a good spot in the shallows, a small trough a foot deeper than the surrounding water. He inched forward, focusing all his concentration on this one place, visualising the cast that he would make.

Getting into position some five yards in stream of the lie, he crouched as low as he could and delivered the flies upriver of it. As the flies came back down, he retrieved the slack line.

The take must surely come.

It did, the dry paused and even before it had fully dipped under, he lifted into the trout. Surprised to find that his net was less than adequate, he drew the trout into the shallows and beached it.

There should be poetry written to describe the landing of a beautiful speckled brown trout. It should be poetry that would task the brains of Ireland's finest, and burn the image of sparkled water, the struggle of wits between fish and angler, and the joy of success into the hearts of its readers forever. Sadly, James P. Brennan is a fisherman, not a poet.

'Bloody stockie, drooping belly,
tattered fins, of little beauty.
Sterile clown, unwelcome freeloader,
in my stream how dare you swim.

Squatter trout, you took my fly,
nose to tattered tail, I'll not bother measure.
If no more I catch, this God-given day,
a blank, my fishing diary shall display.

44

Squatter trout, of un-natural flesh,
I dispatch you now, so take your rest.
To Mick Casey's pig pen next you go,
to swim in pig muck, where no rivers flow.

When Egan next on bacon dines,
I pray to God he gasps in pain.
when a squatter's fish bone,
his tongue impales.

Stupid Egan, with your stupid bees,
by seasons end,
I'll bring you to your knees.
Amen.'

A further three stocked trout came to hand. All three were dispatched and treated with the same disdain. Replacing the heavy point fly with a much lighter one, he fished only the shallows. Just before he came to the neck of the pool, the dry was taken. Without fuss, a wild trout of eight inches came to a wetted hand and was carefully returned. He watched it vanish from sight and continued to stare at the spot long after. *On the ninth day, J.P. Brennan caught one of God's trout, and it felt good.*

He stopped at Casey's farmyard before going home. When he handed Mick a bagful of heathen trout and told him to feed them to the pigs, Mick seemed surprised. Clearly, he'd grown accustomed to catching the stocked fish. Staring into space for a moment, he turned to the priest.

'Hmmm, James, you're a strange, wonderful fool. I had forgotten. Most of us have forgotten what we once had. I've got it! Nine across, six letters, 'ALIENS'.'

Now, that he fully understood the gravity of the situation, James became even more stubborn. His thirst for revenge on Jimmy Egan was now unquenchable.

Chapter 12.

'Father, this package arrived for you earlier,' announced Maggie, putting a carefully wrapped box on the table beside his lasagne. He opened the package. It contained a beautifully hand crafted wooden clock, its face a carved trout. A small card was enclosed. 'Father, I'm home. Sean and Marites Lavelle.'

Spring is definitely in the air, a time of change, a time for renewal. Without ceremony, he swapped clocks on the mantelpiece, and when Maggie came back in to clear away the dishes, he handed her the old clock. 'Here is a present for the bin.'

Maggie gleefully took the clock from him. 'Father, that's the worst clock I've ever seen, the bin's too good for it. If you don't mind, I'm going to bring it home and throw it in the fire. We have to be sure it never ticks again.'

Evening Mass and a short meeting with the parent's committee at the school demanded his presence. Afterwards, he would meet Liam in Lavelle's.

* * *

The pub was still closed, but the inside lights were switched on. As usual, he went to the side gate and knocked at least a dozen times. The apparition that greeted him left him a little dazed. Sean, wearing a tee-shirt, shorts and sandals, tanned from head to toe, and he'd lost at least three stone in weight. James hardly recognised him. In fact, if he'd met him on the street, he would have been hard pushed to put a name to the face.

'Sean, is it Sean Lavelle? Or is it Sean Connery, perhaps? Did you have a facelift?'

Sean attempted a bear-hug, but realising his arms were too short, a handshake had to suffice. 'James, it's good to see your ugly face. I could say that I missed you, but that would be a lie. Come on in and meet Marites, Marites Lavelle.'

James just settled onto his stool when Liam arrived. Sitting quietly, they discussed the opening day on the river. Liam had fared

46

well, catching over twenty trout, all stocked fish. On hearing that news, James's temper rose.

'Liam, from now on, you will kill any stocked fish that you catch. We have to rid the river of those vermin. That's an order not a request.'

Liam seemed puzzled. 'Why would we do that, James? If we kill them there will only be small trout to catch. That's why the river is stocked, isn't it?'

Lighting a cigarette, the old priest looked to the rafters. 'God forgive them, for they know not what they do. Liam, those trout are half tame. Where is the challenge? Where is the thrill of the hunt?' Reaching behind the counter, he grabbed the photo of his great trout and thrust it into Liam's hand. 'See that trout, as wild as the wind. How do you think it got that big? I'll tell you how, by being clever, smarter than other trout. That trout came from the same gene pool as the one that you claim you discovered under the Willow at Casey's. Do you remember the thrill of discovering it, learning how and when it fed?'

Liam nodded.

James smiled. 'I bet you do. Few, if any stocked trout, have what it takes to learn the skills to survive that long and grow that size.'

Like a child being chastised, Liam shrunk into the stool, unable to defy the wrath of James.

'This river produced plenty of big trout. You had to hunt for them, had to develop the necessary skillset and had to be as clever as they. Egan's father had none of the skills, so he cheated, stocked the river with big trout and thought himself to be a great angler when he caught them. If you stick with me, before I die I will pass those skills on to you and you'll experience fly fishing far beyond anything that you have enjoyed so far.'

They hadn't noticed Sean arrive at the counter. 'He's right. I wasn't as good as James, only because he'd God on his side. I quit soon after they started stocking. At first, I thought it great but I soon grew tired of catching finless trout after finless trout. I could catch a dozen with one eye closed and the other reading a newspaper. Isn't that right, Father?'

'Lads, I might have no idea what you're talking about, but I'm willing to take your word for it,' said Liam.

'If after three seasons you don't appreciate the difference, I'll stock the river myself. Deal or no deal?' James offered Liam his hand to shake.

'Okay, Father, you win, deal it is. Sean, where have you been the past five months? James has nearly died of thirst in your absence. Are the rumours true?'

Wearing a most mischievous grin, Sean poured two Ballygowan and shouted, 'Marites, come down and meet my friends!' Turning towards the two lads, he whispered. 'No cursing, she hates bad language, and no smoking either.'

Moments later, Marites appeared behind the counter. Slightly shorter than Sean and at least twenty years his junior, and that would offend some people, but not his friends. Her warm smile lit up the room. She shook hands with Liam, and then looked long and hard at James before she finally offered her hand. 'Father, I have heard a lot about you. I'm pleased you're not drinking.' She pointed at the glasses of water.

He noticed the obvious glint in her eyes was shrouded by fear. This puzzled him, but he thought no more about it, putting it down to shyness.

'Marites, your English is excellent and you're a welcome sight. Too long Sean has been talking to himself, and as you well know, he is not the liveliest of conversationalists. I always feared he would bore himself to death. You'll bring him to Mass on Sundays?'

'We shall see.'

He'd little doubt as who would be the boss in the Lavelle household and smirked as she returned upstairs.

'Father, sorry about going to Rome, but she wanted a blessing from the Pope. What does money matter as long as you're happy?'

Feigning being hurt and let down by his friend, James protested loudly. 'I suppose I'm not good enough to oversee a wedding of such international importance. Maybe I embarrass you, do I, Sean?'

'If you're that upset, I'll let you do the christening if we're blessed with a child, and you're not too busy. Of course, you'll have to be nice to Marites in the meantime.'

The thought of Sean Lavelle changing a nappy was too much. Luckily, the mention of the Pope prompted him to turn the conversation to more pressing matters.

'We will worry about that when the child is born. The first competition of the season is only three weeks away. It's time to set our traps for Egan. I presume the web site is ready?'

Liam nodded. 'The fish tank is in place in Sean's shed and we have our merchandise.'

'Excellent, that reminds me, I must pay Frankie.' James reached into his pocket for his mobile phone and rang Jimmy Egan. He explained that he'd been on the river and as usual, caught nothing. He begged Jimmy to take him out the following day. Jimmy agreed and arranged to meet at ten the following morning at the weir pool.

Let the fun begin!

Chapter 13.

A small fall off snow during the night had left a light dusting on the road. Winter drew his last breath, a final rally before yielding to the spring. James waded up the weir pool at first light. He did not bother with his usual routine and focussed on extracting as many of the stocked trout as possible, from the easier water.

The Pope's golden Celtic cross sparkled in the early morning light. He smiled with immense satisfaction as he started to cast with his five weight, 9ft Pope's Dry Fly rod. Made from an expensive Sage blank, it handled the heavy nymphs at the end of his tippet with ease. With each cast, he varied the way the nymphs drifted.

On the sixth, he'd a take, and repeating the same manipulation, another trout took the fly. By eight o'clock, seven trout lay side by side on the bank. Laying down his rod, he carried them to the car and placed them in the boot. By nine o'clock, he'd made several more trips, and at nine thirty he returned one last time with two more trout. A total of thirty four rainbow trout, quickly and efficiently extracted from the river.

Satisfied that the pool now contained few if any stocked fish, he drove to the local shop and purchased a breakfast roll. He returned to the river and dined in the car. Whoever fried the egg had been in a hurry. Streaks of yolk stubbornly clung to both the front of his waders and the floor of the car. Despite his best efforts, most of his beard had turned a strange shade of yellow.

He grinned as he looked in the rear view mirror. Jimmy parked the Ferrari behind him at ten AM. His waders had dried quite well from the heat in the car, and he prayed that Jimmy would not notice that his boots were damp. He smirked, opened the door of the car and faced his adversary.

Jimmy Egan also had donned his waders before leaving home. If there was a catwalk for fly-anglers, then he would be a supermodel for Simms. He wore the latest waders, boots and jacket and his hat still had its label attached.

'Good morning, Jimmy, a touch cold, I hope the trout are not put down by the snow. Fair play to you, taking the time to show a poor old priest a trick or two, it's a very kind deed. Last week I told the parish sexton what a decent young man you were. "A chip of the old block," he said as he remembered your father with fondness.' *Fondness indeed, a pair of sewer rats.* He'd tried for years to get rid of the sexton, but failed. 'Jimmy, I suppose you have a good plan to attach a fine trout to my flies.'

Jimmy exuded confidence. The fact that the weir pool had received its delivery of fifty trout a week ago, guaranteed good sport.

'Father, if you don't catch at least ten, I will eat my hat. I have just the flies to make it happen.' Jimmy took a fly box from his pocket and handed it to the priest, 'A small gift, twenty of the finest Bees that I have ever tied. It's our little secret. Let me set up your rod.'

'Please be careful with that rod, it cost me a small fortune, nearly my life savings. A priest's income and an engineer's salary are worlds apart. The internet informed me that this rod is the best money can buy. After too many whiskeys a fortnight ago, I went online and used my credit card for the first time. Shock struck me down when the rod arrived, for the events that surrounded its order were a little hazy, if you follow me?'

Jimmy held the rod, examined it. Obviously a little surprised that he'd never come across the brand before. Everyone said that he made a point of keeping abreast of all developments in tackle, yet somehow this one had evaded him. He swished it back and forth a few times, before declaring, 'Father, you bought well. That's a finely engineered rod and the logo is wonderful, a work of art. 'The Pope's Rod', an apt rod for a priest. I might have a cast with it later.'

Taking the tippet he tied on two gold head Bees and four foot above the top dropper he inserted some siliconised yarn into a loop. 'C'mon, Father, let us catch some trout.'

When they reached the river, Jimmy guided James onto the run which hours earlier the wily priest had raped and pillaged. 'This is a great spot, one of the best on the river. See that gentle stream. Look how it twists down from the weir. I can assure you it's stuffed with trout. Off you go, Father, I'll follow you up and will keep an eye on your progress.'

'Jimmy, this is a little bit embarrassing. Would you mind if I sat and watched you fish for a while. I could say it's the arthritis, but that would be a lie. Fact is, I haven't fished in a long time and I would rather observe, and learn. Just till I feel a bit more confident, that is.'

Offered an opportunity to show his many skills to a willing audience, Jimmy Egan could not decline. Unhitching his flies from the keeper ring, he stripped some fly line from the reel and commenced casting. The bees landed with a large splash and the yarn indicator settled on the stream. All the while he gave a running commentary. 'Track the flies with the rod. Watch for bubbles or foam and make sure the yarn is not moving faster. Do a little mend like this. When the yarn dips or pauses, lift the rod and strike.'

Cast after cast, the yarn came back to him without pausing or dipping under. James sat quietly on the bank, smoking one cigarette after another, grinning mischievously as Jimmy's confidence evaporated with each fishless cast.

'It must be the cold weather, Jimmy. Are your flies heavy enough to get down deep?' Jimmy put on heavier flies, then tried lighter ones. Thanks to the plundering priest, the outcome did not change. After each cast, the flies returned to his feet unmolested. Dumbfounded, soon his rhythm went to pot. A new tippet had to be tied on when he hooked his lovely Simms hat.

He might be eating that hat before the day is out. James fumbled in his pocket for his phone. He needed a picture of this to show the lads.

Two hours later a crestfallen Jimmy Egan stumbled ashore and sat down awkwardly. James slapped his back. 'Bad luck, Jimmy, those trout must be asleep. I may as well have a go. Maybe one or two will wake up when my clumsy casts slap down on the water. I'll try that little spot up by the weir near the shallows. It should be safe enough there for an old fool like me to wade.'

'Good luck!' muttered Jimmy.

James was now within casting distance of his chosen spot. A little patch of calm water, the size of a pool table lying amidst the chaos of the rough water that tumbled over the weir. With his back turned to Jimmy, he removed the bees and tied on one of his own. He adjusted the position of the yarn and readied himself. Not an ideal situation, for no man could concentrate after the hilarity of watching Egan for the past two hours. He aimed for a point in the rough water just above and with a single cast he propelled the flies forward to land in the bubbling water.

The yarn bobbed amidst the foam and found its path downstream. Just as it moved into the calmer water, it was driven sideways. James struck. 'Jesus! Jimmy, I've caught one. Bloody hell, it's huge.' Jimmy raced upstream, unslung his net and deftly secured a heavily spotted, wild brownie of about eleven inches.

'Thanks, that was fantastic. Is that not a fine trout?' Quickly he cast out his flies again and caught a second of similar size. After releasing the second trout, he urged Jimmy to have another go. 'I'll wager there is another one there. I took off your Bees and tied on two of 'The Pope's Nymphs' that I bought. By God, they are good flies.'

The guest had turned guide and issued daft instructions to Jimmy. 'Try by that rock, a bit to the left, no a bit more upstream.' Like an automaton, Jimmy responded to each instruction. Despite his best efforts, no trout came to hand.

When they returned to their cars, James consoled a dejected angler. 'Beginners luck, Jimmy, I have been blessed by beginners luck. I'll tell you something, that Pope's Rod and flies are the best I've ever spent a Euro on.'

Jimmy reluctantly nodded, seemingly convinced that the only explanation was the Pope's Rod and Pope's Flies. 'What web site did you buy them from?'

James winked at him. 'It's a bit of a secret, but I'd be glad to let you in on it. Send me an email, fatherjpb@gmail.com and I will reply with the website address. Our little secret, tell no one.'

Chapter 14.

Thanks to a crash course earlier that year from Maggie, James had joined computerised society. He loved his iPad as a new found friend. Researching modern fishing techniques, learning the new lingo, the volume of information available on the internet intrigued him. It wasn't a surprise that an email had arrived from Jimmy before dinner time.

'Thanks for a humbling day on the river, Father. I enjoyed your company. If you get a chance, can you email me the address for that secret website? Jimmy.'

He could picture Jimmy, sitting at home on a posh armchair, a glass of malt in hand, eagerly awaiting the reply. Doing as he'd been instructed by Liam, he traced the IP address of the sender. That was all Liam needed to ensure that outside of the three musketeers, only Jimmy could gain access to the website. He emailed Liam the details and suggested that he open their online shop at six pm. At seven, he mischievously sent his reply to Jimmy.

Up to recently, he received few emails, despite offering his email address to all his parishioners. If they were sick or infirm, and unable to get to Mass, they could send a confession by email. God knows what hot water that would get him in with Rome. He would cross that bridge should any problems occur. Only a few had used the facility. Old Mary Sweeney at the ripe age of eighty-three had confessed to having a crush on James and suggested a sexual romp behind the altar. He advised her to say three Hail Mary's and charge her wheelchair. If she could drive it alone as far as the church, he would be happy to oblige.

Once a month he sent out what he called the Parish E-Letter. The miracle of technology allowed him to contact everyone, especially those who could not be bothered to sit their arse on one of his pews on a Sunday. He'd even offered a bounty and advertised it at the end of the Newsletter. '**Should you know of any sinners that don't attend Mass, a reward of €15 is offered for their email address.**' To date his wallet remained closed, but the eternal optimist remained confident of getting a result.

By chance he gained access to a stream full of sinners. During his research, he'd joined a few fishing forums, and the behaviour of many of the members astonished him. His father would have said, 'Half of them should've been drowned at birth.' That was fine for his father, he wasn't a priest. So he took a chance and posted his email address online. Every day his inbox was full and his parish had doubled in size overnight. To speed things up, he'd a few templates in Word that he pasted into the emails. 'Say three Our Fathers, a decade of the Rosary and stop buying a new fly line every month. The ones you have are fine.' 'Say two decades of the Rosary. Flies made from UV materials are the work of the devil and the trout cannot see UV anyway.'

It was Champions League Football night, so he settled on the couch, leaving his iPad on the coffee table after checking his emails. With no financial interest in the outcome, as matters of a piscatorial nature had taken over from his normal habits, he watched as a neutral.

Every few minutes he checked his email. Jimmy's order, if he'd read the man correctly, should arrive at any moment. The match bored any that watched, barely a single shot on target in the first half, and now midway through the second, it had not improved. He almost dozed off, shaking himself awake each time with a loud grunt. When the referee blew for full time, he checked the iPad one final time before going to bed.

'Bingo,' he shouted when he saw the email in the inbox.

Subject: Popes Order

Sender: trouthunterjimmy@gmail.com

Text: 1 Popes Dry fly Rod 9ft €1500

1 Popes Secret Nymph Selection € 120

1 Popes Secret Dry Fly Selection € 230

He almost choked when he saw the email address, 'Trout hunter'. Jimmy was an even bigger idiot than he'd supposed.

Chapter 15.

James had not fished the Liffey since he was a novice. A chance meeting with another priest, Father Hegarty, provided him with an opportunity to do so. The Pope's delivery to Jimmy had been collected the previous day and everything was going according to plan. Anticipating a return to his old stomping grounds sent his head spinning.

Clane was only twenty-five minutes away from Castlebridge. Driving through this thriving village, he marvelled at how modern it looked. Like most villages within Dublin's commuter belt, the incessant through traffic pulled along as though on a never ending conveyor belt. Contemplating stopping for a coffee, he found himself dragged towards the outskirts, destined for the next centre of man's desire to live in enclaves of concrete, brick and mortar. A desire he could not understand.

An angler stood on Alexandra Bridge, peering over the parapet into the Liffey. Pulling alongside to what he assumed was the other angler's car; he hopped out and joined him.

'Doc, I presume, I'm James Brennan.'

Doc, a slim forty year old, turned, offered his cupped hand to James and opened it slightly, revealing a Large Dark Olive. Born in the river, this delicate fly, in its final life cycle it would find a mate and fulfil its destiny.

'If they are coming off this early, there should be a good hatch later. I'm glad you could make it.'

He smiled as Doc released the Olive, both of them watching it flutter over the top of the bridge and drift on the gentle morning breeze, battling down towards the river and the sanctuary of bushes.

'I'm pleased to meet you, James. Have you a rod with you?'

'I have, it's in the car and already made up.'

'Good! We will take my car.'

'Doc, I hope I'm not being cheeky. Can we start at Monaghan's Island? My fondest memories of the Liffey are from that stretch, the best trout always came from there. '

Doc seemed surprised. He'd probably assumed that he would be babysitting a part time angler, one that had never fished the Liffey before.

'No problem. If you're up to the walk, then so am I.' Doc opened the door of the car.

James grabbed Docs arm, preventing him from getting out. 'Drive around the other side, where we can cross the fields at Connell's.'

Doc turned. 'Sorry, James, there is no parking over there. We will have to go the long way.'

'Don't be silly.' He reached into his pocket and withdrew a Disabled Parking Permit, and showed it to Doc. 'This will cover us, and if anyone complains, I'll threaten them with purgatory. Off you go. Great invention that permit, you can park anywhere with it. '

Driving down the country lane, James interrogated Doc, occasionally commenting, 'That house is new and I buckled me bicycle in a pothole at that bend.' Reaching the last straight near the end of the road, he ordered Doc to stop. 'Pull her in there, tight to the fence and put this permit on the dash board.'

While Doc climbed into his waders, James surveyed the barbed wire fence. Finding a suitable spot, he placed his rod on the far side, and attempted to vault over. He'd miscalculated. The barbed wire almost tore the arse out of his waders and he fell heavily on the far side. Standing up, no major damage done, he rather embarrassingly grinned at Doc. 'Someone should tell the farmers to make the ditches lower.'

Doc nodded, gathered his gear, walked twenty yards down the road and crossed the stile into the field.

'Stiles are a great invention, what do you think, James? Are you coming?'

One-Nil to Doc, and to ensure he inflicted maximum pain; he strode down to the river, leaving James trailing behind. Doc stopped at the fence that ran along the Liffey at Connells Strand, lit a cigarette and waited for James to catch up.

'I need to give up the fags,' announced James, panting. His leg still throbbed from the fall. Surveying the river, his face lit up. 'Connells Strand, by God she has widened a lot. In my day, she was stuffed with small trout. Many a good trout I caught below that rock over there.'

Doc nodded. 'I had a 14" fish there two weeks ago.'

After James had gathered his breath, they moved on downstream. Doc led the way, pausing occasionally, allowing James all the time he needed to reach deep into his memories and map the current river to his dim recollections. Much had changed, new ditches, mature trees that were mere saplings the last time James had walked alongside the Liffey.

Passing Hoban's rocks, shoulder to shoulder with Doc, he asked a million questions. Reaching a high impassable ditch, they turned and followed the line of the ditch back towards the road, until they reached a gate.

I'll take your rod, we will cross here,' said Doc.

James, in his haste to get to the Island, didn't notice the electric wire that ran along the top of the gate. The shock, when it came, assisted his crossing, and once again he ended up flat on his back. He looked crossly at Doc who grinned back at him. 'Watch out for the electric fence. Did I forget to mention it, sorry.' Two nil to Doc.

Again he trailed behind Doc, holding back a mouthful of expletives and grimacing at the stabbing pain in his back. Reaching a wire fence, Doc lifted the bottom strand, beckoning James to slide underneath. A little wiser now, he cupped the strand of barbed wire with his free hand, ensuring that if Doc's grip on it failed, he would not receive an unwelcome blessing. Doc slid under, strode down a hollow and through some bushes, whose thorns only had eyes for James. James appeared moments later and rubbed the blood off the scratches on his cheek, swearing loudly. 'Thank God, the river. Are we near the island yet?' he pleaded, all the while panting from his exertions.

'You are standing on it! It's not an Island anymore. You just crossed what was the inside channel.' Three nil to Doc.

They remained silent for ten minutes, both anglers content to survey the river and tuning into the task ahead. He rarely enjoyed fishing with another angler, but he relaxed, allowing himself to absorb everything as though he were alone. Doc also exuded a calmness that's a prerequisite to being a good fly angler.

Doc broke the silence. 'Nymphs, what do you think?'

'That sounds good to me. I'm keen on learning more about the modern methods which I have researched. Most seem bullshit, but heck, I'll try and be open-minded. Do you French Nymph at all?'

Doc glanced at the river, as though seeking an answer. 'I do occasionally. I'll set up my rod to French Nymph and you set up yours for a Klink and Dink.'

'What the hell is Klink and Dink? It sounds like an exotic cocktail.'

'Nymph under a dry fly.' Doc handed James a matchbox. 'Try these, black nymph on the point.'

'Nice flies, Doc. Off you go. Let us see if the Irish are as good at French nymphing, as the French are at producing fine wines. Can I have a peek at your setup first?'

Doc showed him the braided indicator, then stepped into the river; waded some twenty yards downstream and started casting, explaining the technique to James. After several casts, Doc beckoned James to join him and they swapped rods. Standing at James's shoulder, Doc guided him up the stream.

The nymphs landed where he intended, and apart from the indicator, little differed with his own methods. One badly timed cast caused a tangle, which he dealt with quickly, despite Doc laughing out loud and teasing him.

When the indicator dipped and James did not strike, Doc sighed. 'You missed one.' This happened several times and Doc grew more agitated. 'You have to strike when the indicator dips or pauses.'

James ignored the advice. 'Sorry Doc, I didn't see it dip.' His casts now covered the eye of the pool and his concentration, total. Just as the indicator passed the edge of a large rock, it moved ever so slightly off its line of drift and he lifted the rod, bending into a good trout.

As he played it, Doc teased him. 'Not bad, one hooked out of eight takes.'

'Stop yapping, Doc, and net this trout for me.' *Time to put this whippersnapper back into his box,*

'About a pound,' said James as the fish came over the rim of the net. 'Nice trout. Ignoring all the takes from the small fish ensured this fellow wasn't put on guard by their splashing. I'm not the fool you thought, eh, Doc?'

Three-One to Doc, the old dog had responded to the challenge of the pup.

After wetting his hand, Doc reached into the net for the trout. Noticing that it had taken the point fly, he seized the opportunity to regain the upper ground. 'Nice trout, but it would have taken my black nymph, even if you had played every other trout in the pool.'

Hooked, now strike, James hadn't expected a bonus point.

'It would take a better trout than that to take your black nymph.' He opened his cupped hand and handed Doc the black nymph. 'I swapped it for one of my own when I had that tangle.'

Doc stared at the hare's ear nymph as he unhooked the trout and looked up at James, his growing admiration etched on his face. With a few miles of river left to fish, this competition would test his mettle.

Three-Two to Doc, a slender lead and both anglers knew it.

As Doc outlined the water ahead, James listened intently. 'It sounds like the river has not changed too much. I should be okay on my own.'

They had decided to leapfrog each other up the river. James would fish first, with Doc coming behind. Then they would alternate on the next stretch. It remained unsaid, however both knew that to score a point would require the catching of a good trout from water that the other had just fished. Each recognised the skills of the other and knew few points would be scored.

Try as he might to concentrate on fishing, Doc seemed distracted. It was uncanny the way the old priest quietly waded from each prime spot to the next and extracted one good trout after another. James had now reached Hoban's Rocks. He exited the river and sitting, he lit a cigarette and watched as Doc moved upstream, taking a few small trout on the way.

James had not covered the best lie. Bemused at the intense concentration with which Doc approached, he muttered, 'May God forgive me.'

Almost within range, Doc paused and adjusted his setup. Edging slowly forward, his eyes focused on the tiny seam of water that snaked between two rocks. As he readied to cast, James coughed. 'This is your chance, Doc. I left the best spot for you, make it count.'

Doc looked up at James, growled and made his cast anyway. The nymphs landed two yards below the intended target with a heavy splash.

'Not to worry Doc, I'll try and locate another good trout for you. Hopefully you won't scare the next one.' He could not contain himself and burst out laughing.

Doc groaned as he wound in and joined James on the bank. Outwitting this priest proved difficult. Doc would need to dig deep just to stay in touch. Stalemate!

'As far as I recall, there are a lot of holes here,' said James, as they crossed the shallows above Hoban's rocks, cursing loudly each time he stepped into one.

'You're right. Did I forget to mention that?' said Doc.

Doc glanced at his watch. 'The hatch, if there is a meaningful hatch of large dark Olives today, should be starting soon. I think we should move to the upper rocks and take a break. Good place to watch the river come to life.'

James nodded. The upper rocks were one of his favourite places on the river. A high bank overlooked Hoban's Strand and the rocks above. This offered a vantage point to sit and observe.

'James, you obviously know this river better than most.'

James did not need a second invitation and recounted in fine detail his exploits on the Liffey. Those memories were as fresh as though the events had occurred only last week. Occasionally, he threw in a humorous story, recalling other characters that searched her waters, many long since dead.

'One incident stands out above all others,' he recalled, laughing as the memory came flooding back. 'It was the end of April. Following a flood, I fished a heavy nymph at the bottom of Drury Byrnes. I stood beside fast water, working the edge when the line paused. I struck hard and all hell broke loose. That fish raced to the top of Drury's.

'Twice I fell in, and nearly drowned as I struggled to cross the river. Only when it surfaced, I realised that it was a Salmon. As I lifted the rod high to try and beach the fish, I noticed my Nymph dangling in mid-air, three feet above the Salmon. The Nymph had hooked through the eye of a swivel. Someone fishing worms had already hooked that fish and had been broken off. As much as a Salmon steak for supper appealed to me, I broke off the worm hook and released her back to the river. She wasn't for me. She hadn't been caught fair. What would you have done with her, Doc?'

Doc replied, 'That's easy. Broiled with fresh parsley sauce. But only if she was real and not a figment of your imagination.'

Both men laughed.

'Oh, she was real alright.'

The sun had broken through the light cloud cover. In unison, they sensed the change and turned their attention to the river.

'Doc, I don't know about you, I have had the best days fishing for many a long, fishless year. To continue any longer, may be tempting fate and could spoil what has been a perfect day on the river. Let us call it a draw.'

They walked back up the fields, shoulder to shoulder, nattering as though they had known each other for years. Reaching the top, Doc guided them to the stile. 'After you, James, and watch your step.'

Driving back along the road, they arranged to meet at least once a month, agreeing that in future they would only compete with trout. Before James drove away, he handed Doc back his matchbox. 'Try these ones and don't show them to anyone else, not in this world or in the next. There is also something else in there. I want it back the next time we meet.'

* * *

Doc stood at the bridge, watching the old Clio splutter up the road. Curiosity demanding the immediate opening of the match box, he tipped the contents out on to the palm of his hand. Rarely prone to expletives, his 'Holy Shit!', so loud in its delivery, sent any wildlife in his vicinity scuttling for cover. In his hand, lay three flies and a rusty swivel.

Chapter 16.

James's inbox was full. One day away on the river, and in his absence the world had almost ground to a halt. Cutting and pasting from his standard replies, he managed to respond to all the emails. One however caught his immediate attention. Nestled snugly between two E-confessions was one with a subject of 'The Pope's Rods'

'Jesus! I hope he's not broken the sage blank already,' he shouted as he clicked on the email.

'Dear Father Brennan. Thanks for the heads up on the Pope's site. Best kit that I ever purchased. See you Sunday at the competition. Jimmy E.'

'Good God! Sunday, the plan,' he grabbed his phone, rang Liam and arranged to meet at Lavelle's that evening.

Whilst most of the E-confessions were the usual common ones, some were a little more interesting. He filled a small Scotch and read the crème de la crème of confessions, from a fine English wordsmith named Simon Everett.

By God, these foreigners have a good command of English. He wondered should he start an angling E-story club. It might raise a few Euros for the parish.

Dear Father Brennan,

I have to confess. The guilt has been keeping me awake at night for years and I yearn for a good night's sleep. I must get this burden off my chest.

It was many years ago now. I was a young, impressionable lad when old Bill taught me the ways of the water and the field. These were his ways, the ways of the true hunter, not those of the sportsman. Bill had a family to feed and he went to the river to bring back fish to eat. Just like when he went to the woods or the fields, he came home with a rabbit, hare or partridge – and not a single shot was fired.

His shaggy coated lurcher was deft at picking up a clamped bunny or hare. His homemade nets, dragged across the fields at night procured many a tasty partridge. It was from his teachings that I learned to pluck a salmon from the river. That was when the trouble started. I became fond of running dogs, too, and he let me have one of his pups. I still have one from the same line today, called Fly.

I was about 26 or 27, home on leave and I was itching to get down to the river and see the familiar sights and smell the scents of the wild garlic in the woods that grew alongside. The West Country River produced some sizeable sea trout, my best was 16lbs, but I have to confess, while it came to a rod and line, it did not take a fly or spinner. This is not my confession, because nobody saw the fish until I placed it on the kitchen table! No, my burden is from a day or two later. The water was getting lower and the fish were getting easier to find, stuck in the deeper pools, unable to continue their journey upstream.

It was early morning. The steam was still rising from the surface of the now warm river, as it fell from the wilds of Dartmoor over the moss covered rocks towards the sandy estuary, where it poured out into the sea. It's lower section slow and slightly meandering as it cut through flat water meadows, where mullet, bass and flounders would meet the resident trout and sea trout. I was on my hands and knees, bent over the undercut of one of the pools close to the tide, a stick in one hand and a child's beach bucket in the other, with the bottom knocked out of it. At the end of the stick a brass rabbit wire was fastened by its cord, and the wire wedged in a split in the end, to make it easier to guide over the tail of the waiting salmon.

The bucket took the ripples off the water and allowed me to see more clearly into the depths. I couldn't quite reach, so I lay on my stomach and extended my arm into the water, my shirt sleeve, wicking the slightly warm water up the fabric and into the main body of the garment, making me chill. I didn't shiver though, my hand was steady and the loop of wire was gently eased over the spade-like tail of the resting fish. Once I had it in position I steadied myself before lifting the stick to close the noose. The fish gave an almighty thrash and soaked me to the skin, it kicked and thrashed as I struggled to drag the mighty fish over the bank. I had just got it onto the grass when a voice called out, 'Finally. I've got you red-handed this time!' I looked up to see the fresh faced young keeper from the estate striding towards me.

I kept my composure as I straightened my soaking clothes and slid the wire off the tail of the fish, which still lay kicking on the grass. 'Got me red handed at what?' I replied.

'You're poaching salmon,' Martin, the young keeper, retorted.

'I'm not poaching salmon. I am not doing anything of the sort,' I replied. 'If you're referring to Sammy here, he is my pet salmon and I have just brought him down for his daily swim in the morning.'

Martin was taken aback by this and demanded, 'What do you mean, his daily swim?'

I explained that we kept him at home at the pond in the garden and I brought him down to this pool so he could have a proper swim, because he couldn't exercise properly in the pond. I gave him an hour and then whistled him and he would come back, so I could lift him out and take him home.'

Martin didn't believe me, so I offered to prove it to him. I took the salmon and placed him gently in the water, once again up to my armpits in the water. After a minute or two he revived and started to give a few wriggles, preparing to launch himself from my gentle grasp.

'Well, go on then,' encouraged the young keeper, 'let's see him go for his swim.' So I let him go and then sat back on the bank and waited. After about 15 or 20 minutes, Martin said, 'Now, let's see you whistle that salmon up then. I have got to see this.'

I turned to the young keeper and asked, 'Salmon? What salmon?'

I understand when he got back to his boss and recounted the tale, he lost his job. I have always felt guilty for that.

Father, please forgive me.

James struggled to type on the iPad keyboard, hard enough to use at the best of times, but nearly impossible when you're shaking with laughter.

This is a wonderful confession, Simon. Seventeen Hail Mary's, one for each of my belly laughs. As further penance, write a new tale every month until you have been purged of your sin. That poor young keeper, you should be ashamed of yourself.

Father James.

Chapter17.

James made no comment to Sean regarding the metamorphosis of the back room in Lavelle's. Knowing that Sean itched to hear his appraisal, he welcomed the opportunity to have some harmless fun. When Sean arrived with a bottle of Ballygowan water, James instigated some meaningless conversation. 'Nice weather we're having for this time of the year.' The idle chat lasted for ten minutes, covering current affairs, the state of the economy and sport.

Wiping the counter for a second time, Sean could not contain himself. 'Well, James, what do you think?'

Perturbed, he looked him straight in the eye. 'What do I think about what? I may be a priest with many skills, but a psychic I'm certainly not, and nor am I the possessor of a third eye.'

Sean shook his head. 'The decor, Father! Are you blind?'

Liam arrived and caught the tail end of the conversation. Seeing James wink in his direction, he joined in the fun. He sat on the new bright leather stool and shuffled around on it. Without commenting, he stood up and down several times, and then pushed it to one side and stood at the counter. 'Nice morning, lads. A pint of your finest ale please, Sean.'

Sean grunted and retreated to the main bar, returning moments later with a pint. 'Liam, you're a family man! What do you think of the new decor?'

Obviously feigning complete surprise, he surveyed the room. A flat screen television hung on the back wall. Two new stools stood proud on the new wooden floor, and the walls had been painted in bright pink. The pièce de résistance, though, was the sign that hung over James's head. In large bold red writing, it could not be ignored. *NO SMOKING*. Marites had been busy stamping her authority and righting the years of wilful neglect.

'Sean, that will improve the ambience a thousand fold,' he said, pointing at the sign. 'Shame though, the rest of it more resembles a nursery than a bar. If a man could bear to stay here more than ten minutes, he would get piles from sitting on those stools.'

Knowing that Sean prepared to explode and just needed a further gentle nudge, James obliged. 'Sean, any chance you could get me a glass of milk and a packet of nappies?' He hopped off the stool, just as Sean lost control and attempted to punch his lights out. When Sean calmed down and they had praised his great work, they came to the order of business.

'I spoke to Gerry at the trout farm. Sean, those trout will arrive tomorrow. Make certain the tank out back is ready; put the aerator going this evening. We don't want them going belly up before Sunday,' said James.

Sean nodded, 'Okay, boss!'

'Liam, the competition starts at ten o'clock. Egan usually arrives at the car park about a half hour early, you collect me at eight thirty?'

Opening the holy-grail, his note-book, he double checked that all angles had been covered. All nodded, they understood the plan for Sunday, and toasted their success with three glasses of whiskey of unusual quality.

'Revenge! May she be as sweet as this expensive malt. I'm off, I will see you on Sunday morning, Liam.' said James.

Closing the door James shouted back, 'Sean, take down that sign before I return or Marites will hear a little bit more of your past, more than you might want shared with her.'

Sean growled and threw a beer mat in his wake. 'Bloody priest!'

Chapter18.

If anyone had spotted the two men dressed in olive fly fishing jackets, waders and balaclavas, crossing the fields early on Sunday morning, they would have called the police.

James and Liam crouched low, hidden in the trees that surrounded Jimmy Egan's property. They had a clear view of the house and of the fish tanks. Liam switched on his video camera, and he took a few practice clips, which he replayed, ensuring that each showed the correct date and time stamp. They had the appearance of a couple of school kids about to rob an orchard, sniggering away, apprehensive that they would be caught.

Jimmy raised the camera when Emma Egan, attired in a nightdress, opened the curtains on an upstairs window.

'Put down that camera. Have some respect,' whispered James. He gasped for a cigarette, had a cramp in one leg and his bladder demanded relief.

'Is there no man left in you? Priest or not, you cannot deny that she is a fine looking lady.' Liam smiled as he lowered the camera.

Hearing a noise from the back of the house, the pair of voyeurs stiffened. Jimmy Egan crossed towards the fish tanks. Liam lifted the camera, focused on Jimmy, and giggled as he pressed record. Jimmy took a bucket from a storage area under the largest tank, and climbed the ladder to the top. Taking handfuls of fish pellets from the bucket, he tossed them in.

'Pellets for pellet pigs, oink, oink,' whispered the padre.

Egan fed those in the smaller tank, then went behind it.

'Crap, where is he gone?' said Liam.

Moments later, Jimmy re-appeared, carrying a long handled landing net. He dipped the net into the smallest tank and secured a large trout. They got a good view when Jimmy lifted it out of the net and dispatched it with two blows from the handle.

'Five pounds, maybe five and a half,' whispered James.

They stopped recording after Jimmy placed the trout in the boot of his car and returned to the house.

James sent a text to Sean 'Bring a six shooter. JPB.'

They scurried back across the fields and sped down the road. Still giggling, they stopped at a petrol station, bought two breakfast rolls and drove to the car park where the anglers met before the competition. As James scoffed back the last piece of sausage, Jimmy Egan's Ferrari rolled into the car park.

'Here he comes,' said Liam, Jimmy 'Pierce Brosnan' Egan. I cannot wait for the premiere of his latest movie.' Both howled uncontrollably.

James strode over to the Ferrari. 'Nice horse you have got there, Jimmy. Looks like it will be a good fishing day.'

They shook hands.

'I don't know whether to fish the Bees or the Popes Nymphs, maybe one of each. What do you think, Father?'

Laughing out loud at being asked and still grinning wildly, he replied. 'I haven't a clue, Jimmy, what could I tell an expert like you? I'm only here for a bit of fresh air. By the way, I robbed the poor box and bought another one of the Popes Rods, the French Nymph one. I read a bit about French Nymphing in a magazine and decided that I needed to get modern. Good luck and if you catch a few extra, you might slip one into my bag.'

Jimmy winked. 'Fish the bees and you'll not blank. By the way, is that egg yolk running down the leg of your waders? Ten o'clock lads, off ye go!'

After Liam had dropped him off, James walked downstream from the graveyard. In no particular rush, he enjoyed the stroll, noting the budding spring flowers and the first flush of growth in the hedgerows. It was a good time of the year to be out in the fresh air, rejuvenating after the long dark oppressive days of winter. Missing little of nature's beauty, as he crossed a stile, he spotted a hare at the far end of the field, its ears raised and alert to the sounds of his footsteps. 'Be gone or I will have those ears,' he shouted, grinning, as the hare scarpered, twisting every which way towards a gap in the far ditch. *The March Hare!*

On reaching his chosen pool, he took the braided sighter gifted to him by Doc, and attached it to his leader. Two medium weight nymphs were tied on five foot of fine tippet. He casually fished the shallows, working the nymphs occasionally, allowing his muscles to train themselves to this new method of fishing. The sighter was a godsend to his tired eyes, and when it dipped or paused, he struck. Several precocious salmon parr were landed and some small trout also came to hand. This pleased him, as they confirmed that despite the interlopers, the river was indeed healthy.

Now at deeper water, he changed the point nymph to a much heavier one and then fished in earnest. In less time than it took to say a few Hail Mary's, he hooked three rainbows and placed them in his bag. Job done, he retired to the shelter of a tree, lay back, and pulling his cap, drifted off to sleep. At about three o'clock, he awoke to the sound of a text arriving on his phone. 'Mary O'Neil's cow has calved. Sean'.

God almighty, is that the best Sean could come up with?

He sauntered back upstream to the graveyard and leaned over the wall. Certain that it was deserted; he clambered over and meandered between the headstones. Overgrown with brambles and ferns, he followed the path to the oldest part and searched for Mary O'Neil's grave. 'Mary O'Neil, Departed this life. 12 May 1926. RIP'. After a prayer for the souls of the departed, he retrieved the package that was concealed behind the headstone.

Fin perfect, he laid the six pound brown trout on the grass. Even an expert would struggle to identify it as a farm fish. He placed it in the bag alongside the rainbow trout and made the long trek back to the car park.

One by one the anglers returned. Leaning against Liam's car, a young angler that he did not know approached him. 'Hello, Father, nice to see you at the competition, I'm Davy, Davy Hughes. You might remember my father, Seanie.'

James beamed. 'Are you really Seanie Hughes' son? I haven't seen you since you were a nipper. One of my best friends, and a better angler than your dad would be hard to find. Your mother, Davy, is she well? I lost track of her when she moved from this parish.'

'She is still with us, though not in the best of health.'

Feeling guilty at his neglect, James whispered a reply, 'Davy, I'll visit her before the month is out.'

Lost in thought, remembering his old friend, he muttered, 'By God, your father stalked trout with a determination that bordered on insanity. Do you know that he watched a single trout for a season and a half? Such was our friendship he showed me her lie below the graveyard. Isn't the poor devil at rest, not a stone's throw away from that lie?'

'He is, Father.'

'Every chance he got, he watched her, until finally she made a mistake. During a hatch of large Caddis, she lost her sense. Taking one pupa after another, in her greed, she edged out into the stream, away from the submerged tree trunk. When your father's fly drifted towards her, she grabbed it.'

He could see that Davy was enthralled, his face flushed with excitement on hearing of his father's exploits. The sharing of them was so cruelly taken away by his untimely death.

'That was a magnificent trout. When hooked, she bored for the weeds and broke free, leaving your father staring at the shrivelled nylon. To his credit, he never complained once. In fact he was happy, as it confirmed her as nearly the greatest trout that ever swam this river.'

'Nearly?' said Davy.

Lighting a cigarette, James grinned. 'Aye nearly, there was a better one, two field's further down. I guessed she weighed around eight pounds, maybe nine. I felt sorry for your old man, so I revealed her location. He'd her out within a week, clipped off the top corner of her tail and handed it to me after Mass. I told him that I would have the tip off the bottom of her tail before the end of the season.' He paused again, allowing Davy the time to respond.

'Did you catch her, Father?'

Tipping his cap sideways, he beamed, remembering it as though it were yesterday, 'I did! Two months later and I clipped her tail. But it was a shallow capture, for your father had left us and I have never told anyone till today.'

He lightly slapped the priest on the back and laughed out loud. 'Father, my mother was right. She said you were an awful man for telling fairy tales, especially when it came to the fishing.'

As usual when confronted, he raised his hands to heaven. 'Lord, another unbeliever, what have I done to deserve this?'

Taking a package from deep within one of his zipped pockets, he laid it on the bonnet of a car. A crease of a smile crossed his face, as he removed the plastic cover and the aged brown paper underneath, revealing a small sheaf of paper which he unfolded. What remained could be best described as a fossil. Nothing was left of the piece of the trout's tail, but the imprint was unmistakeable, etched for all eternity on the paper.

'Do you believe me now? I never had the pleasure of showing it to your father. You keep it and someday show it to your own lad.' he said.

Davy was speechless, a tear running down his cheek, he accepted the gift and stowed it away. 'Father, I know now why my father loved you more than his own brothers, thank you. You fished when the trout were all wild, would you like to see that day come again?'

He greeted this with an immediate reply, 'I would, Davy, more than anything. What have you in mind?'

Davy's face lit up. 'I have tried for years to convince the committee to stop the ridiculous stocking. Every year, despite my efforts we are thwarted. It's decided by secret ballot. Last year we lost by one vote, one miserly vote. Will you join the committee? Jim Breslin quit last month. With you and God on our side, maybe we can convince one other member to see common sense. Well, Father?'

James stuck out his hand. 'You are your father's son, Davy. We will see it done.'

'Right, lads, let us weigh these trout,' shouted Jimmy Egan. He stood behind the Ferrari, and a weighing scales lay on the ground at his feet. Blissfully unaware of the impending shock, he bore a confident grin.

Mick Murphy responded, 'You go first, Jimmy, and put us out of our misery.'

A few more shouts. 'Go on, Jimmy, you first.'

Jimmy Egan obviously revelled in being the centre of attention. He took his bag of fish from the car. One by one, he laid the rainbow triplets on the scales and with great ceremony, took the last fish out of the bag. A few gasped, as he placed a fine 'wild' brownie alongside the others.

Mick feigned to walk away. 'We may as well go home. The committee should pay someone to cull all the brown trout out of the river, only then will the rest of us have a chance.'

James wondered how many of the anglers believed this nonsense. *Jealousy, she is the greatest enemy of common sense.*

The brown trout, weighed separately, was a massive five pounds four ounces. Jimmy beamed at the rapturous applause. Each came forward in turn with their trout. James, stunned that only Liam had matched Jimmy with four trout, scratched his beard.

Liam shouted across the crowd, 'Father Brennan, did you blank?'

'I did no such thing,' he said in mock indignation. He walked to Liam's car, returned and tossed a bag at Jimmy's feet. The look on Jimmy's face, when he took out the trout was worth recording, and Liam had done just that. Camera phones can be very useful.

All eyes were on the scales. Mick leaned over the stunned Jimmy and called out the weight. 'Mother of god, he's caught Jonah's whale, six pounds and three ounces.'

Jimmy, gathering his wits, looked up and searched for James in the crowd. He failed to locate him, but he shouted anyway, 'Great trout, Father, it's a shame she is alone.' He almost stumbled when the three rainbows landed at his feet. Liam got a photo of that as well.

Liam took one more photo for posterity, Jimmy shaking James's hand, as he handed him his trophy.

Chapter 19.

James put the trophy on the mantelpiece, to the left of the new clock. He placed it backwards in recognition of the fact that it had been secured by wilful cheating. Today, he would be busy. As expected, a new order had arrived from Jimmy, two Pope's French Nymph Rods, leaders and Secret French Nymph flies. Armed with such magnificent equipment, Jimmy would surely secure the trophy at the next competition.

Davy Hughes' suggestion that he join the committee was a very welcome surprise. He'd envisaged that he would have to engage in some political manoeuvring in order to wiggle his way to the top table. Davy's invitation fast tracked everything, and that would allow him plenty of breathing space to analyse each committee member. Opening his diary, he contemplated his plan, scribbled a few notes and duly satisfied that all was in hand, he went to church.

Two funerals and an unexpected visit from the Bishop took up all his time that week. As he drove to the hotel on Friday evening, he contemplated his approach. Deciding that the best option was to keep low key, he relaxed. The committee meeting was due to start at eight sharp, so he timed his arrival for ten past eight. Opening the door, he surveyed the room. Jimmy and Davy immediately stood up, welcomed him and ushered him to the vacant seat.

As he settled, the other members nodded in his direction. Mick Murphy laughed out loud, banging his fist on the worn table. 'Good man, Father, after your display in the competition, it's only fitting that you took that seat, so that we can keep an eye on you.'

He retorted with an equally loud bang on the table. 'By God, Mick, you have it all backwards. It's because your wife asked me to join to keep an eye on you. I have no other reason to be here. I thought the committee met once month, but she seemed to think that five meetings took place.'

Mick blushed. If only he knew that James chanced his arm, he would not have had to reveal his indiscretions.

'It's only a small white lie. Even Charlie, there, has to tell his wife the same one. How else could we escape their clutches for a bit of peace? A few nights a month is hardly a sin?'

Jimmy Egan regained control of the meeting and the various items on the order of business were discussed, voted on and laid to rest.

Davy fidgeted with his biro as matters came to a conclusion. When Jimmy asked the inevitable question, 'Any other business?' he stared into space before blurting it out.

'Are we going to revisit the stocking policy this year?'

Mick groaned. 'Here we go again, annual torture time. Davy, have you a death wish or something? If we stopped stocking, we may as well take up golf. What would we be able to catch?' A few laughed, their names duly noted by James.

'Mick, in your case, it would make no difference at all.' Davy's response left Mick seething with anger.

Jimmy had to intervene before it came to blows. 'Lads, it's a fair question. It will be on the agenda for the meeting in September, a week after the last competition. As usual, it will be a secret ballot to ensure that there are no bad feelings afterwards.'

All agreed, and when calm returned, Jimmy closed the meeting and they all went their separate ways.

* * *

Lying back on his couch, James mused over the evening's proceedings. Since there is no point in trying to move a mountain, he struck Mick off his list of people that could be swayed. Apart from Jimmy Egan, and obviously Liam and Davy, the rest had question marks beside their names. Out of the nine man committee, three were against stocking, two definitely for, and four unknown. Two of the four must be turned, but which ones?

Mary Kelly, unelected chairwoman of the parish busybodies, stuck her nose in everyone's business. Outwardly at least, the most virtuous woman in the parish, Mary had one vice that she kept hidden, her daily consumption of copious amounts of vodka.

The following morning, he called on Mary and placed a large bottle of Smirnoff on her kitchen table. Understanding he'd a job for her, she didn't protest when he supplied her with four names.

'I need a written report on each. Leave no stone unturned and you have two weeks to do your work.'

A bottle of Vodka and being able to delve into the hidden lives of four people, two addictions served in one go. She attacked the job with gusto. By the time the bottle was empty, she'd made her report, and a second bottle sat on her kitchen table.

Saint Teresa
Pray for Us...

Saint More
Pray for Us...

Saint Line
Pray for Us...

Saint Kolbe
Pray for Us...

Saint Fisher
Pray for Us...

Saint Clitherow
Pray for Us...

Saint Bede
Pray for Us...

Saint Alban
Pray for Us...

itant, a barrister, a mechanic
m. If Mary could not find any,
g had honed his instincts, and
his opening gambit. Joe Daly,
prefer stocked fish and would
s priest.

der board showed James 10
be allowed to win the second
ng something unpredictable.
again, Liam on camera, they
l of netting his illegal trout.
,' said James, confident that
y would be his. Jimmy was
unders found their way to his

tion as they left the car park.
g back a distance, he followed
the narrow lane, he pulled in
going to Casey's and he would

cted, see the top of Joe's head
op of Casey's field. Moving
ea of fast water and caught his
upriver and sat at the opening
access for cattle to drink from

. Another smoker, it reminded
uld make a few casts, retire to
fter an hour he moved up and

any luck yet?' he said, as he

noke and grinned. 'No keepers,
ed?'

bag down on the grass. 'Four

hough he seemed completely
said Joe. 'I haven't weighed in a
at it really.'

eemed a competent caster, but
below, Joe had not ventured
that he wade out a bit further

and cover the deeper water. Not for the first time in his life, he'd come across an angler unwilling to take advice. As they sat and watched the river, a small hatch of olives started. Several of the rainbows rose in unison, and soon all up and down the river, the rings of rising fish were visible.

'Off you go, Joe, here's your chance to fill your bag.' Urging him a second time, Joe waded out slowly and moved upstream. He paused, changed his fly and glanced over his shoulder at James. When a trout rose in the shallows on his side, he turned towards it and cast. James tracked the dry fly, and within two yards it disappeared in the rings of a rise. Joe never struck. He casually wound up his line and walked ashore.

'Jesus, Joe, I see your problem, you have to strike when you get a take.'

Joe lit another cigarette before responding. 'That was a wild trout, probably eight or nine inches. What would be the point of playing it, when I had no intention of taking it home, or weighing it in at the competition.'

'I see!'

Joe looked James straight in the eye. 'No, you don't, Father, I don't strike for fear of having to land one of them stupid stocked trout.'

James slapped Joe heartily on the back. 'Oh, I do see! I think you're a man after my own heart.'

Joe and James were deep in conversation; their noses stuck in each other's fly boxes, and barely noticed the other anglers arrive back to the car park. James weighed in his trout first, followed by Liam, and both noticed the grin of satisfaction on Jimmy's face.

Mick made his usual singular contribution to events. 'Well done, Jimmy, more vermin wild trout removed from the river.'

As Jimmy received his trophy, he winked at James. 'French Nymphing using the Pope's Rod.'

74

He stared at the reports, an accountant, a barrister, a mechanic and a farmer, and no dirt on any of them. If Mary could not find any, then none existed. A lifetime of gambling had honed his instincts, and having little else to go on, he decided on his opening gambit. Joe Daly, the farmer, was the least likely one to prefer stocked fish and would be the first to receive attention from this priest.

* * *

With one competition over, the leader board showed James 10 points, Jimmy 9, Liam 8. Jimmy would be allowed to win the second one, no need to panic him into doing something unpredictable. Peering out through the trees once again, Liam on camera, they giggled as Jimmy went through his ritual of netting his illegal trout.

'Bet it's at least six pounds, Liam,' said James, confident that Jimmy would make sure that the day would be his. Jimmy was making sure all right, two fine four pounders found their way to his car.

Competitor's cars jockeyed for position as they left the car park. James started his old Clio, and keeping back a distance, he followed farmer Joe to the river. Driving down the narrow lane, he pulled in and sat smoking a cigarette. Joe was going to Casey's and he would allow him plenty of time to start fishing.

Crossing the stile, he could, as expected, see the top of Joe's head as he waded up the run at the top of Casey's field. Moving downstream, he stopped at the first area of fast water and caught his four stocked trout. He sauntered back upriver and sat at the opening where the wire fence stopped to allow access for cattle to drink from the river.

Looking upstream, he observed Joe. Another smoker, it reminded him that he needed to cut back. Joe would make a few casts, retire to the bank and light another cigarette. After an hour he moved up and joined him just as Joe lit another.

'Good morning Joe, have you had any luck yet?' he said, as he approached.

Joe looked up through the haze of smoke and grinned. 'No keepers, yet, Father Brennan. How have you fared?'

'I have my four,' he said, laying his bag down on the grass. 'Four stocked fish, as would be expected.'

Joe offered his congratulations, though he seemed completely disinterested. 'Don't worry about me,' said Joe. 'I haven't weighed in a trout in many years. I'm not much use at it really.'

This comment surprised him. Joe seemed a competent caster, but he'd noticed whilst he'd watched from below, Joe had not ventured out into the stream. James suggested that he wade out a bit further and cover the deeper water. Not for the first time in his life, he'd come across an angler unwilling to take advice. As they sat and watched the river, a small hatch of olives started. Several of the rainbows rose in unison, and soon all up and down the river, the rings of rising fish were visible.

'Off you go, Joe, here's your chance to fill your bag.' Urging him a second time, Joe waded out slowly and moved upstream. He paused, changed his fly and glanced over his shoulder at James. When a trout rose in the shallows on his side, he turned towards it and cast. James tracked the dry fly, and within two yards it disappeared in the rings of a rise. Joe never struck. He casually wound up his line and walked ashore.

'Jesus, Joe, I see your problem, you have to strike when you get a take.'

Joe lit another cigarette before responding. 'That was a wild trout, probably eight or nine inches. What would be the point of playing it, when I had no intention of taking it home, or weighing it in at the competition.'

'I see!'

Joe looked James straight in the eye. 'No, you don't, Father, I don't strike for fear of having to land one of them stupid stocked trout.'

James slapped Joe heartily on the back. 'Oh, I do see! I think you're a man after my own heart.'

Joe and James were deep in conversation; their noses stuck in each other's fly boxes, and barely noticed the other anglers arrive back to the car park. James weighed in his trout first, followed by Liam, and both noticed the grin of satisfaction on Jimmy's face.

Mick made his usual singular contribution to events. 'Well done, Jimmy, more vermin wild trout removed from the river.'

As Jimmy received his trophy, he winked at James. 'French Nymphing using the Pope's Rod.'

Chapter 20.

Multi-tasking is the art of being able to juggle three balls, cook breakfast and do a crossword all at the same time. James could no more multi-task than the Pope could surf. Consumed to the point of obsession, he thought about nothing else but fishing, Jimmy Egan and impostor rainbow trout. Single-minded stubbornness has its advantages, but a quick temper is not one of them, and when Pups arrived at his door, he flew into a rage that sent him scurrying away.

'Come back!' he shouted, regretting his outburst.

Pups edged past him into the hallway, furtive glances ensuring his behind was safe from an unwelcome boot. James shut the door. Seeing fear on the poor lad's face, he ushered him into the sitting room. Pups relaxed, hopped from one foot to another and excitedly waved a sheet of paper. James grabbed it, read the contents and snorted. *Free Greyhound Trials at Newbridge Stadium– All day Wednesday.*

In order to qualify for anything, other than an open race, Castlebridge Lad had first to do two trials over his preferred distance, after which he would be graded and deemed eligible for racing. Deferring every request from Pups to organise trials, using every conceivable excuse, James had run out of track, and his shoulders sagged. Hopefully, this would be the end of any notions Pups had of becoming a pro.

'Okay, Pups. Are ya sure he is ready?'

'He's been doing twenty sprints a day in front of my new racing bike and has to slow down for me to catch up. I'll eat me ca, caa, cap if he doesn't get in the top three grades in the sprint.'

'You have my word. I will collect you on Wednesday. Now, feck off, I've work to do,' said James, tiredly.

Pups stood his ground, scratched his belly and looked confused.

'What? Go on, off with you.'

'Fa, Father. Today's Wednesday!'

'Feck!' James grabbed his coat and car keys, pushed Pups out the door and his temper flared when he noticed Castlebridge Lad bounding around on the back seat of the car.

'Put a muzzle on that hound at once, or I'll put one on you,' commanded James, an order that Pups obeyed after he hopped in and cuddled his pet.

Snuggled up close to the hound, Pups looked so content that James remained silent until they reached the greyhound stadium. Inside, huddled groups of trainers chatted, hounds barked and officials raced to and fro.

'Pups, whatever talking is to be done, let me do it. Okay?'

Pups drew his fingers across his lips, and they remained shut while they wandered around. Leaning over the fence that surrounded the track, Pups couldn't contain his excitement. Pointing to the traps, he yipped and he yapped, hollered and cheered, as dogs sprung out and chased the electric hare, ignoring James's pleading for him to quieten.

Conscious of other trainer's smirks and their whispered laughs growing louder, James wished he could hide. Duty bound, he'd no choice but to see this through to the bitter end, and be there for Pups when his dreams were shattered. 'For the love of God, give me his papers and I'll get him signed in.' Registration was a simple affair, the papers were in order, and Castlebridge Lad drew trap two in a sprint, that would start twenty minutes later.

Ready to enter the arena, Pups took a sweet from his pocket, gave it to the Lad and whispered in his ear.

'What's that all about?' said James, exasperated, as though speaking to a child.

Pups sniggered, patted the Lad, and without any hint of a stammer, 'James, I know you think me a bit of a fool, a stammering gobshite that doesn't know his arse from his elbow. That dog understands me better than you do. My fa, fa, fahs and my da, da dahs ensured I was bullied at school, wiped my self-confidence and left me open to constant ridicule. Today, when that dog proves his speed, so will my worth be proven. You having shown me love will show me respect. As to the sweet, the Lad isn't thick either. If he runs as fast as he did on the road, the full packet will be his to scoff.'

Gobsmacked, James stuttered, 'Ho, ho, holy feck!' He leaned against the rail along the track, fumbled for a fag, and watched Pups stride confidently to the enclosure. *The meek shall inherit the earth. Never was a truer word spoken.* He looked towards the heavens, watching the cigarette smoke spiral upwards towards a cloudless sky. In that instant, he knew a greater hand had taught a valued lesson; one he would not forget.

Pups led the hound to the traps, removed the muzzle and leash and gave the Lad a final hug before guiding him inside. James waved. Pups nodded and strode to the finishing line, clearly confident that his belief in his hound would be rewarded.

'They shouldn't let young lads with their pets into the trials,' muttered a craggy faced spectator beside James.

'Nor cranky old fools, either,' said Brennan, ready to defend Pups against all comers. 'Do you have a mutt out there?'

Craggy snorted and spat on the ground. 'No! I have a half-share in Dancing Dan, and if he is half as good as his father, the bookies will weep.'

'A betting man? Are ya willing to wager, or is it only your mouth that opens?'

'Dancing Dan against a pet, it would be the same as robbing the poor box. I'll put some loose change on it, just to make it more interesting for an amateur like you.'

James grinned and pulled a wad of notes from his inside pocket. Under Craggy's watchful gaze, he placed five one-hundred euro notes on the rail and weighed them down with his lighter. Seeing wariness battle against greed in Craggy's expression, 'I'll make it easy for you.' He added another three notes to the wager. 'Pet versus pedigree, and since I'm a generous priest with the poor box in his pocket, I'll give you two to one.'

Greed won, spitted hands were shaken and Craggy's four-hundred sat alongside James's money.

Lord, send down one of your Angels and make the Lad fly. Amen.

The hare whizzed past. Traps flew open. James roared with excitement. 'C'mon Lad! C'mon!'

Castlebridge Lad, first out, neck arched, powered to the first bend, took it tight, holding his line like a seasoned racer. Craggy's shouts dissipated into groans as Dancing Dan, aptly named, waltzed over the line in last place.

'Beginners fucking luck!' screamed Craggy.

'Maybe your mutt needs proper training. As a man of God, I can't take that money for myself.'

Disbelieving his luck, Craggy lurched for his wad of cash, and gasped when Brennan grabbed his wrist and seized all the notes. 'What the hell?'

'My conscience allows ..., actually it insists I take it for the poor box. God bless your generosity.'

Craggy grimly watched his money disappear into Brennan's pocket, spat once more and stomped off toward the bar.

At the finishing line, Evan buried his face in his hands, flung his cap in the air and grabbed the panting hound. By the time James had joined him, the times were displayed on the neon board. Both gawked at it, unable to comprehend they had a grade-one sprinter on their hands.

'I told ya, James. You will, qua, qua, quadruple your money.' said Pups, as he hugged the astonished priest.

'Any more sta, sta, stammering and I'll leave me boo, boot so far up your anus that it would take a sur, sur, surg ..., a doctor to remove it. Pups, go get your grading papers.

'Yes, Sir! By the way, my name is Evan, always has been. You already know I have a PHD in Physics. From now on, in polite company you may call me Doctor Evan O'Leary.'

'One question, Doctor EMC-Squared. The subterfuge, I think I understand why you played the fool, but how did you manage to carry it off all these years? How did you get rid of the stammer that you were born with?'

Evan flicked away some flies that buzzed around Castlebridge Lad, 'Not only hounds can be trained. Patient tuition from a wonderful actress, that's how.'

'Emily Jane?'

'Yes, James. Pup's still stammers, always will. Under Emily's tutelage, I can switch from Puh, Puh, Pups to Evan at will. She once told me that given enough time, she could even train you to say please.'

'The feckin witch!'

Chapter 21.

September now, the seventh and last competition was on the horizon. The scoring could not be closer. Jimmy, Liam and James were equal on 54 points. The final competition would be the decider.

The revenge committee had their final meeting in Lavelle's, the evening before the great event. Sean, in a flamboyant mood, had even organised some finger food to go with a bottle of champagne that he'd been minding for several months. Cabled into the flat screen television, Liam's laptop paused at the opening scene of their video. Sean collapsed laughing as he read the title, 'The Outlaw Jimmy Egan.'

'Hang the bastard. When you show this to the committee, there will be hell to pay.'

Liam had done a fantastic job editing the nine minute long movie. He'd added a little comedy by reversing some of the sequences, showing Jimmy walking backwards from the car and putting the trout into the tank. With such incriminating evidence, Jimmy could not deny his dastardly deeds.

James waited for Sean to calm down before speaking. 'Great job, lads. We will deliver the coupe de grace at the committee meeting after the last competition. Speaking of which, the winner is yet to be decided.'

Taking a coin from his pocket, he tossed it in the air and caught it. 'Heads you win, Liam.' Opening his cupped fingers, Sean and Liam leaned over to look. 'Heads it is, Liam, our very own Liam O'Brien will be angler of the year,' said James.

Sean shook Liam's hand, 'Fair play to you, I always knew you were good enough,' winking at James. 'Our own cheating bastard.' All three howled with laughter and sunk the last of the champagne.

Chapter 22.

D-Day, 10th September, once again the intrepid pair hid in the trees alongside Jimmy's property. They did not bring the video camera. Enough footage had already been recorded. Jimmy, with a spring in his step, carried four trout to his car, each about four pounds weight. Victory seemed certain.

The text went to Sean, 'Mary O'Neil needs 15lbs of sugar in three bags to make her jam.' Sean did not disappoint and the outcome would favour the conspirators.

Jimmy's hands shook as he readied the scales for the weigh in. It had been harder this year, yet the Angler of the Year award would find its rightful place on the shelf in his fishing basement. Confidence written in his every action, he weighed his own mighty bag first. Sixteen pounds and two ounces of 'wild' brown trout glistened on the scales.

James whistled and made a comment before Mick had a chance to make his usual quip. 'Well done, Jimmy, wonderful wild trout, we are so lucky to have such a productive river.'

Jimmy grinned. 'Indeed Father, you just need a little skill to find them.'

'Indeed, Jimmy, you need to know the river like you know your own back yard.'

Liam had to turn away, as he was unable to keep a straight face at this comment.

When Liam retrieved his bag from the car, he was greeted by a hushed silence, all realised that Liam had a fine bag of trout. One by one, Jimmy's trembling hands placed the trout on the scales and with a distinct tremor in his voice he called out the weight, seventeen pounds and two ounces.

Mick raised a mighty roar. 'The greatest bag of trout ever to come out of the river ... And three of them are wild! Who would have believed it possible?'

An obviously crestfallen Jimmy whispered. 'Are there any more trout to be weighed in, lads?'

James nodded, walked to his car and returned with his bag. 'I only caught one,' he said, as he lifted his trout and placed it on the scales.

Liam stared at the scales, dumfounded, unable to fathom where the trout had come from. Seven pounds and one ounce, bigger than any trout they had put in the tank at Lavelle's. With an incredulous look on his face he turned to James.

'A beauty Liam, she is as wild as the wind. It's a fine river that can produce a trout like that.'

Liam shook his head and stared at the trout. They all stared at the trout.

'That's it for another season. Well done, Liam' said Jimmy. 'Committee meeting next Wednesday, eight PM.'

James and Liam watched the Ferrari accelerate up the road.

'Wednesday night, the premiere of 'The Outlaw Jimmy Egan', our revenge will be complete,' said Liam.

James placed his arm around Liam's shoulder. 'Not quite Liam. The vote on the stocking is more important than revenge. We will visit him to-morrow night and ensure that he votes against it.'

Liam protested, unpleased at this deviation from the plan. 'Despite the great fish that you caught, I'm unsure whether the river has sufficient wild trout to ensure good fishing.'

'She bloody well can, and you'll vote to make sure no more vermin trout are ever placed in the river.' He tossed Liam a coin and told him to examine it.

Liam gasped, both sides were heads. 'That's why you won, Liam, and that's why you'll vote with me.'

Liam looked at the old priest. 'By God, I have been dancing with a devil. Is no one safe from your deviousness?'

'I have told you on many occasions, Liam, the divil is in the detail. When it comes to detail, I'm a master craftsman. When I teach you about real fly fishing next season, you'll thank me. Tomorrow evening, Jimmy Egan's house at eight o'clock, be there and bring the movie.'

Chapter 23.

James carefully placed the bottle of 1957 Brora on the front seat of the car. It had cost a small fortune, money that could have been used for work in the parish. With the profit from the Popes Angling Emporium, he could have bought shares in the distillery, so the expenditure incurred left his conscience intact.

In the infamous words of his hero Colonel Hannibal Smith of A-Team notoriety, 'I love it when a plan comes together.' The question of which came first, the Chicken or the Egg was very relevant here. In James's less than humble opinion, it was a clear case of plagiarism. In copying his unique talents, they merely swapped the priest's robe with a military uniform. Jimmy Egan, God bless him, would receive worse than the wrath of Khan, and James salivated at the prospect of delivering it in person.

The marble pillars at the door of Egan's house were a fitting entrance for this colossus of a man. Standing there, erect, confident and with the authority of the Almighty in his back pocket, he pressed the door-bell twice. When Jimmy answered, he strode past him into the entrance hall, as though Jimmy was a butler and he the lord of the manor. Liam stood just inside holding a glass of malt. Turning to Jimmy, he showed him the bottle that he carried.

'Glasses, Jimmy, your fishing room would be a suitable place to savour this king of malts.'

Jimmy seemed as if he was about to protest, but like an obedient pup, he led them down to the basement and filled three glasses.

Delighted, Jimmy grinned. 'Wonderful, Father, it slips over the pallet like the caress of a gentle breeze. What is the occasion that demands the partaking of such nectar?'

Grimacing at such poetic nonsense, James looked to the floor. *The caress of a gentle breeze. What a load of ...'*

'Jimmy, we are here to view the premiere of the finest movie ever shot in this parish. Liam looked after the camera, and I directed. Knowing that you're a connoisseur of the fine arts, we thought it fitting to get your appraisal, before presenting it to the world. Liam, set up your laptop on the fly tying table!'

They sat on the luxurious swivel chairs, James on the right, Liam in the middle and Jimmy on the left. Liam switched on his laptop, James quietly sipped the whiskey and they watched the screen. It seemed to take an age for it to boot up.

'What is the movie about? Fishing I presume,' said Jimmy.

'Yes, Jimmy, you're correct. It's about fishing, but it's much more than that. It's about the capture of the most devious of fish, one that has avoided capture for many years. In fact one that hid in the deepest water, a foul grotesque creature thrown up from the very bowels of hell.'

Jimmy sat on the edge of his seat, shaking with apparent anticipation. His excitement turned to horror when the title came up. Hands shaking, he gulped back the remaining whiskey and sunk into the chair, still staring at the screen. As the video clip played, James and Liam watched every reaction, each facial muscle registering Jimmy's utter disbelief that he'd been caught. He whimpered as the video clip ended. Sitting silently with folded arms, reminiscent of a common criminal in court, he awaited the inevitable judgment of his peers.

'Not pretty, Jimmy, not pretty at all. What madness possessed you to do it, I will never understand. What pleasure did you gain by cheating on your fellow anglers? Look at all those trophies on your wall, each a deceit, each a testament to your despicable nature. When St. Patrick rid this Island off snakes, he surely missed one and you're its descendant. Have you anything, anything at all to say in your defence?'

Jimmy could not even look at them. He stared straight ahead and after an age he murmured, 'No defence, I'm at your mercy, forgive this sinner. Though I know I don't deserve it.'

For the first time that evening, James smiled. He almost felt sorry for the wretched fool that sobbed pitifully on his own leather chair. 'Jimmy, we entertained the idea of playing this movie at the committee meeting on Thursday night. It would be only right that those you deceived, were aware of the wrongdoings of one they considered a friend and a fly fishing brother.'

Jimmy sobbed out loud. 'Please, is there no other way?'

James shook his head. 'I have no option, unless....'

'Unless what, Father?' Jimmy sat up straight, his eyes pleading for an alternative.

'There's only one way out of this. You must vote against the stocking policy.'

His sobbing ceased, 'I will. I will vote against it, anything, Father. Please don't tell anyone about this, my life would be in tatters.'

Good cop, bad cop, Liam intervened. 'I think this is too soft a punishment, but if you think it's the best way forward, then I will keep silent.'

Chapter 24.

First to arrive for the meeting, James chose his position carefully, sitting directly opposite where the chairman always sat. He wasn't taking any chance that Jimmy would get a sudden burst of bravery. A wounded animal is a dangerous beast, only a fool would turn their back on one. Knowing that he broke the law against smoking inside a hotel, he lit a cigarette, left the cigarette packet on the table, and beside it, a small envelope. Would any challenge his illegal smoking? If any did, he would deal with them. When the vote came, they would not dare cross him a second time. *The divil is in the detail James, in the detail.* He laughed out loud as he lit a second cigarette.

A few spluttered, a few waved their hands around, but only Mick commented. 'Priests and politicians are the same the world over. They think they are above the law. Just as well I smoke myself, Father.'

Ignoring the comment, he concentrated on Jimmy, who had just sat down and opened his folder. It was a good omen that he looked nervous.

Liam sat beside James and whispered. 'I reckon he is with us. If you farted loud enough, he would probably jump.'

'Right,' said Mick. 'Since the chairman seems occupied with papers, I'll start the meeting. There is only one item on the agenda. The quicker we vote on it, the sooner I can acquaint myself with a pint of Guinness. Has anyone got anything new to say on the stocking? Not that it's likely that there is anything new to say.'

Everyone looked around the table. When no one spoke, all eyes turned to James. 'Father, you haven't had to listen to the nonsense for the past few years. Here's your chance to air your views, and then we can get to the voting.' Mick as usual liked to get straight to the point.

James opened the envelope that he'd placed on the table. Removing the photographs, he handed two to each committee member. 'Just a small reminder of what a real brown trout looks like. My recent capture and one I caught many years ago. Look at those fish and compare them to those tame rainbows that you call trout. Look at them and make your decision.'

Jimmy stepped up to the plate and honoured his deal, more than honoured it. 'Lads, I have decided that I can no longer manage the stocking. My wife is fed up at looking at the tanks at the back of my house. Will you look after it, Mick? You have plenty of time on your hands.'

James nodded at Jimmy.

Mick had been put on the spot. 'Lads if you asked me an hour ago, I would have said yes, but looking at those photos got me thinking. Father, half of us could not catch a wild trout if you paid us, we can barely catch the rainbows. If I vote no, will you teach me?'

This was more than James had bargained for. 'Of course I will, Mick, and anyone else for that matter. We will call it Father JP's Wild Trout School.'

'Good,' declared Mick. 'Let's vote and feck the secrecy, raise your bloody hands. All those in favour of having only wild trout, say aye.'

Hands that had stayed down for many years were reluctantly raised. Not a single member opposed the motion. James wasn't finished yet and taking advantage of the advent of common sense, he struck. 'As we really are unsure of how healthy the stocks are, we need to show restraint. I would suggest that next season we exercise a strict catch and release policy. Shall we vote on it?'

Mick responded before the others could even think. 'No need to vote, if I see anyone killing a wild trout, they will have to answer to me. Agreed?'

Everyone nodded.

'One final matter,' James knew this could cause problems. 'We cannot have any further competitions. I know we have a long and rich history of monthly competitions. I'm as competitive as any man here, but they cannot continue in the current form. I suggest that instead of a monthly competition, we hold a monthly social, at which we will fish, and learn from each other. The trophy, each month will go to the person that has done the most work that month for the river and its inhabitants. This can be the finest wild trout fishery in the country.'

This request resulted in a stunned silence, as each digested the implications. Mick again came to the fore, quashing any possible dissent. 'By God, Father, you should be in Rome, Pope J.P. Brennan. I have a few good ideas on how to improve our river. Put my name on the first trophy next season. Is everyone in agreement?'

Jimmy stood and reclaimed his control as chairman. 'Gentlemen, this is the finest committee that ever sat at this table. I will do anything that's required to ensure that James's ambitious dream come true.'

Each member left a little perplexed at this sudden and unexpected turn of events.

James caught up with Jimmy in the car park. 'Thanks for going beyond the call of duty. You have honoured your debt. It will never be mentioned again. Your Father was a mean spirited man. I understand how that would have affected your judgement. He started the stocking. You have balanced the scales by putting an end to it. The circle is now closed, Amen.'

Jimmy smiled. 'He was a mean man! I hope that in time, you'll realise that all my life I have tried to make amends for his meanness.'

James shook Jimmy's offered hand. 'I have always known that, Jimmy. Next season, we will spend a lot of time together. You can count on that. By the way, the proceeds from the Popes rods will be going to the poor box.'

Chapter 25.

Monday morning, James's plan had come together and life would never be the same for the Shereen Anglers' fishing club. He walked over to the mantelpiece and turned the three trophies the right way round. They were testament to the greatest prize of his angling life. He called Maggie and asked her to dust the mantelpiece. With a renewed zest, he strode towards the church. The thought of a quick gin and tonic before saying Mass never crossed his mind.

* * *

'The Mass has ended, go in peace, Amen.'

Almost finished his duties, he strolled over to the confessional. About to sit, he noticed something on the seat; a ball of tangled nylon with a single fly attached to one end. Rather puzzled, he stuffed it in his pocket, assuming a parishioner had found it along the river and decided to leave it there for him.

A quick visit to the barbers to trim his beard, and after that, he left Clio at the garage for a long overdue service. Returning to his house, he groaned because he faced the arduous task of dealing with two months of neglected paperwork. Midway through the pile, disturbed by someone knocking on his front door, he cursed.

'Someone with a sense of fun, Father,' the postman announced as he handed over a package, pointing to the address.

He closed the door and read the address. Written in bold, black, printed letters, 'Father Sherlock Brennan. The Presbytery. Castlebridge. Co. Kildare.'

He felt the package, tracing the outline of something firm, and of unusual shape inside. Curious, he sat at the dining room table, opened the sealed bag and tipped the contents onto the table. A beautifully crafted Calabash pipe rattled, as it fell onto the surface. Astonished, he lifted it and examined the finer detail. The fishtail mouthpiece caught his attention and it brought a smile to his face. Moving down, he examined the silver band, cursing that the hallmark was too small for his aged eyes, but the stamped impression of the unique Sherlock Holmes profile made his heart skip a beat.

Sitting back, he lifted it to his lips and scratched his beard, before examining the package. No letter or note inside, nothing to indicate the sender of this rather puzzling gift. The postmark was however very clear, *Baile Atha Cliath,* Dublin in English. That narrowed it down somewhat, one and a quarter million possibilities. When you add the daily commuters and visitors, it became a proverbial needle in a haystack.

He returned to the dining room and placed the package on the mantelpiece, out of harm's way. Reaching into his pocket for his cigarettes, he squealed, as something sharp pierced his finger. The fly and the ball of nylon, he'd forgotten about them. Sucking pain and a dribble of blood from his finger, he tossed the fly and nylon on top of the mysterious package, and returned to his paperwork.

Unable to focus on the job at hand, he regularly glanced at the mantelpiece. He shoved the paperwork out of the way. Then he placed the pipe, jiffy bag and balled up nylon side by side on the table. Clearing his mind of all other thoughts, he assessed the situation. A package addressed to Sherlock Brennan, a Sherlock Holmes pipe and a ball of nylon with a fly attached. Was there a connection?

Many years earlier, he'd regularly sat at this table, playing Monopoly with old Father Mc Shane. Passing Go and collecting their two hundred, wheeling and dealing in the property market, the winner decided upon when the bottle of Scotch had been emptied. Monopoly soon became tedious and their attention turned to Scrabble. But the effects of the Scotch resulted in strange words been concocted and arguments ensued. Cluedo replaced Scrabble, and, so began James's love affair with the art of amateur detective work. 'Colonel Mustard, with the Dagger in the Dining Room. Am I right?' Soon after, he became an avid reader. Agatha Christie, Raymond Chandler, P.D. James and many others added to his growing library. His passion however was the work of Arthur Conan Doyle and his hero, the flawed Sherlock Holmes.

Lifting the pipe to his lips, he pretended to light it, inhaled and blew a spiral of imaginary smoke slowly out. *What would Holmes make of this evidence? What are the relevant details? Is it co-incidence? Or is it the work of a great criminal mind?* Placing the pipe back on the table he chuckled, *Brennan, you're not the full shilling. However the pipe might be used when I retire.* Turning his attention to the fly he examined it closely. A well tied Snipe and Purple, nothing remarkable about it. *Enough distraction!* He sighed, before he placed them back on the mantelpiece and thought no more about them.

Thursday morning, another exciting day at the altar almost complete, he happily entered the confessional booth, confident that his exit would be as swift as his entrance. All of his audience this fine October morning were of the virtuous type. The last of the Mass goers turned and wondered where the shout had emanated from. James, standing erect, reached down and lifted the latest gift off the seat. He stared at the top four inches of a fly rod. The broken second ring stuck out at an angle, the root cause of the pain in his now throbbing arse. 'Where in the name of Jesus did this come from?' he shouted before bursting out of the confessional.

He scanned the church, only to find two old ladies staring at him, their mouths wide open in shock at the profane language used by their priest. Such profanity in the house of God, they shook their heads, whispered their disdain at such irreverence and quickly left. Alone now, he sat tentatively on the nearest pew. *A bit of fun is fine. Attacking my arse with a weapon, this is war!*

Clutching the broken rod tip, he strode back to his house. About to open the door, he turned. Something clung to Clio's windscreen. He lifted a small envelope from under the wiper blade, raced indoors, and banged the door shut, sealing himself from any prying eyes.

Once again, sitting at the dining room table, he lay the envelope and rod tip down side by side. *Right Holmes, what can be deduced from this?*

He opened the unstamped envelope and teased out a folded, unremarkable piece of paper. As expected, it had been printed on a laser or similar printer.

A four inch rod is a suitable tool, for a celibate Priest fool.

M&M

He laughed at the unoriginality of the signature. Moriarty, Holmes' arch enemy.

A double M, so I face, not one, but two Fiends. That's interesting, eh Holmes? After reading the single line, he growled at the impertinence of their less than subtle reference to his manhood. He dispelled any suspicion that it was merely a disgruntled parishioner.

Laying all the evidence on the table, he went upstairs to his fly tying room and fetched his magnifying glass. Back at the table, he took out his note-book, the Holy Grail, turned to a fresh page and began his appraisal of the evidence.

Two suspects, though this may be a ruse.

A good knowledge of fly fishing. Narrows the field.

Coarse wit. That does not narrow the field much.

One at least, a refined taste and probably wealthy. The pipe is exquisite and expensive.

They are known to me.

Using the magnifying glass, he examined the fly, twisting it slowly in his hand and ensured every detail was perused. Something about the knot caught his attention. Once again he raced upstairs and returned with a needle. He teased the knot open.

Gotchya!

The divil is in the detail. Amen.

* * *

The following morning, he wasn't surprised that no further gifts lay on the confessional seat. As he waited for a penitent, hoping none would come, he pulled out one of the photos that were still in his pocket since the committee meeting. He smiled, as any angler would. It was a year since Liam had walked into the confessional and sought forgiveness. What a year it has been. Hearing the door open and close on the other side, he waited a moment and then coughed.

'Bless me, Father, for I have sinned. It has been many months since my last confession.'

James leaned a little closer to the grille. The voice had a certain familiarity, a tonal inflection that could not be disguised.

'Have you, my son, what is your sin?'

There was some shuffling the far side. 'I have lied and cheated.'

About to suggest three Hail Marys, when he heard a second voice, he stopped.

'Me as well, Father, I'm guilty of the same sins.'

This was most unusual, two people at Confession at the same time. It was rare enough to get two people in the one day, two at the same time, never. 'Are there any other sins?' he probed.

There was silence for a moment. Then they both spoke. 'The divil is in the detail, Father. We conned someone.'

'Who did you con, my sons?'

A loud laugh came from the other side. 'We conned you. Remember the oath of the confessional. What you heard here cannot be revealed. Are you coming to Lavelle's, Father. We owe you a pint?'

James flung open the door of the confessional and found Liam and Jimmy Egan falling out the other door. They looked sheepishly at James.

'Sorry, Father, we had to be sure that the stocking came to an end. Sean Lavelle suggested that you were the only man capable of getting a result, so we conned you into conning me. What do you think?' said Jimmy.

'Why all the subterfuge? Why didn't you ask me for help?'

Liam answered, 'We were previously let down by others who had claimed they were against stocking. Jimmy had threatened on several occasions to quit doing it. Those who had volunteered to take over were likely to stuff the river with diseased and unhealthy fish. We could not allow that to happen.'

James burst out laughing, 'What do I bloody think? I suspect the pair of you should've been priests. I also think that we need a drink. You pair of con artists are paying for them.'

* * *

When the pub door opened and they walked in, Sean stared at Liam and smirked when he received the thumbs up signal.

'It's a fine morning, lads! Three pints, is it?'

James banged his fist on the counter, 'Make it three and three large, and those scallywags are paying for them.'

'That would be four and four large, James, and this conspirator says they are on the house.'

James nodded, almost looking disconsolate, 'Now why does that not surprise me, Sean?' He said nothing further until the pints arrived.

Sean lifted his pint, sipped the cool Guinness and finally broke the silence, 'Fair play to you, James. With great guile and skill you put an end to the stocking. We knew you would.'

'I did, Sean. It was a job well done.' All nodded in total agreement. No more stocked, finless trout would reside in their river.

'The Sherlock bit was my idea,' Sean laughed at his own ingenuity. 'I bet you twisted and turned in your bed this past week, wondering about the M&M's. You would not have figured it out in a month of Sunday's.'

James reached into his pocket for the Holy Grail. He opened it at the last page of writing and laid it on the counter for them all to see, 'That's the difference between you and me, Sean. I have the grey matter of Hercule Poirot, you the brains of an ass.'

Liam lifted the note-book and read the page out loud. The three conspirators looked at each other, clearly wondering how he knew. Liam bravely posed the question.

'Liam, the knot on the fly you left in the confessional, you were the only one that I showed that knot to.'

Sean placed four liberally filled glasses of brandy on the counter. 'James, you're a bloody genius, but no Einstein. You figured out the Sherlock bit, fair play. As sure as a pig grunts, you never knew that you were being conned.'

James raised his hands up in mock surrender. Then lifting them to heaven and in the finest of melodic chants, he replied. 'Lord, you created Adam and Eve. You sent your only son, Our Lord, to save sinners. Then, in your finest hour, you sent your servant James P.

Brennan to educate gobshites. Sean, king of the gobshites, there is an envelope behind your till that I placed in your safe keeping a year ago. If you can read, please open it and read it out loud.'

Sean reached behind the till and pulled out the forgotten envelope, opened it and read from the page that it had contained.

'Gentlemen, for now you remain nameless.

I shall play along with your masquerade.

Liam, the divil is in the detail. By now, you know that to be true. The weeds under the willow at the bottom of Casey's field never held such a trout, and never will, for it's too close to where the cows drink.

I know not your purpose. YET!

James Brennan. November, the year of Our Lord, 2010'

James raised his almost empty pint. 'Cheers! Luckily success is not a measure of the result, but of the journey. Still, winning, too, has merit. Isn't that so? GOBSHITES! Tomorrow I'm going greyhound racing. Pup's hound has more brains that you fools.'

Chapter 26.

Mé do rug Cú Chulainn Cróga, "I gave birth to brave *Cú Chulainn*", proud words from the crest of the historical town of Dundalk, nestled to the south of the Cooley peninsula. While the peninsula is famous for the first century raid by Queen Maebh from Connacht, *The Cattle Raid of Cooley,* dogs rather than cattle were the reason for James's visit. If Castlebridge Lad lived up to the potential he showed at the trials, this priestly son of Connacht would raid the bookies.

Pup's Evan O' Leary, holding Castlebridge Lad on a tight leash, led James and Emily into the greyhound stadium. With all the appearance of a seasoned trainer, he jostled and fought a path to where he had to sign in for his first ever race.

'Father, mind the Lad while I see to the paperwork,' said Pup's.

Emily giggled as the hound tried to follow Pup's, dragging James, pulling him off balance. A sharp tug, followed by a command to sit, had other trainers turn their heads in surprise. Only an idiot would train a hound to sit. Realising his error, he grabbed the dog's collar and held firm. As if to inflict further embarrassment, the Lad sniffed James's crotch, cocked his leg and attempted to mark his territory.

'Sit ya little ... or I'll send you to hell,' he yanked the leash so hard that the Lad whimpered.

Leaning heavily on her walking stick, Emily kept a tight grip on her handbag and perused the crowd. Trainers, gamblers, vagabonds and chancers mingled, poor and wealthy alike. 'Watch out for those two by the door, pick pockets or my mother was a goat,' she said, spiting a curse in their direction.

'They, I wager are politicians handing out election leaflets,' said James. 'Watch their eyes light up with false promises, overly positive is their body language, and, there just now, watch the older one. See his head drop and his lips snarl a whispered curse. He's just been told to feck off, or worse.' A perfect gent when the mood took him, Brennan doffed his cap to two elderly ladies as they approached.

One linked the other, and possibly they had two good legs between them. Either could have been *Little Red Riding Hood's* grandmother,

94

with their eyes twinkling below wispy grey hair, they tottered towards James.

'My, my, Mary, that is a lovely dog. I wonder ...' said the one in the lemon cardigan. She grinned at Brennan and Emily. 'Oh, my, what a handsome couple and their lovely hound. Mary, the camera.'

Mary, though her eyes were wide and alert, her skin was pallid, a thin almost translucent sheath covering her ancient frame. She fumbled in her handbag and stepped closer to James. 'Young man, is there any chance, you would take a photo of your lovely wife standing with the dog and my sister? I'm too haggard, and would ruin a photo but Catherine is only ninety three, and still has her looks.'

Of all the skills learned by a priest, sweet talking the old dears flowed as easily as beer from a keg. 'I was just saying to my elderly wife that if I was ten years younger, I'd be asking the pair of you to a dance. Isn't that right, Emily?'

'Why, Horace, of course you would, and wouldn't it be a kindness to me and my poor toes. Devil knows, it was you prancing on them that left me crippled. Hand me the leash and take the camera from Mary, and take one of your tablets to settle your shakes,' said Emily, inching forward to take the leash. Leaning close to Catherine, she whispered, 'He hasn't been right since he caught a dose from a prostitute.'

'God bless you, Horace,' said Mary. She stood behind James, directing the shot. Wobbling forward, she nudged the Lad to lie down, asked Emily to remove her hat and generally acted as would a professional pain in the arse. Several minutes passed until she announced, 'Perfect! Lights, camera, action.' She stood directly behind James and waited.

With consummate skill, he pressed the auto focus button, closed one eye and positioned the camera for a perfect shot. You would swear he knew what he was doing; anything to impress the ladies. 'Say cheese!' Catherine's false teeth peeped between her lips. She raised her eyes and directed a smile straight at the lens. Emily stuck out her tongue, smiled momentarily, lunged forward and lashed out with her stick, catching James on the shoulder. A second strike whacked Mary across the head, drawing blood and a curdling scream.

'What the feck. Emily, have you lost your mind,' he said, grappling with her. He grabbed the stick as she aimed another blow.

'Let go you idiot. Where's your wallet?' she released her grip and stood defiantly between him and Mary. 'Well?'

A small crowd had gathered, circled them. Some scratched their heads, while others grinned, enjoying the unexpected entertainment.

James reached into his back pocket, finding it empty, he gasped. Raising the stick above his head, he towered over Mary. 'Do you want another?'

She rasped a curse, spat at him, and tossed his wallet on the ground. A security man burst through the crowd, still nattering into his walkie-talkie, he grabbed Mary. A second, many years his senior, buttons straining from his bulging beer belly, he grasped Catherine by her collar. They spat, they kicked and they hollered all the way to the gate.

Noticing an authoritative figure weave through the crowd, Emily stifled her mirth from seeing Brennan in a tizzy. Drawing a hand across her forehead, she moaned, swooned, and fell into the arms of management.

Poor man, he panicked, looked around for help. Supporting all of Emily's weight he shouted, 'Security, doctor ..., someone get the doctor.' He eased Emily onto the ground, took of his jacket and placed it under her head.

James raced forward and dropped to his knees. 'Emily, Emily do not leave me. My tortured soul forgives you those affairs with the gardeners, the football team and any male in uniform. Stay, Emily, I could not bear to be alone.' He sobbed, he groaned, he raised his hands to Heaven. 'Merciful God, leave her a while longer.'

A lady in the crowd wiped away tears that streamed down her face, leaving a mascara streak that melded with her lipstick. 'So sad, so sad,' she said, over and over again, till others joined the sea of sympathy that washed over those gathered.

Touched by such an out pouring of collective grief, James leant over Emily, held her wrist and whispered in her ear. 'Get up or I'll loosen your blouse.' Only a slight quickening of her pulse indicated she heard him. 'Okay, you asked for it.' He shouted, 'Give her air, for pity sake, step back. At the touch of his hand on the top button of her blouse, her eyes twitched, opened, she shot upwards, gasping for breath.

'She's alive, thank God, she lives,' shouted mascara face.

The crowd clapped, management man smiled and Emily demonstrated the most miraculous recovery ever witnessed by man or hound.

She stroked the back of the manger's hand, so light a touch that he reddened and placed his other hand over hers. 'Let's get you up to the executive lounge to wait for the doctor.'

'Oh, my kind boy, I'm so grateful. No need for a Doctor. It's not the first time the light beckoned me. I told God to feck off. Though he seemed gruffer than usual, he faded and I returned. He won't be annoying me again for a month or so. Perhaps a large brandy to celebrate my return, maybe two since I have so little time left.'

James watched her, ever amazed at her charm, her verve and bloody cheekiness. Warmth, love unfulfilled, he could do little but smirk and wish her a few more years to keep him company.

Pup's carried his papers, reading them as he meandered towards James and Emily, ignoring the grunts of those who scattered out of his way. *Beamed like Pup's*, it must surely become a cliché, for the grin he wore could not be matched.

'Fa, Fa, I mean Father, Emily, the Lad has drawn the inside trap,' said Pup's. Only then did he notice the manager, and the staring crowd 'Wha, what's going on. Is the Lad okay, is he hurt?'

'Nothing Evan, nothing at all. The Lad is rearing to go,' said Emily, winking at James. 'Give me a hug and go show them that's the best hound in the land.'

Hugs all round, even one for the confused manger. Pup's led the hound to meet their destiny, and the manager guided his strange guests to the executive lounge.

Pups became a man that evening, and Castlebridge Lad a champion. Emily lived on to taste all that life could offer, especially the brandy. James wondered if this was truly paradise, for his wallet, so nearly lost now bulged with his winnings to be shared with his friends.

Chapter 27.

A cold north easterly had been blowing incessantly for several days. James stood waist deep in the river Liffey, wishing he'd worn a second pair of underpants. Why nature chose to send such inclement weather during the first month of summer always perplexed him. Though his teeth rattled from the biting chill, he happily braved the elements, tense with expectation at the first signs of a hatch of elusive Iron Blues.

These dainty fragile insects for some obscure reason never failed to excite the curious and predatory trout. A few fish were already up and snatching the early hatchers. Soon the river would burst into song and he would hunt. Seasons could pass without presenting such an opportunity. Today, however, God smiled on his lowly servant. Rod ready, he awaited the crescendo that he knew would come.

As though a conductor had waved his baton, the river erupted. Everywhere he looked, the rings of feeding trout confirmed that this would be the highlight of his season. Just as he lifted into a back-cast, the river calmed, not a trout to be seen though an enormous hatch took place. Aborting his cast, his eyes transfixed on the river, he waited for it to begin again. All over the river the slate blue wings were visible as the flies emerged from the depths and took flight. He lit a cigarette, and through the spiralling smoke watched as the hatch diminished. Distraught that the opportunity was cruelly wrenched from his grasp, he tossed the half smoked cigarette into the river and cursed.

'Quit smoking! They are bad for you.'

Startled, James looked to-wards the bank. Standing with folded arms another angler grinned down at him.

'Where in Hell's name have you come from? Have you been there long?' James waded ashore towards the stranger, inwardly seething, now knowing why the trout had suddenly gone down.

'Not long! A few minutes I would guess. Are you a visitor? Did you catch anything? I'm Otter, by the way.'

Glaring with an intensity that would have soured butter, James exploded, 'I'm James. How many do you feckin think I caught?'

'If I fished during a fine hatch like that, I would have expected a bagful of trout. It's inexplicable why sometimes we are thwarted,' said Otter, offering a hand to James as he climbed up from the river.

Inexplicable, my arse! This idiot stands at the top of a pool and wonders why the trout have vanished. James was about to unleash his terrible temper when he noticed a glint of mischief behind the innocent smile. 'You are wrong. The trout vanished and the reason is clear. A furry gobshite called Otter scared them. Why, is the question?'

'That's easy. You're standing in my pool, Father.'

Hitting another nerve, the look on Otter's face suggested that he expected a volcanic riposte, but the word 'Father' rang Brennan's alarm bell.

'My dear furry friend, I am not of the water, not of your kind and certainly not the water dog that spawned you. Why do you call me Father?'

Otter calmly replied, 'If you were an Otter, the pool would be emptied of trout and your belly full. Though your foul tongue belies your profession, I believe you to be a disciple of Christ and a soldier of Rome. Am I correct?'

He lit a cigarette to allow time to think. Unable to see beyond the mask into the mind of this creature, he said, 'You are correct. If we were standing here during the inquisition, I would have you hauled away and tortured until you prayed for death. By what foul means have you discerned my profession and my faith?'

'I have a message for you.'

Ears perked, he rubbed his dribbling nose with the sleeve of his wading jacket and nonchalantly replied. 'What message, postman Otter and from whom?'

Taking a step forward, Otter offered his hand and laughed loudly, 'Ah, James, the message is simple. One–nil, to Doc!'

'Jesus! I should've guessed that Doc would have at least one friend. I'm James Brennan. May I shake your paw?'

'You may, and then get your arse into my pool. The trout are feeding again. I will wander downstream a bit and allow the trout to test your skills.'

For the next hour, James enjoyed fine sport. Well satisfied, he joined the watching Otter. They sat and discussed everything and anything to do with fly fishing. When Otter enquired about James's own river, the flood gates opened on thirty years of fishing stories.

After an age, when he finally ceased, Otter clapped, 'Did you really do that to Jimmy Egan?'

'We did, the best year of my life if the truth be known.'

Otter tossed a stone into the river and watched as the rings spiralled outwards. Deep in thought, he turned to James. 'All my life I

99

have yearned to write a book, but unsure of my skills, and of the tales I could tell, I never did. The conning of Jimmy Egan is too good to remain the sole property of the conspirators. Would you allow me the pleasure of narrating it, presenting it as a work of fiction to the world?'

James jumped to his feet and paced around, 'Would I let you? I'd pay you to do it. When can you start, my furry Shakespeare?'

Otter took a Dictaphone from his inside-pocket and spoke. 'To savour the delights of an artery-clogging breakfast fry-up, one must do the job properly. After dispatching a few crumbs and stray grease from his lips with a swift wipe from his sleeve, James Brennan lit his first cigarette of the day. A concerto of belches, farts and spluttering coughs confirmed him ready to face the monotonous duties that were the daily life of a parish priest.
'

He switched of the voice recorder and turned towards James. 'The opening paragraph of your opus, what do you think, James?'

Chapter 28.

'Sean, will you stop picking your nose and pull three of your finest pints. We have some business to discuss, and it's hard to concentrate when the barman is picking and flicking,' said James.

As usual, on his days off work Liam passed an hour or two in Lavelle's. Three years ago to the day, he'd been put on a three day week and still he hadn't told his wife. Quiet men can get away with anything, never attracting too much attention, adept at thinking before speaking. 'What is on your mind, James?'

James glanced at his watch, 'All in good time, Liam. Where is Egan? The bloody golf is always interfering with important matters.'

Sean guffawed when Jimmy sauntered in, sunglasses perched high over his well-tanned forehead, pink Pringle sweater over white golf slacks. 'Jesus! It's Rory. He looks even more a wanker in real life than on television. Late as usual, did your home made battery die on the golf buggy?'

'It's only a prototype. Eleven hours is far beyond anything on the market. When I get it to last for sixteen, production will begin and I will reap the rewards.'

'Amen,' said James, 'If Einstein can stay awake a little longer he will be delighted to know that I have some good news for my brothers of the Con.'

All immediately turned, they had not heard that word in a while, and silence reigned as if they were awaiting the patron saint of conmen.

He related his chance meeting with an Otter a year earlier. They listened intently, an occasional gasp as they grappled with the idea that their simple story had been transformed into a book.

When he'd finished, Sean leaned across the counter and whispered into his ear.

'That's the truth of it. Sean, you're going to be famous. There is a small problem. 'The Con', she needs to be on paper, lads. Otter did a fine job writing our story, but it's lost in Cyberspace. We have to find a publisher and I refuse to self-publish. Either it's good enough or it's not, simple as that.'

'With all due respect,' said Liam. 'Conning you into saving the river was a piece of cake, compared to getting a book published.'

'For mere mortals, yes, but for men with special skills, it's not beyond achievement.'

Sean looked blankly at the others before asking, 'What skills, Father? Does it involve murder or espionage?'

'Conning, you daft bollox. Conning skills, and we are masters. There is a website where fledgling authors can display their books. Each month they pick the top ten books and the editors make a decision to publish or not.'

Jimmy flicked a fly off his slacks. 'How do you get into the top ten?'

'It's a bit like the X-Factor or American Idol. You need votes to get to the top.' James was proud of this comparison, though not quite the truth, he knew it would catch their attention, especially Sean's.'

Busy washing some glasses, Sean remained quiet, and then he blurted, 'I once queued for the X-Factor, but chickened out at the last moment.'

'Thank God for that. I have heard you sing. Lads, Otter has put the book on the website. Register and login, locate The Con, click on 'Support the book'. Facebox the link to your friends and if they like it, they can register their support. Be sure to leave a review and no swearing or causing trouble. When the time is right, I will put a request for assistance on the fishing forum. Lads, if we don't go viral, I will give up the fags.'

Liam grinned. Every day in this priest's company involved one exciting adventure after another. 'Father, you're as daft as Basil Fawlty's brush. This will be great craic. I'll send a link from Facebook to everyone I know. It would be like having our own number one hit, count me in.'

As usual, Sean looked a little confused, but after a second explanation, he grasped the plot and sniggered like a schoolboy reading a dirty magazine, 'Mighty, another con, count me in. Hold on a minute, how much will it cost me?'

'Not a farthing, Master Scrooge, you won't have to open your safe or touch your communion money,' said Liam

Sean nodded.

'Pulitzer, Sean,' said James as he tossed a beer mat in his direction.

'Pulitzer what? I pull pints. What's a Pulitzer? Sounds like one of them girlie vodka drinks.'

'Oh, never mind,' said James raising his glass. 'To the Con, may her rise to number one be as good as a brown trout's to a mayfly.'

Liam opened the website on his phone and whistled, 'She is ranked at 5513 in the charts. Reaching the top ten will be difficult, even if we get the fishing lads supporting us.'

James banged his glass on the counter and kicked Liam's stool, 'Have I ever let you down? Please stop being as negative as a bishop. Now that the fishing season is well under way, all the lads will be in great form. This will give them something to do during the day, and won't it be better craic than discussing mad fly fishing theories, theories they have heard a dozen times before?'

'A small problem,' said Liam.

'What problem?'

'It could be a bit short, James. A novel needs to be double that size!'

James reached into his pocket and pulled out his black note-book, the Holy Grail, and placed it on the counter. 'Otter already spotted that one. The devious little furry critter has a solution. If the fishing lads pull in behind us, Otter will write our quest to reach number one into the book, as we go along. It will be like a reality TV show. Liam, the devil is in the detail.'

'Bullshit,' said Sean, 'The devil is sitting on my stool, drinking and conspiring. We may be going to hell for this.'

'James, if our aim is to get the book published, the publishers will not be impressed by our campaign. Even if the book is good enough by the time it gets to the top, they are not likely to find any humour in our approach.'

James contemplated this for a moment. He'd been so carried away on a wave of enthusiasm that he'd not reflected on this at all. 'Liam, if a trout is sipping down every mayfly that passes overhead and your fly is a perfect imitation, are you guaranteed success?'

'No, Father,' Liam replied tentatively.

'Good, would that prevent you from trying?' James leaned a little closer to Liam, demanding an immediate answer.

Liam groaned once more, 'No, James. Okay I'm with you. Let The Con Part Two begin.'

Chapter 29.

Sean hopped up out of his marital bed, rubbed his eyes and tried to figure out the source of the banging. It sounded as though it came from the back gate. He glanced at Marites as she lay on the bed, sleeping like a lamb. Immune from Sean's incessant snoring, only a bomb, or Jedward screeching on the radio, could waken her. Sean cursed as he put on his slippers and made his way down the stairs.

It had been a late night. Castlebridge had won its first championship football match in eleven years. More importantly, they had beaten their sworn enemies, the neighbouring parish of Elmwood. The heroes and their bruised and battered supporters had made their way to Lavelle's for the celebrations. Marites had to administer ice packs to several of the walking wounded and all but Larry 'The Boot' Byrne's' black eye benefited from her treatment. He wore his shiner with pride, and had refused treatment, thus ensuring, his badge of honour would not fade for at least a week. Larry had scored the winning point eleven years earlier and enjoyed being the parish hero ever since. Yesterday, however, he'd been elevated to the status of legend. Larry 'The Legend' had, with a single punch, floored the Elmwood manager. In the resulting brawl between the supporters, a few Elmwood players joined the melee and were sent off. The party had lasted until three in the morning, and Sean was knackered.

'I'm coming, for the love of God, stop banging.'

Sean made his way through the yard, opened the rusty gate a little and peered out. James shoved his way past, almost sending the startled barman flying over some empty kegs. Sean stared in astonishment as two men carrying an enormous cardboard box followed James into the yard.

'Sean, take your hands out of your pockets and help us. Right, lads, follow me.' James cleared a safe path up through the yard, all the while guiding the men. 'Left a bit, the other left, you idiot. Steady as it goes. Watch that crate of Bulmers.'

Step by careful step, the entourage made their way to the back door. The cat had retired to the flat roof over the kitchen and watched the priest, ready to flee should any missiles come in her direction.

Sean followed, remonstrating loudly. His protestations fell on deaf ears, as James was on a mission. The men came to a sudden stop at the back door, the outside step almost catching them out.

'Tilt her lads and watch the step,' One hand on the box, he reversed into the kitchen and guided them into the back room where they lay the box against the sidewall. 'Well done, lads. Sean, a pint for everyone. By the way, those are nice pyjamas. Did Marites pick them for you?'

Red faced from both embarrassment and temper, Sean did as bid. When he returned to the counter with three pints, he gasped. They had opened the box and discarded the cardboard.

Settling onto his stool, James opened the manual before grinning at Sean. 'A 64 inch, flat screen Smart TV.'

'I can see that it's a television, but what is a Smart TV? What is it doing here?'

'A Smart TV is for less intelligent people and I thought you deserved a belated wedding present. What do you think?' James wore his saint-like expression as demurely as a debutante going to a ball and waited for Sean's temper to explode.

Though not quite fully awake, he'd seen through the cloak and quietly responded. 'Father, that's very kind, though I think the living room would be a better resting place for it. Why do WE need a Smart TV?'

'The Con is climbing the charts and I thought we would make this room the centre of operations. We can get the internet on it and watch the books progress, reality TV at its best. If we can get enough people interested, you could make a fortune providing drink and food. If it goes according to plan, I will have TV crews here within two months, and you'll be the most famous publican in Ireland.' James knew that Sean required time to digest this information, so, he began to read the manual. After two pages, he was confused and texted Liam. 'Get your lazy arse over to Lavelle's. We need your technical know-how.'

One of the workmen left and returned moments later with his toolbox. Sean came around front with a bowl of cornflakes and watched their progress. They measured twice, argued incessantly and reaching a decision, they made four marks on the wall. The beefier of the two seemed to be in charge and after fitting a bit into the drill, he aimed for the first mark. He was about to drill when he turned to Sean, 'Is there any pipes in the wall?'

Cornflakes left Sean's mouth like a shower of confetti, most landing on James and the manual. 'Christ, Father, if you go through a pipe I'll never forgive you.'

'Go ahead lads. Barney Mulligan, the plumber, lives around the corner.' The drill started on James's command and Sean grimaced as they bored each hole. They had not noticed Marites arriving at the counter and once again cornflakes flew when she spoke.

'Sean Lavelle, what is going on, why all the noise and where did you get that TV?' Marites snarled in anger. Her sleep had been rudely interrupted and she'd a face on her like a cornered rat. Sean pointed to James as he shovelled another spoonful of cornflakes into his mouth.

She glared at James, 'I should've known you were behind this. You're barred for good.' As usual, she disappeared before he could respond. Once again he'd failed to get in the last word with her. She challenged him every chance she got and always remained elusive.

As the last screw was inserted into the wall, Eamon, the larger workman, turned to James and Sean, 'We require help lifting her onto the support frame.' After much heaving, grunting and cursing, they managed to fit the television. Just as James pushed the plug into the socket, Liam walked in.

'Need any help, lads?' He stared at the screen as it flickered, wondering what was going on, knowing full well who was responsible. Before James could make a speech, he cottoned on and grabbed the manual.

While Liam scanned through the pages, James paid the workmen. 'Here is an extra fifty each. I have scribbled a website name on the back of these. When you get home, Eamon, log in, sign up and support the Con. If you don't, I will be talking to your wife about the horses. If you get another twenty people to vote for it, then there is a hundred Euros for each of you.'

Liam played with the remote, going through one setting after another. Finally a box appeared on the screen.

'Sean, have you WiFi in here?'

Sean puzzled over this technical question for a moment, then grinned, 'I need to switch it on.'

James winked at Liam, 'Penny pinching again. You cannot teach an old dog, new tricks or is it a leopard ..., whatever.'

Now munching on a slice of toast, Sean returned, 'Try it now, Liam.'

Liam lifted the remote, 'WiFi passphrase please, Sean.'

Bits of toast landed on James's lap. He spelled it out one letter at a time. 'I L O V E B A R B I E' Liam keyed it and within seconds up popped Google on the screen. They howled in delight.

Liam tossed back the rest of his pint, 'Another round please, Sean. Does Marites know about Barbie?'

It took some time for Liam to get to grips with Internet viewer. After an age he brought up the publishing site in all its glory. Proudly displayed across the enormous screen was their story.

Staring at it, Sean howled, 'Look at the ranking; it's up to 3203, that's good, James, isn't it?'

'To the Con Part Deux,' James raised his empty glass, 'now let us get some support, from any quarter. I'll make sure Otter gets his furry paw out and edits the book.'

Chapter 30.

Another morning in the command centre, James was in great form. A twenty to one tip had won by five lengths, and his secret parish coffer had been blessed with nearly five grand. When he received a text his rather short fuse ignited, and he cursed so loudly that Sean almost knocked over the tourists keg, the one all the slops go in. 'What is wrong Father?'

'The book has had an agent by the name of Jack evaluate it. Jesus! There was a typo on the first line, so the agent rejected reading any further. Switch on the television. Otter has screwed up the story. I warned him that the free Irish-English translator was a false economy. He is a bloody skinflint, same as you, Sean.' He grabbed the remote, logged in to the website and showed the response from Jack. *'Interesting pitch. I'm cranky today, so the first line typo 'of/off' put me over the edge.'*

'Those English Protestants are as particular as the Irish ones. Look there, Sean, the first line, a man cannot eat his breakfast in peace.'

Sean read the chapter about ten times before he finally copped on. 'Holy St. Arthur, I see it now, he is jealous of you having a housekeeper.'

As was his habit and his prerogative, James raised his hands to heaven, 'Lord, you healed the blind, the lame and the infirm; but sent me amongst brain-dead gobshites. Finished OF, Sean, it should be finished OFF, like when the stupid jockey at the Grand National fell OFF the horse. Do you get it?'

Sean laughed, 'I get it now, similar to every Thursday when you give up drinking, by Friday you have fallen OFF the wagon. What do you intend to do? Jack is only doing his job. See his picture, he does not look like a protestant, no protestant would have a picture with a fag hanging out the corner OF their mouth, or is that OFF?'

'Sean, if he does not give our story another read, ignoring the fecked up translations and arse about tit grammar, I'll have him at confessions before the month is out. If I asked him whether he would like a pint of Guinness or a pint of Guiness, he would still bloody drink it. I will get Otter to rewrite that first paragraph. If anyone is looking for me I'm gone to the river.'

* * *

Walking downstream, he paused occasionally and poked his head out between bushes, trees and other vegetation that concealed him from the river. When his blood pressure was bordering on heart attack territory, a good walk and locating a fine trout was a far better cure than any of the chemical concoctions prescribed by the doctor.

This, as is usual, proved to be a Catch 22 situation. Locating the larger trout required stealth. Patience is a prerequisite to stealth, normal blood pressure, a prerequisite to patience. It was a test of endurance; two miles were walked before locating what he guessed was a good trout. She lay tight to the bank on his side. Peering through a bush, he watched the gentle rings each time she rose; all thoughts of Jack and grammatical correctness evaporated.

The clues were in the rings of the rise, a gentle sip as the trout leisurely took its food from the meniscus, something small and dead, probably a tiny midge. He continued to watch, noting that she fed each time the breeze ceased. She lay a yard out, just inside a few strands of weed that offered some refuge from predators. It would be an easy cast.

He withdrew, and opening his fly box he selected a suitable pattern; tied it on carefully; tested the knot and tuned into nature as only a hunter knows how. Quiet, keeping low, he edged back towards the river and poked his rod out slowly. All it would require was a gentle flick of his wrist and the fly would reach the unsuspecting trout.

Waiting for that small window of opportunity when the breeze would cease, he tensed with anticipation. Staring intently at ripples on the surface and feeling the caress of the breeze on his weathered face, he silently prayed for a positive outcome. It was a magical moment. The river transformed, as though the hand of God had decreed calm. Just as he prepared to cast, the phone announced the arrival of a text. 'Ouch!', his head struck a branch as he shot upwards.

'Sorry, Father, a lot of commas missing, will fix ASAP. Otter'

Every trout for five hundred yards scuttled for safety as James exploded into a tirade of abusive language, his blood pressure at a record high. *Commas, bloody missing, misplaced commas. Otter wouldn't recognise a comma even if one jumped up and bit him on the arse.* He furiously typed a return text and shoved the phone back into his pocket.

'Go back to school comma learn some grammar comma eat commas comma drink commas comma or I will shove my boot comma up where the sun does not shine FULL STOP'

Walking back upstream, he contemplated the boundaries of his universe, shocked at the realisation that it was an insignificant corner of an insignificant island on the edge of Europe. Their story wasn't receiving worldwide acclamation at the pace he expected. Clearly, his myopic view of how it would be received beyond his world had been ill conceived. That his central position in his own parish held little sway elsewhere shook the foundations of all he held dear. Dropping to his knees, tears freely flowing down his cheeks, James actually prayed, well, almost. Staring up at the darkened sky, 'Lord, please guide this old fool. You were friends with fishermen, and must have had a few tales to tell. Shine your light upon your servant and guide our book to the printing press. Amen.'

Light, glorious beams of sunlight, streamed from the heavens and shone down on this humble priest. A booming voice behind startled him such, he almost shat himself.

'Father, you dropped your fags.'

He leapt to his feet, wiped away the tears and turned. 'Jimmy, you nearly gave me a heart attack. I was searching for them, thanks.'

'Was that you screaming like a wounded fox, less than half an hour ago? I thought someone was being murdered.'

'Murder, screaming, not I, but I could murder a pint. I haven't had a chance to have a chat with you recently. What do you think about the book? You have an enormous library! Could it grace the shelf of one such as yours?'

Strolling back towards their cars, Jimmy responded, 'A million dollar question, James. Anglers will easily identify with the story, a bit of fishing and a bit of craic. They are used to reading 'How to Fish' books. A fishing story? Yes, it would be highly prized during the close season, when the long dreary nights see anglers dreaming of caddis flies dancing on a summer breeze.'

'I'll meet you in Lavelle's. We will discuss this further.'

* * *

Daydreaming, he walked in the front door of the pub. James chastised himself for being so careless. Sean was leaning on the back counter, and working furiously at the remote control. James caught only the merest glimpse of two busty naked females just as the screen changed to Google. Sean, as would a guilty school boy, muttered incoherently, placed the offending remote control on the counter and began filling a pint.

'Make that two pints, you dirty little barman. What were you looking at?'

'Not a thing, Father. Terrible, the adverts they put on television these days. I'm having awful trouble with the gout to-day.'

'Is that so, the gout, swollen big toe, is it? I might be a priest, maybe a useless priest, but don't take me for a fool. That smart television is for watching The Con, not for the satisfaction of your sexual appetites.'

'Sex did you say, Father, I have been meaning to talk to you about that,' said Jimmy. Neither had noticed Jimmy's arrival. 'Our story has plenty of fishing, but we need some sex for balance.'

Furious, James shook his head, 'Lads, you're two married men. You should be ashamed of yourselves. No sex, that's final.'

Jimmy casually asked, 'Why James? Are carnal appetites too much for you? I was thinking, if we had a durty sex scene we could tick more boxes and would entice a few more readers.'

Sean retreated towards the till. A barman's instinct warns when a storm is brewing. Not for him to interfere. James plucked at his beard, knowing that this was a realm of human experience in which he was an outsider for too many years. Jimmy's point was well made, justifiable perhaps.

'Jimmy, you talk to Otter, Sean and Liam. I will trust you to make a decision. I cannot be involved, nor should I be.'

Sean edged a little closer to the counter, 'I thought you would invoke the Saints and send us to eternal damnation. There was a sexual act out on the lane this morning. I was changing a keg around 2 AM, when I heard all sorts of panting and puffing outside the back gate. The Disco would have just ended, and a bit of cuddling in the lane would not be unusual. This sounded a bit more robust, so, being the good citizen that I am, I chose to investigate. We have to make sure the young fellas behave themselves, don't we, Father?'

'Voyeur, more like,' suggested James.

Sean stiffened at this libellous comment.

'Let me finish the story. I could not believe that they were doing it in the lane. It wasn't natural what they were up to. I was gobsmacked and I had to put an end to it. Was I right to do that, lads?'

'Good for you, Sean. Thank God you were out the back yard. What did you do?' James was sitting on the edge of his stool. Biting at the bit to find out how Sean dealt with the situation.

'I did the only thing I could do as they ignored my shouts. I gave the buck a kick up the arse and they ran away.'

'Well done,' James shook his head. The morals of the parish were going to ruin, a sermon next Sunday would be necessary. 'Did you know who they were? If I have a word with their parents, we can put a stop to it. Maybe they were only drugged up and losing the run of themselves.'

'No! It wasn't the drugs. I recognised them all right. I don't know who their parents are, and I doubt they know either.'

Hearing this, James's heart softened a little, 'Were they orphans? Or possibly they were from a broken home? That could explain such behaviour in public, who were they?'

'I know that both are from good homes. They are over-loved if anything. You know them as well, Father. I don't know if it would be fair for me to tell you.'

James leaned over the counter, grabbed Sean's arm and twisted it violently, 'Tell me or I'll snap your scrawny arm.'

Sean pleaded for him to let go, 'Stop, I'll tell you, let go, Father. It was Josie O Malley's Alsatian having a go at Agnes Clohessy's poodle.'

'For fucks sake, Sean, you're a right clown,' shouted Jimmy, as he and James convulsed with laughter.

When they calmed, James resumed rubbing his beard. 'Sean, you're barking mad, yet, possibly the cleverest hound in the parish. A solution to our problem; a sex scene for the book, another genre ticked.'

Sean beamed, obviously choosing only to hear the compliment. While James and Jimmy discussed this addition to their Opus, he brought up the publishing website. The ranking was static, had been so for a few days.

'No movement, Father, she is like a sheep bleating, trying to be heard amongst thousands of similar bleats.'

James did not seem overly concerned, 'Lads, Otter has a lot of work to do as the book is in its infancy. Like presenting a dry fly to a trout, timing is everything, stealth equally important. Otter will interact with his literary brothers. They are the key to getting to the top. When the book is ready we will cast our own die and unleash our brothers of the angle. Jesus! I'll be late for Mass.'

'Tragedy, Father, another genre, it would be tragic if you were late for Mass,' Jimmy watched as James hurriedly made for the back door, bemused, amused and utterly confused. 'Sean, I need a holiday!'

* * *

Sleep wasn't coming easy to James that night. He tried counting sheep, swapped pillows; hid under the duvet cover, had a fag, and considered a gin, but all to no avail. Their quest to try and reach the top of the pile; the fellowship of The Con was floundering on an ebbing tide. Something needed to be done, but what?

At all costs, he'd avoided following the fickle world of celebrity, but no matter how one tried, it could not be avoided. Adverts, newspapers and chat shows were daily feeding the masses. He flicked on the bedside light and thumped the pillow, his shout echoing around his small bedroom 'That's it! Controversy, we need controversy.' On a small scale, it had followed him all his life. The solution was as alarming as it was exhilarating. 'Scandal! We need a scandal,' he exclaimed out loud, as he punched the air.

* * *

The following morning he went to the newsagents to buy a packet of cigarettes. When the proprietor, Una Mahon, asked how he was, he grunted, 'Not well at all! Someone has put out a malicious rumour that I had an affair with a married woman and that I'm about to become a Father for the second time. What would I know about fathering a child? To make matters worse, there are rumours that some gutter press reporter is going to write a book about it. He turned and quickly strode out the door before a shocked Una could respond.

God knows what he'd just unleashed, for she could carry news as quick as the internet, certainly faster than a carrier pigeon. Grinning as he strolled home, he contemplated his next move and decided that Sean, Jimmy and Liam would be contacted first, and the Bishop last.

He sent Jimmy and Liam a short text message, 'AWOL for at least a week. Any1 asks, you don't know where I am. Any1 asking about me or the book, you know nothing, OKAY. Father B.'

He then rang Sean. Twice, he gave the same instructions and added one additional order. 'If any stranger comes into the pub enquiring after me, get their name and text me.' Finally, he sent an email to his Eminence, stating that he'd a bad viral infection and would be out of action for a fortnight.

Jesus! I nearly forgot about Maggie.

He rang Maggie, told her that some nasty individual was spreading untrue rumours about him, and that he was going away for a week. Maggie started sobbing. It took an age to calm and assure her that it was all a mistake. She believed he was innocent, yet she feared the inquisition of the gossipers. Knowing that he could not allow this to happen, a spontaneous and daring offer was made. 'Maggie, will you come on holidays with me?'

Chapter 31.

May 19th.
Like the soft, barely audible rustle of bronzed leaves caressed by an autumnal breeze, it began! Penetrating the acutely aware minds of the adepts, its hosts and carriers, it gathered form. Empowered now, the rustle grew stronger, becoming a whisper, stealing up alleyways; into homes and shops. It knew no favour, and Castlebridge was its epicentre. With each cycle of the moon, the whisperings grew, reaching outwards, gathering strength. Forever mutating, its progress relentless, uncontrollable and random, for not all minds could be carriers. Within days, the neighbouring parishes of Elmwood, Longthorn and many others had succumbed to the growing infection.

10 AM May 24th.
Kate Kelly, the postmistress in Elmwood, paused as she expertly counted a wad of notes. It was Friday, pension day and a queue of four almost reached the front door. 'What did you say, Eileen? Someone has written a book about Father Brennan from Castlebridge?'

Eileen nodded, 'That's what I heard yesterday at the hairdressers in Castlebridge. I was getting a perm when I overheard one of the assistants telling Agnes Quinn. The drier was on. My hearing, the way it is, I could only make out small bits of the conversation.'

Kate finished counting, stamped the pension book before handing all back to Eileen. 'Here you go. Will you be at bingo tonight?'

'I won't, Kate, the knees are at me. I'll stay in and watch the Late Night Show on the television.'

Slowly the queue dwindled until Emma Ahern finally arrived at the counter. 'Good morning, Kate, soft day! I'll have another money transfer for Mikey, fifty Euros, please.'

Kate prepared the documents for the money transfer. Emma had been sending money to her useless son for over four months. The idle layabout Mikey, like his father before him, bled Emma dry.

'Has he still not found any work in New York, Emma?'

'No, times are hard out there as well. I lit two candles at Mass this morning, God will see his way to finding him employment, wait and see.'

This was very unlikely. Mikey could smell work coming a mile away. Allergic to it, he would be long gone before it arrived on his doorstep.

'Speaking of Mass, did you hear someone has written a book about the priest in Castlebridge, Father Brennan?'

'No, what is it about? I hope there is no sex or scandal in it, is there?'

'There could be, for all I know, maybe he is having an affair with a married woman.'

A devout Catholic, Emma blessed herself before carefully placing what was left of her pension money into her purse. 'That's shocking, a priest and a married woman, what is the world coming to? Goodbye, Kate.'

After leaving the post office, Emma shuffled up the street towards the small supermarket, calculating how much she could afford to spend on groceries. Lost in thought, she almost bumped into Noeleen Lynch, Paddy the bus driver's wife.

'Sorry! Noeleen, I was away with the faeries, in another world I was.'

'Not to worry, Mrs Ahern, sure don't we all have our own worries? Poor Paddy does not know from one week to the next if he will have work. It's a struggle, no denying that, but worrying only produces wrinkles and solves nothing.'

Worry had followed Emma all her life, yet she still managed an occasional wry smile. 'You are right, Noeleen, and you should tell that to Father Brennan of Castlebridge. The poor man has the weight of the world on his shoulders.'

'Why? I'm keen to hear what ails that vile man.'

'Oh, a married woman, and someone is writing a book about it.'

Noeleen's eyes lit up, leaning a little closer to Emma, she whispered, 'Is there a love child?'

'There might be, I suppose there must be, if a book is coming out. I'd better be going. Goodbye, Noeleen; tell Paddy I hope his job is safe.'

Noeleen bit down on her lip. Her own brother Samuel had been an altar boy and a victim of child abuse. Fourteen long years her family had battled for justice, it came, but too late for Samuel. He was at peace now, in the cemetery in her home parish, at the top of the hill

115

that overlooked the church where he'd been abused by another Father.

7 AM, May 25th.

Paddy Lynch had been a bus driver for twenty six years. A people person, he enjoyed the company of his passengers, and they, his. Nuala O'Grady travelled to Dublin every Monday, returned on Friday evening and always occupied the front seat near him. She was a waitress at one of Dublin's finest hotels and a daughter of one of Paddy's closest friends. Despite the generation gap, conversation flowed easily between them.

'Nuala, have you heard about Father Brennan of Castlebridge?'

'No, who is he? You know I never go to Mass, boring!'

'They say he'd an affair with a married woman.'

She looked up, her eyes bleary and bloodshot from staring at her Smartphone, 'Soooo yesterday, a priest using his willy for more than pissing rubbish from a pulpit, boring!'

'They say there is a child involved and someone is writing a book about it.'

'Love child, imagine being a priest's son or daughter. How boring is that. Now, if there were some raunchy sex scenes in the book, it might be worth investigating. What did you say his name was again? Father Bunyan? OMG, maybe he is a transvestite. That would be so cool!'

Paddy laughed, 'If only your father knew half of what went through the mind of his little angel, he would be shocked. Nuala, you're depraved. His name is Father Brennan.'

'Right, Brennan as in Brennan's bread,' she texted all her friends, 'Anyone come across true book about a raunchy, transvestite priest from Castlebridge, fathering a child with a married woman, Father Brennan.'

7:30 AM May 25th

Padraig Gallagher walked through Ryanair's departure gate at Dublin airport, ready to board a flight to London Heathrow. Carrying only a bottle of water and his phone, he hurried across the concourse and secured a good seat near the front. This was his eleventh business trip to London this year, the first year of his working life. The novelty had long since worn away, and a mind blowing hangover wasn't the best start to the week. As the plane filled, any hope of having a row of seats to himself quickly evaporated.

When a tall, middle aged, silver haired man slid into the adjacent seat, he inwardly groaned. He wasn't in any humour for idle conversation. *Fuck the weather, fuck politics and fuck this hangover.* While the air hostess, carrying her cardboard grin and tatty lifejacket, demonstrated the complicated process of pulling a cord and blowing into a tube, he checked his text messages. The two from colleagues could wait until the hangover rescinded, as could the three from customers. Nuala's brought a welcome smile.

He watched as everything shrunk, ant-like cars in a long progression, carrying their commuters to their daily toil. The Irish Sea beckoned. How many trawlers and ships could he spot before the clouds sealed them from the world below? He traced the progress of a lone trawler, and when a ferry, probably bound for Liverpool was spotted, panic took hold. He could feel it developing deep in his bowels, a slight cramping of the muscles, his worst nightmare. Eight pints of Guinness on top of a Chinese meal had an inevitable outcome, wind.

As the pressure built, he contemplated a trip to the toilet, grimaced when he noticed his way both fore and aft were blocked by the air stewards and their trolleys. His degree in physics only made the situation worse. In any contained system, the valve will be designed to withstand a precise pressure. His valve was at breaking point, and the more he tried to squeeze it closed, the faster the pressure built. Turning the cheeks of his arse towards the window, the valve failed. The long thunderous fart gave immediate release and embarrassment was instant and unavoidable. Without turning, he knew that dozens of eyes cast in his direction, seeking out the perpetrator.

'Better out than in, I always say,' the silver haired man whispered without turning his head.

Reaching across with an outstretched hand, he introduced himself, 'Father Xavier. It's not common knowledge; even the pontiff has to fart occasionally. Too much garlic with his pasta, I fear.'

A very self-conscious Padraig reluctantly turned, shook hands and grinned, 'Sorry about that, Father. You know the Pope, like personally? I'm Padraig, by the way.'

'Good name, after St Patrick, I presume. I love the Gaelic version, more musical than the anglicised one. Yes, I know the Pope quite well. In fact I will be meeting him this evening. After a short stop in London, I travel on to Rome. Perhaps I will tell him that I met St Padraig on a flight from Dublin, and that he suffers from a similar affliction, flatulence. The Pope has a good sense of humour, and sadly, few know that.'

117

Padraig relaxed, he was obviously in the company of a VIP priest. This was a welcome change from being sandwiched between two overweight, over pressed suits. 'It's an awesome co-incidence that you're the second priest that crossed my path this morning. The first I'm sure would find less favour with your boss, his behaviour, definitely not humorous.'

'Is that so, Padraig, do I know this priest?'

Padraig switched back on his phone and showed Father Xavier the text. From my girlfriend, Nuala, and it's probably a load of nonsense. What do you think?'

Father Xavier nodded and laughed loudly, too loudly, 'Rumours, malicious rumours that are unlikely to be true. If you don't mind, I will close my eyes and rest as I have a long day ahead.'

10 AM May 25th

Father Xavier quickly typed a text as he sat in a black London taxi en route to Westminster.

'Need dossier on Father James P. Brennan, Castlebridge, Ireland. Leave on my desk. URGENT. Xavier.'

Chapter 32.

Father Xavier was pleased to be back in Rome. Before opening the dossier that lay on his desk, he poured a small measure of Jameson Gold Reserve into a crystal glass. As much as he loved Rome, this small vice provided a regular reminder of his Irish heritage.

The orange sticker on the front cover caught his eye as the whiskey slipped over his tongue, gently warming his throat. All the files in his care concerned priests that had transgressed; orange for those whose misdemeanours were persistent, but not a major threat to the well-being of the church. *Hmmm my friend, your dossier seems rather obese; you have rocked the boat more than once I fear!* He shivered, as though some malevolent spirit crossed over him. It had happened once before in similar circumstances. But for him, the Church would have fallen in chaos. *Okay, Brennan, what fires have you started?*

Xavier lifted his silver cross, pressed it to his lips. *Sit incipiam* 'Let it begin. Amen!' Rituals played a vital role in his approach to his vocation as the Vatican's fire-fighter. He placed the whiskey glass on the left of the dossier, his note-book and gold pen on the right. He glided to the front of his desk and looking at the cross motif on the tiled floor, he silently prayed. With the deftness of a ballerina, he walked the outline of the cross, never once misplacing a step. After another silent prayer, he returned to the desk and sat. Inhaling deeply, he cleared his mind of all thoughts. When he could no longer hold his breath, he exhaled loudly. Now he was ready for whatever challenge faced him.

Methodically, he read every single page of the dossier, stopping only when he could not prevent his mirth from turning to outright laughter. He lifted his pen and wrote in his diary. 'James Brennan – ROGUE, guilty of breaking all of the seven deadly sins, regularly!'

There was nothing in the dossier to warrant further investigation yet instinct told him otherwise. The shivery feeling that he'd experienced earlier was a clear warning. Returning to the beginning he read the first page, a synopsis on Father Brennan. There it was, easily skipped over, a single fact. 'Vocation: NO' He admonished himself for being so careless. Xavier understood the significance of that simple fact, for his own dossier contained the same and it was he who had insisted many years earlier that this be included on the synopsis form for every single priest. A priest without vocation invariably needed to channel their angst, their bitterness and inevitable loneliness. *Has Brennan passed from rogue to villain?*

'Augustus,

Father Brennan, Castlebridge, Kildare. Rumours of affair with married woman, love child. Transvestite perhaps – need I be concerned?

Xavier'

He finished his whiskey and sent a second email, addressed to Brennan's Bishop, the Archbishop of Dublin and the Papal Nuncio.

'RE: Rumours circulating concerning Father Brennan, Castlebridge. Don't intervene. The matter is being handled by Rome. Forward any information received directly to me.

Father Xavier,

Nullum sine fumus igne. 'There is no smoke without fire.'

He made a final entry into his diary, 'Father Brennan ???'

Physically and mentally exhausted, he glanced at his watch as he closed the dossier and gratefully made his way to his apartment overlooking St. Peters square.

Chapter 33.

Gus O'Loughlin sat at his desk, typing the last few lines of his latest scoop. An investigative reporter for The Midland Chronicle, his current status was far removed from the illustrious position he once held in Dublin when he worked for a national broadsheet. Still he enjoyed his work, happy in the knowledge that switching to a less tempting environment had saved his marriage.

Week's earlier, three dozen sheep had disappeared from a local farm, right from under the farmer's nose, one Henry Bradshaw. It wasn't unusual for the occasional sheep to disappear under the cloak of darkness, but during the day it was a rare event.

Henry claimed that he'd spent all morning fixing a fence alongside his house. Early afternoon, he made the second of three daily checks on the livestock. Not a single sheep could he find, not even the pet lamb. A full investigation took place, but no one could determine how they could have vanished into thin air. Within a week, various theories were put forward, blaming everyone from an Eastern European sheep rustling ring to the faeries. As usual, a UFO sighting was offered as the most likely answer.

Gus solved it within five hours, at a total cost of one hundred and forty Euros and an unmerciful hangover. He'd visited the pub nearest to Bradshaw's farm at four pm. It was hardly a feat of genius to establish which punter was the local drunk and before long, he was quenching both their thirsts with large whiskeys. Packy had gratefully downed the whiskeys as though water. By the end of the second bottle, his tongue had loosened and a direct question was fired from one very unstable ship across the bow of another.

'Packy, you seem like a man of great intelligence. Where are the missing sheep? That UFO story is a load of bollox!'

'What mussing sheeps? There's no mussing sheeps. Packy noses where they are.'

Packy pointed to his nose and laughed loudly.

'They were only tourists at Bradshaw's and Packy noses that.'

By the time Gus teased the full story out of him, they were both pissed. All in a day's work, someone has to take the pain for the cause.

A cute hoor, Bradshaw had borrowed the sheep from a farm forty miles away, so he could get a subsidy from the EEC.

'Packy noses everythung. Would you have a spare fag?'

Ace reporter Gus had triumphed again. Yet he yearned for a real story, one that would raise his profile to be once again lauded and appreciated at a national level.

Such a possibility was presented sooner than expected as he read the email from his older brother Xavier. Castlebridge was only thirty miles away. If there was dirt to be had on Brennan, no stone would be left unturned in finding it.

2 PM May 26ᵗʰ

Driving twice up and down the main street of Castlebridge, Gus quickly came to the conclusion that it was a typical Irish village. The church commanded the skyline and probably a lot more besides. A small supermarket with its garish neon sign sat alongside the petrol station at one end. The requisite corner shop was exactly where it should be, no doubt peddling newspapers, Mass-cards and sweets. Three pubs, one flanked by a clothes shop on one side, the red and white barber's pole marking the use of the building on the other. It was likely that the undertaker was in close proximity, most likely down one of the side streets.

Gus parked near the church and placed the corner shop under surveillance. It was just after 2 PM and, if his lifetime experience in being a fly on the wall held true, then the lunchtime customers would dwindle away soon enough.

At two fifteen, Una Mahon smiled as the bell on the door announced the arrival of another customer. Gus flicked through a few magazines, acutely aware that the middle aged lady behind the counter held him in her gaze. After a few minutes, he sauntered up to the counter.

'Good afternoon. By any chance, would you stock Hamlet cigars? Surprisingly, they don't have any in the supermarket.'

'Of course they don't! Cheap tobacco and stale bread is all they sell. You have come to the right place.' She took a box from the shelf and placed them in front of Gus. 'That comes to Six Euros and seventy five cents please.'

As Gus counted some loose change, he pointed to an apple tart, 'Would that be homemade? My poor old mother used to bake ones just like that. It's hard to find a nice apple tart these days. All those mass produced ones taste like toasted toilet paper.'

Una beamed, 'Baked in my own AGA oven before I opened the shop this morning. My tarts have won prizes at the county fair, you'll not find better. You have a good eye. Most people don't know the difference. Is your mother still alive?'

'Oh, I wish she were. Cancer took her two years ago and I have not tasted proper apple tart since. My own wife tried to bake one a month ago. Bless her kind heart, but not even the dog would take a slice.'

'I'm sorry to hear about your mother. Young ones, they have it too soft these days. If they spent more time looking after their husbands properly, there would be fewer divorces. I see them every day, pulling up outside the supermarket in their SUV's and filling their trolleys. You would think they had won the lottery. It's disgraceful the way they flounce around, in their high heels and designer clothes.'

Gus responded with a smile that would charm the darkest of hearts. 'You are so like my own mother. God rest her soul! I'm Gus by the way. Thank God the supermarket did not have Hamlet cigars, else I would not be eating apple tart tonight made by a fine looking woman like yourself.'

Una blushed under her layers of mascara as she adjusted her apron and flirted with her aged eyes. 'I'm Una. My poor late husband was a charmer like you, though not as good looking. I'm closing the shop in five minutes and there is a tart warming in the oven. There is nothing more manly than the aroma of a cigar. Go in the back and I'll make you a nice cup of tea and tart.'

Shit! How do I get out of this? Gus winked at her, 'That sounds like a date. I don't know if my wife would approve of me having tart with a fine woman like you. It would make her very jealous, but sure there is no harm in having a little tart in the afternoon.'

Gus lifted his box of Hamlet, moved behind the counter and squeezed past her. She purred as her ample bosom brushed against him as he passed. Gus shivered as he settled onto the edge of a small settee in the backroom. It had been a while since he'd found himself in such a predicament. *All in the line of duty, Gus,* he tried to convince himself of his motives, and lit a cigar.

She glided into the small sitting room. The full length apron was gone, revealing a mature, but yet very sexy figure. Gus could not make eye contact. *Gus, for the love of God, get a grip of yourself.*

'Gus, you make yourself comfortable. I'll put on the kettle,' she purred once more, and with the twirl of her hips, she slid into the adjacent kitchen.

When she returned carrying an ashtray and sat on the settee as close to Gus as possible, he inched forward almost falling off the edge. With the ashtray provocatively balanced on her knee, below her plaid skirt, she whispered, 'Gus, your wife is so lucky to have you all to herself. That's very selfish of her.'

Her hand inched towards his knee. *Use your brains, Gus, not your balls.* 'Una, you seem like an intelligent lady. As much as I look forward to your tart, you may be able to help me,' unable to take his eyes of her slender fingers stroking his lower thigh, moving upwards.

'Yes, Gus, anything,' her eyes now firmly locked with his, her hands still working as though they had a mind of their own.

'Do you know Father Brennan?'

With a horrified look she sat upright. The ash tray fell off her knee and broke into a thousand shards of glass when it shattered on the tiled floor. Panicked, she raced to the kitchen and returned wearing another apron and swept up the glass. The moment had gone and all Gus could think was *Thank Fuck!*

Standing in the middle of the room with her arms folded, she glared at him. 'Father Brennan, did you say? That dirty old man, a child with a married woman half his age. Imagine that, a married woman and he, a priest. The scandal has rocked the parish and poor widows like me have to lock our doors at night in fear.'

Afraid of raising her passions once more, Gus took a gamble, 'That's terrible! Afraid and locked up in your own house because a sex fiend is on the loose. Have you ever thought of taking in a lodger? That would protect you from that animal. Has he done anything like this before?'

She was lost in thought, her mind obviously chewing over the possibilities of having a male lodger. Eventually, she returned to reality and with much venom, she spat, 'He is the devil himself, a wolf dressed as a priest. Half his life is spent in Lavelle's pub, the other half gambling and whoring and up to God knows what other debauchery. You did not hear that from me. I hate gossips, but the world ought to know about that vile man.'

'Where would I find him?' asked Gus.

She looked at her watch, 'Mother of God, look at the time, the shop should be opened.' She strode out to the shop with Gus following like a lap dog. She bundled two tarts and another packet of Hamlet into a shopping bag and handed them to him. 'Tell your wife thirty seconds in the microwave is just right. Try Lavelle's pub.'

Gus leaned across the counter and gently kissed her on the cheek, 'Una, you're a wonderful lady, if I were single ...'

3 PM May 26th

Kicking off his sandals, James lay down at the base of a sand dune, enjoying the warmth against his cheeks. He tipped the brim of his straw hat downwards, cutting out the strong sunlight, and looked over the tips of his wiggling toes. All along the beach, families frolicked, building sandcastles, fathers playing ball with children; kites rising and diving on the sea breeze.

He smiled as he spotted a Springer Spaniel race through the foam and launch into the breakers. Only its head and back were visible, as it swam outwards with purpose. Its progress was watched by a young boy, who stood by the edge of the sea. The bobbing head moved outwards until it surged and turned, carrying something in its jaws. The spaniel almost surfed back on the coming tide, racing forward with each breaking wave. Dancing across the dark damp sand, it shook the water from its fur into rivulets of sparkling diamonds. Ears flapping wildly, it dropped the Frisbee at the lad's feet.

Turning to his side as warmth not experienced in years washed over him, he spoke quietly, 'Maggie, I think I'm falling in love!'

Maggie giggled as she leaned over and punched him affectionately, 'James, it's never too late, but the collar will have to go!'

'Ah, Maggie, the collar is welded to me. A wild, steamy affair is about all I could offer. What do you think?'

Lifting up her sunglasses, she leaned towards him and raising up an elbow, she gazed at the grizzly old man thirty years her senior.

'God knows, the chins are already wagging at our joint absence. James, you should never have been a priest.'

She lay back, staring across the beach and laughing.

'Here comes Joseph and the kids, with the ice-cream cones. My goodness, look at Elise. It's dripping all over her chin.'

For the first time in all the years he'd come to Enniscrone on holidays, he shared an ice cream and the simple delight almost made him weep with joy. Asking Maggie and her family to accompany him had been a masterstroke, but his ingenuity had not anticipated that it would affect him the way it did. Hopping to his feet, he rubbed away the ice cream that clung to his beard and shouted, 'Come on kids, time to fly the dragon kite with Uncle James.'

Chapter 34.

3:30 **PM** May 26th

A bundle of tissues lay on the front seat of Gus's car. He'd devoured one of the apple tarts. He wiped the last streak of apple from both chins and tossed the tissue on the growing mound. A glance at the mirror confirmed that he'd cleaned the crease between them, and licking his lips he thought, *that was nice. I'll give the second one to mother.* He hopped out of the car, brushed away the stray crumbs from his clothes and strode towards Lavelle's pub.

The outside facade suggested that it was a traditional man's pub, untouched by the Celtic Tiger and Bacardi Breezers, his type of establishment. Inside the dimly lit and sparsely furnished bar, a single customer at the counter slouched on one elbow over a glass, his other hand to his rear, scratching his behind. He looked up at Gus, grunted, then took a sip of air from the glass and banged it on the counter. Gus smiled. This would be too easy. He walked past him and pulled out the adjacent stool, its cast iron legs grating on the stone floor. The mark looked up through his glazed alcoholic eyes and spat on the floor in front of Gus.

'That's Gerry's stool.'

'Oh, sorry, is he gone out?'

The mark's was the only glass on the counter.

'Nope, he won't be in today. His dole money has run dry. No mon, no fun!'

Gus leaning on the stool quickly replied, 'Dole day was only yesterday, wasn't it?'

The mark gagged and spat again, 'That's the truth. Try telling the government fuckers. You couldn't get half a hangover on what they pay us. Shower of lazy bolloxes.'

'You're right about that, I lost my job three months ago and I haven't got a cent out of them. Can I rent Gerry's stool? It looks well-worn and experienced. Would a pint and a half one cover the expense for an hour or two?'

The mark opened his mouth and grinned through his single tar stained tooth, 'A temporary arrangement while you keep the stool warm for Gerry.' He banged his glass on the counter and shouted, 'Marietta, a pint and a Paddy, and whatever my friend, GT, requires. I'm Mouse, Mick the Mouse. What name will I put on the rent book?'

Before he could reply, Marites arrived. With elbows sticking out defiantly, she glared at them. 'Mouse, if you ever shout like that again, I'll tie your tail to the back of the bread van.

Mouse doffed his imaginary hat. 'Begging your pardon, Marietta, but the taxman here has a rebate for me and insists on me buying him a drink with it.'

Gus struggled to keep the apple pie below deck. Laughing, he ordered two pints and two Paddy's.

Marites looked at Gus suspiciously, shook her head in resignation, poured the drinks, took payment and glanced back over her shoulder before returning upstairs.

'Cheers, GT,' said Mouse, as he did a Houdini with the whiskey before Gus had placed the change into his pocket.

Gus sipped, weighing up how best to proceed. He decided to play it by ear and seize an opening when it came. Mouse was a strange fish for sure, but Gus had detected a sharpness and underlying intelligence that suggested that he would not be a pushover. This diagnosis was quickly confirmed.

'Have you lived in Castlebridge all your life?'

Mouse replied, a steel resonance to his squeak, 'Who says I live here?

'Do you?'

'I might, depends who is asking.'

Gus inwardly groaned. It was going to be a long afternoon and his stomach did not feel in the best of order. 'Only making conversation with my landlord's drinking partner. Where is the harm in that?'

'Are you from the dole office?'

'No'

'Prove it!'

'How can I prove it?'

Mouse scratched his tooth as he seemed to consider GT's identity crisis. 'Show me your hands.'

'Feck off, what would that prove? Go away and eat some cheese.'

He stood and raised his fists, 'Fucking dole man, show me your hands or I'll beat the bejesus out of you.'

Gus could have knocked him over with half a feather, but acquiesced for the sake of peace. Mouse carefully examined Gus's hands before making his judgement, 'No biro marks, but your hands are soft. Are you a priest?'

Gus pounced on the Mouse. 'Lord, no, if you want me to prove it, we can go up to the church and ask the local priest.'

'Can't.'

'Can't what? Would you spit it out, Mouse?'

Mouse spat on the floor and grinned, 'Can't, Father Brennan isn't around.'

'How do you know? Were you at Mass this morning?' *not bloody likely.*

Mouse rasped, coughed for at least a minute and spoke as though laryngitis had set in, 'I need a packet of fags and a pint to wash it down. Any chance of some rent in advance?'

Marites was summoned, cigarettes and drink purchased, and while Mouse polluted the street, Gus loosened his tie and hung his jacket on the back of the stool. He'd finally met his match.

'You were saying something about Father Bacon,' said Gus when Mouse returned.

'Was I?' double spit. 'Father Brennan you mean, are you half deaf or something?' a third of a pint sunk. 'What about him?'

Gus took off the tie, stuffed it in his jacket pocket and opened the top button of his shirt.

'What are you doing? Marietta doesn't allow strippers in this joint. You're not going to get frisky or something. I'm no queer.'

'Who said you were? What about Brennan?'

Mouse looked long and hard at Gus, opened his mouth, rolled his tongue over his tooth and looked as though a lengthy speech was imminent. Gus leaned a little closer, ready to receive data, be it intelligent or otherwise.

'Back in a minute, I need a fag'

For fucks sake!

Mouse returned reeking of cigarettes, which happily concealed the numerous other odours that emanated from this particular rodent. 'GT you ask more questions than a priest, are ya a bishop?'

'Mouse, if you want any further rent, then tell me about Brennan or I'll move to the stool the other side of you.'

'You can't do that! That's Larry's stool and a much more valuable property as it has a cushion. Rent is double on that one.'

Unable to take any more, Gus rose and went to the toilet. Urinate he did, relieve himself of frustration he could not. *Enough, I'll try another pub!* Returning to the bar, he pulled on his jacket, grasped his glass, and staring straight ahead, he sunk the last drop.

'See ya Mouse, find a new tenant this one has to go.'

Mouse grabbed him by the sleeve, 'Brennan has done a runner. Every morning after Mass, he usually has a few pints in the backroom, but not these past few days.'

Gus settled back onto the stool. 'Why has he vamoosed?'

128

Mouse spat regular before replying. 'The priest has fathered a child with a married woman, and he old enough to be her father. I knew he would come to no good when he stayed...'

'Stayed?'

Lips were closed and permanency stitched across Mouse's face. Gus called Marites, another two pints secured, he changed tact. 'Is he a womaniser?'

Like the parting of the red sea, Mouse's barriers came down and his tooth vibrated as each charge was levelled at Father Brennan.

'He is, and a bad bastard as well. Some clever-shite is even writing a book about him, full of sex and dirty pictures.'

Mouse blessed himself with his cigarette lighter. 'That poor woman, Maggie, feeling sorry for him after all the gossip that travelled the parish, she has let him into her knickers.'

'That's terrible! Who is Maggie?'

'Sure, she is his housekeeper. The two of them packed their dirty bags and left a few days ago. Even the sheep aren't safe with a randy priest like him around.'

'He likes sheep?'

'Aye, and goats; hates cats and mice. Fish as well. He spends that much time at the river, I expect he gets a blow job from any willing old trout. He is a tranny as well, a feckin weirdo.'

'A radio?'

'No, ya clown, a tranny likes wearing women's clothes.'

Gus called Marites. Mouse's glass needed fuel. They had moved onto gay orgies when Sean arrived at the counter.

'Good afternoon, gents. What are ya blathering about, Mouse?'

'Nothing at all, this fella here, GT, was asking about Father Brennan and I was just telling him what a fine priest he is.'

'GT?' enquired Sean.

Gus stuck out his hand as he rose, 'Gus O'Louglin, I'm doing a piece about village priests, for the paper. Shame he is not around, no matter, I'll try the priest over in Elmwood.'

7 PM May 26th

'James, Gus O'Loughlin, reporter, had drinks with Mouse, talked about you.' The text was sent a few minutes after Mouse received a mother and a father of a telling off from Sean.

8 PM May 26ᵗʰ

The view over the bay from the hotel dining room was breath-taking. Maggie's Lobster Thermidor invited immediate attention, but rather than eat, she took a photo of all the dishes on the table. This would be added to her growing repertoire. Joseph smiled lovingly and patiently at his wife and winked at James.

'Father, you must be the best fed priest outside Rome.'

James rubbed his middle aged spread and raised his glass, 'And you the best fed husband. I suggest we have a toast to our very own master chef in the making. I have some news concerning our elopement!'

After taking a second photograph of the Lobster from a different angle, Maggie turned her attention to the living and her own plate of food, 'Good news, I hope?'

'That remains to be seen. The bush telegraph has made it all the way to Rome,' James replied.

Maggie stopped dead in her tracks, her fork hanging in mid-air, 'Rome! How do you know that? Merciful Jesus, what have you done?'

'Relax, Maggie, I will deal with it, you need not worry.' *Xavier O'Loughlin, an unexpected bonus. The Lord works in mysterious ways and has delivered an opportunity to right the wrongs of the past.*

Gus had not sobered up enough to send his report to Xavier, nor was he aware of the imminent storm that brewed in a quaint seaside village.

11:30 PM May 26ᵗʰ

Three trips to the toilet and a sleep on the couch left Gus feeling slightly better than the queasy semi-drunk state when he'd arrived home. He lay back, cuddling a mug of strong coffee, watched the steam rise and contemplated his bizarre visit to Castlebridge. Una's version of events were confirmed by Mouse, but how much of the rodent's aspersions were believable? That single tooth, washed over by daily doses of alcohol, was capable of allowing fact and fiction to pass in equal measure. Knowing that Xavier had a temper only matched by an eruption of Mount Etna, he had to respond.

'Xavier. Visited Castlebridge today.

Fact: Brennan enjoys a sexual affair with a married woman.

She is pregnant.

He has eloped with his housekeeper – unclear if they are one and the same.

His reputation as a womaniser is unequivocal.

A book on his sexual indiscretions is imminent.

Innuendo: Possibly involved in gay orgies and sex with animals.

Rumours are rife that he is a transvestite.

My appraisal: GUILTY, almost certain.

Gus.'

* * *

For the first time in many years, Gus didn't double-check information received. *Fuck, that email might do more damage than the belly busting apple pie, if that's possible.*

Chapter 35.

'Good luck, Father, you're a brave man to stand at the altar this morning,' said Maggie.

'By the end of Mass, the chin-wags will be unsure of themselves. Your own good name will be restored, and the rumours concerning me, will turn back on the mongers that allowed them to creep as far as Rome. When a priest bites back, Maggie, he bites with a purpose. This priest could rip a rabbit from the fangs of a hungry wolf.'

'God help them. I think I will skip clearing up and sit at the back of the church. This episode is one that I dare not miss.'

James stood in front of the altar with his arms folded and inwardly smirked as the church filled. *A scandal fills an arena quicker than free tickets to a U2 concert.*

Many heads were bowed. A few leaning to one side, whispered and nodded. Several men brazenly held their stare when he caught their eye. It was obvious those who never came to Mass considered this to be as good as a football match final. Mouse sat right at the front, pawing at his tooth and drew an imaginary knife across his throat before tittering loudly. A hushed silence greeted Maggie when she entered, and James held back the laughter behind his stern face.

'I'm delighted to find the church filled following my short break with my housekeeper and her family. Maybe it's something all priests should consider doing once a month. Maggie has cooked for me for many years. Her husband and I agreed that she deserved a treat away from dirty plates and greasy frying pans.'

He paused, watching the reaction, noting the defiance in some, acceptance that the rumours were untrue in others.

'One of the fundamental tenets of Christianity is the selfless act of forgiveness. I prayed long and hard this morning and asked our saviour to...' he stopped mid-sentence, as Mouse squeaked all too loudly.

'Bet you did. You like it when you're bending down or on your knees.'

He ignored this and the guffaws from those in the front rows.

'I prayed that the church would be full this morning and it has been answered. I see in front of me, many that should've been christened Judas. Yet, who am I to judge others? That I have been wronged by malicious gossip is the work of the devil. To doubt my celibacy hurts me a great deal, but that you would cast aspersions on my innocent housekeeper, is a disgrace. Who amongst you cast the first stone?'

He slowly looked over the audience, pausing, staring at those he knew to be the stokers of the fire he'd started. *Fair play, they did a great job.*

'In case any are in doubt, let me make myself clear. I'm as virgin as Our Lady. If any think or know otherwise, speak now.'

He paused, giving ample time to any that would be brave enough. Mouse fidgeted and looked as though he was ready to stand. Nature being what it is, bravery failed him and he gnawed at a finger nail.

'As I expected, bleating sheep with nothing other than gossip on malicious lips, and you call yourselves Christians. The confessional will be open after Mass. You know who you are. Be certain that I do also. I expect every adult here to queue for as long as it takes, and confess before God. If your Sunday roast burns, that's a better outcome than the fires of hell.'

When Mass ended he watched as Maggie and Emily Jane stood, and with Maggie's aid they shuffled towards the door. They turned, cast a glance back toward him and both winked and smiled. *God bless them! Now for the sinners, penance fit for murderers will be dished out this day.*

Mouse, overcome by thirst, stood defiantly. He spat on the consecrated floor, turned and staggered down the aisle. For good measure, he paused several times, shook hands with any that were brave enough to do so.

James struggled not to smile. *Mouse, you're one of a kind. Alcoholic or not, you alone have the balls to stand your ground.*

Mouse slammed the church door shut, the thud reverberating around the packed church.

Head held high, as he strode towards the confessional, James caught sight of someone moving in the shadows, behind a pillar near the back. A tall silver haired man that he did not recognise, head bowed, moved swiftly towards the door and left.

James sat within the confessional, took out his phone and searched the internet. Before long, he was rewarded with a photo of his unknown guest. *Xavier! The shadows hide you for now. Eager I am for when you choose the light.*

'Bless me Father, I have sinned. I have gossiped and been indiscreet.'

'Now why isn't that a surprise? Say fifty Decades of the Rosary, and keep your gob shut in future. Amen'

Confessions took seven hours. This was definitely a record for the parish, possibly a world record. If chins wagged before Mass, they now sagged in the mire. James might be less than pure, but few of his parishioners now had the stomach to discuss his private life in public. For most, it was back to business as usual. The more religiously inclined had penance to occupy their free time for the foreseeable future.

With the thirsty work of confessions out of the way, he walked in the front door of Lavelle's for a liquid lunch. Mouse ducked, but the blow caught him on his right ear.

'Ouch, bloody priest, what was that for?' as if innocent was his middle name.

'You were blabbing to a reporter while I was on vacation.'

Mouse tried to rub the pain away. That made the red blotch even larger.

'Sean, did you see that? The sex-fiend has attacked me and should be barred.'

'See what,? All I see is an idiot rubbing his lug.'

He did not see the second blow arrive and now he rubbed both throbbing ears.

'Balance in everything is my motto. Next one will be in the beer storage area. What did you tell the reporter?' asked James.

Mouse climbed down from his stool and stole over to the corner nearest the window. His path to the door and freedom was blocked by James's burly frame. 'What's it worth?'

'Your life, if I feel generous. Maybe a pint might be considered, if you're honest with your answers.' Brennan moved a little closer, folded his arms and glared.

Life had long since lost any meaning for Mouse. Though self-preservation was somewhere on the radar, drink consumed his every thought.

'A large one as well. Deal?'

'Deal.'

'Twenty fags, a pint and a large one, will get everything I remember. Deal?'

Mouse blurted. James threw twenty Euros on the counter and rounded off their encounter with a kick in the arse, as Mouse raced to grab the loot.

Enjoying the comfort of his own stool in the back room, he waited for Sean to come with a pint. The back door had a jagged hole in the bottom panel. As Sean placed his drink on a beer mat, James pointed to the door.

'Attempted break in?'

'No, break out. We had a Poitin event last evening.'

'Gerry?'

'No, Father, Mouse drank half a bottle, down at the pond. When I tried to get him to go to his nest and sleep it off, he kicked the shite out of the door. I'll have to get a new one made as it's an unusual size.'

'That gut rot is dangerous stuff. I've warned Gerry a dozen times, but I may as well be talking to the Mona Lisa. Jimmy Nagle has a lot of strange stuff at the back of his joinery. If I'm not mistaken, a stack of doors from the old convent are lying there for years.'

Sean blessed himself, 'Is a pub a suitable resting place for a convent door?'

'It's as good a place as any. Doors don't tend to be particular where they are hung, though straight is always preferable to keep draughts out. Have any more strangers called in my absence?'

'I will visit Jimmy Nagle to wrangle a free door from his miserable paws. Nobody called. Wait, just one and he said little. Sat on your stool and drank a small Jameson, asked where you and your girlfriend were gone.'

'Was he tall, silver haired, and had the demeanour of a priest?'

'Now that you mention it, yes, he was hung like a proper priest. Unlike another priest that is my misfortune to know, he was very polite. He wore a cap and could be bald for all I know. I haven't slept a wink since you left. Is there any truth in all the gossip?'

'There is and there isn't.'

Sean could not contain his laughter as James explained all that had happened and his reasons for doing it.'

'Scandalous scandal, have you no shame at all, Father? Whatever you did is working a treat. The Con-Quest is going up the charts faster than one of them flying comet thingies.' Sean switched on the Smart TV and proudly displayed their ranking.

'Bring up the list of those who have supported the book.'

Sean did as bid and with much mirth, read out the names. 'James, it looks like we are attracting some weird people.'

'They are authors! Scandal has yet to garner deserved attention. It won't take much longer.'

Confused as usual, Sean wittily replied, 'I was right, peculiar ones, just like our ghost-writer Otter. What does the Holy Grail say about our next move?'

James finished his pint. 'Text Jimmy and Liam, meeting here next Sunday evening at Eight PM. Get that draughty door replaced, or all your customers will abandon this watering hole for a less windy pub.'

Chapter 36.

It vexed James that his culinary skills were sadly lacking. Maggie had taken the day off. He grabbed a tin of beans from his kitchen cupboard and searched for the can opener. Dexterity of mind wasn't matched by deftness with kitchen tools, nor with the scissors that he used to cut the bandage minutes later. Still, a few inches had been successfully negotiated and bright saucy beans gleamed below the blood splattered, serrated lid. Burnt toast and cold beans, washed down by a cold beer, hardly constituted a Sunday lunch. This meagre fare was far removed from the delightful meals that he had on his holidays. A performance worthy of a snake saw the last of the beans licked from his lips and the edge of his beard.

Keeping a daily log of events caused him to look deep into his soul, and that was an uncomfortable experience. Later, he would collate all the notes from his diary and email them to Otter.

As he toyed with a piece of incinerated crust, he considered how best to take advantage of recent activities. Many roads needed to be travelled if the book was to reach the publisher's desk. Controlling the inevitable twists and turns was his forte, and he revelled in the challenges presented. *Destiny, James. It's the result of applying yourself to ensure its journey is a work of art.*

Xavier's presence in the church was of immediate concern. Mulling over the possibilities, James concluded that it all fell down to a key decision. His head advised letting Xavier make the first move, his heart as usual won.

Intending to spend the afternoon dealing with some E-confessions and general paperwork, his plans were thwarted when he received a call from Emily Jane. She asked him to drop everything and come around to her house. Afraid that she was ill again, he grabbed a bottle of holy water and a stole. He sped over to her home, jumped out of the car and raced to the front door. It seemed an age before the door opened.

Emily laughed, 'Keep smoking those fags and I will outlive you. Oh, my God, you thought it was third time unlucky. Sorry, you don't need your witch doctor's kit today. Come in, James, I have a whiskey poured and news that may cause your chin to redden beneath your splendid beard.'

He followed her into the sitting-room. Still panting, he slumped onto an armchair and accepted the glass of whiskey. It lived up to its name. The water of life restored his inner balance and a cigarette calmed his troubled lungs. This was one of those rare situations where poison was medicinal.

'Emily, next time I'll kill you with my bare hands and then give you the last rites. What's so urgent that you would risk giving me a heart attack?'

'Ah, James, have you taken your tablets? I fear the coronary is yet to come.'

Gulping back the remaining whiskey, he braced himself for whatever news was forthcoming.

She refilled his glass and settled on the armchair opposite, where she sipped her own whiskey, and clearly she enjoyed his discomfort. 'I have received an email from my niece who works for a newspaper. An interesting article is to appear on the front page tomorrow.'

'The Midland Chronicle?' he whispered.

'Yes. How do you know?'

'An article concerning a reckless priest, am I close?'

Emily leaned forward and held his hand tenderly, 'No, my James, not reckless, alive. Fathered a child, gay orgies and an erotic book; I would more easily believe that the Pope is an alien, than anything that's to appear in the article. Why have you been selected to sell their trash? That's the question that leaves me troubled.'

He stood and strode around the room, stopped in front of a line of black and white photographs of Emily, the dancer and actress. 'Not selected, I volunteered. What price fame? What cost being known by the masses? You lived that life. What toll for vanity?'

Emily was taken aback, 'You orchestrated this newspaper article and the gossip that ran without rectitude through the parish and beyond?'

'Yes, my dear friend. I sowed the seed. The harvest has come earlier than expected and I'm unprepared, can you help me?'

'Answer me first. Why has a priest uncloaked from the sanctuary of the altar? You swore that you would see out your days, no matter the pain. What dangerous game are you playing?'

Leaving out no detail, from the first confession to the last, The Con to The Quest, he told the entire tale and left her in convulsions.

'Holy Shit, you're more outrageous than even I had given you credit for. You think you know me, yet you cannot for I don't know myself. Emily Jane died many years before we met, replaced by an actress that you see before you. You think us friends. Are you sure of that?'

'Yes, certain, beyond any doubt we are. Feck it, I have few enough, so should know those who are my allies.'

Emily smirked, 'True enough, but I have the skills to make you believe it, even if it were not true. If you're to take on the mantle of fame, you need to learn to do likewise. Look at me smiling in those pictures, smiles as false as the value of wealth over health. In the company of those whom you would rub shoulders with, hold your tongue and fetter your temper. Plain talk will bar your way. Flower everything and stroke egos. Doors will open if you stick to these rules. If your quest for fame is to but last a day, be your contrary, loveable self.'

'You are gorgeous, my dearest, Emily.' He leaned over and kissed her hand.

'Fuck off, your eyes did not match your actions, go practice on your mirror, you rascal. If I were you, I would seek to get on a chat show on national television. On that forum, a countrywide audience will be at your beck and call, act first and then revert to yourself. They will fall in love with you, as I have.'

'Okay, my sweet. If your once shapely legs can walk to the computer, then please e-mail a copy of the article. Au Revoir, my goddess, and thank you. I'll let myself out.'

When he returned home, he followed her advice and spent hours conversing with a mirror. By the time he lay on his bed, reading the email from Emily, he'd enhanced his acting skills beyond recognition, and an Oscar wasn't beyond possibility. Tomorrow he would start by practising on those people he disliked, and there were many to choose from.

The article was amusing, and the headline, a standard paper seller.

'Gay orgy priest fathers love child?' The writing, more flowery than his front garden, exaggerated the wrongdoings. Indirectly named and everything written suggested all the rumours were malicious gossip. Gus covered his butt and did so with aplomb. The article ended stating that the newspaper did not condone such tittle tattle and would be investigating to ensure that the priest had every opportunity to clear the air and put the rumours to rest.

Clear the air, my ass! Xavier's hand is all over this. Let thy enemy do thy bidding. If I wrote it myself I could do no better.

Chapter 37.

Ghostly was the reflection in the mirror, despite the semblance of a grin. Its face tilted each way and then, a hand reached up, and stroked its chin. Back replacing front, the image shrunk, as James moved away and placed the talcum powder on the dressing table. *Jeepers, imagine what I could achieve with a real makeup kit.* The kitchen sacrificed an onion, and soon his eyes wept and reddened when he rubbed them.

First scene was set to be played out at the newsagents. Una Mahon took a step backwards and seemed to shrink behind the counter as he closed the door.

'Good morning, Una. I'm here to apologise for my behaviour at Mass yesterday. In case you thought I was including your lovely self in my admonishment, I'm truly sorry. I didn't sleep a wink for thinking you were upset.'

Tension left her face and her mascara took on an angelic hue as she smiled, 'Oh! You poor man and awful is your appearance. The look of you would stir a dying man to take pity on you.'

'A shop keeper must make idle chat with customers and there is no harm in that. My dear, am I forgiven?' He offered his hand in reconciliation.

She flinched, but then stepped toward him and shook hands. All the while, her quizzing eyes made a lie out of her forced smile.

'Nothing to forgive, Father, sure my heart was free from guilt. You put the busybodies back in their chattering cartons and sealed the lid tight. It's terrible! The words that come out some mouths would make one shiver.'

'Nuala, you're a saint. You cannot believe anything you hear. People can look you in the face and brazenly lie. I'll have my usual cigarettes, if it's not an inconvenience.' *Should I comment on her hair? No! That may be a nicety too many.*

She took a pack from the shelf and placed a packet of Paracetamol alongside, 'Take two of these and keep that flu at bay. Get a little rest, Father. A difficult few days have taken their toll on you.'

'That's a great kindness. I'm so glad we are friends.'

If she'd seen the grin on his face, as he walked towards the door, she would not have muttered, 'Poor man,' in his wake.

Chuffed at how well that had gone, he stood outside the shop and lit a cigarette. The hustle and bustle of early morning shoppers enthralled him, as they weaved from one shop to the next, pausing to chat with others on similar missions. His decision to wait outside Una's shop ensured she was idle. All that approached, on seeing the leper priest send spirals of cigarette smoke towards the heavens, crossed and took safer passage. Some people no doubt were destined for Una's. They turned tail and made the long trek to the supermarket at the far end of the village. He contained any feeling of hurt caused by those who chose to avoid him. Any chance of practising his new acting skills in an impromptu setting had evaporated.

His eyes narrowed as the hunter within woke from slumber and scanned those who crossed the street. *Aha, a Banshee approaches.* Agnes Murphy's powers were on a par with Una, the snake. She had the personality of a Rottweiler. Her fangs would leave no tale untold until blood was drawn. He threw the fag-end onto the pavement, squashed it with his foot and timed his crossing so that it would leave Agnes without any escape route.

Mouth agape, her dark hazel eyes glared at the presence that blocked the path a few yards in front. She tried transferring her shopping bag to her other hand and gasped when it was wrenched away.

'Good morning, Agnes. It's high time I practised what I preach. I saw you wandering up the street carrying this heavy load and I said to myself, 'Father James, a good Christian would ease the heavy burden that she bears on her shoulder.' Let me carry this home for you and save the leather of your shoes from scraping away under such a millstone.'

Whiteness of a sheet was replaced by a scowl that yielded to a reluctant smile. 'Ah sure, Father, I'm well used to carrying home the shopping this forty-seven years. There is no need at all.'

'Nonsense, it's the least I could do for you. I'm well equipped to look after the women of this parish. None have complained so far, or refused my advances of assistance in their hour of need. It will be my pleasure.'

Knowing she would be gripped by blind panic, he turned and walked by her side. She stared straight ahead.

'How are all the family, Agnes?'

'They're all well, Father. Joe, please God, will be ordained next spring and Amy is in a convent in France.'

After turning into the cul de sac where her small cottage peered up at the church, he stopped and faced her.

'Do you know I told the Bishop a month ago, that you were a fine example of a hard working Catholic mother and would put some clerics to shame with your religious zeal? I was thinking that we should say a Decade of the Rosary and pray the Holy Spirit keeps your children safe from sin.'

Agnes nodded. On reaching the cottage, she nervously glanced around, turned the key and led the priest indoors.

When James left an hour later, Agnes waved after him. 'The Lord has heard our prayers and my sinless heart rejoices. Father, I'll bake a nice cake for when you call next week.'

A currant trapped between two teeth was released with a matchstick, before he lit up and inhaled deeply. He opened his lips and let the smoke mingle with the expletive that could not be contained. 'Two faced bitch. God forgive me and Agnes as well.'

If saying Mass was thirsty work, performing alongside such actresses as Una and Agnes left a shrivelled tongue, and he gasped for a pint to kill the sour taste that lingered. Turning left, ahead was Lavelle's and sanctuary.

The sight that greeted him in the back room took his breath away and he wished he'd a camera.

'A mouse at work, do my eyes deceive me? Today, I, a humble priest, witness in living colour, the eighth wonder of the modern world.'

He slumped onto his stool, raised an arm to his forehead and then swooned onto the floor. 'Fare thee well, my time has come. Alas, a shadow draws over me and my heart grows cold. Hold me, Mouse. Hold me, my dear friend.' He lay on his back, eyes closed and hands crossed like a fallen Crusader.

'Get up, ya bollox. If you were closer to the door, I would let it fall on you.'

James opened one eye and rolled over, as the spit left Mouse's tooth and spiralled towards him. Getting to his feet, he strode over and stood on Mouse's toe. Mouse squealed as he let go of the door and hopped about the room. The door rocked for a moment, tilted sideways and in slow motion yielded to gravity. A firm hand from James prevented the fall and the second shunted it back into place. Sean roared from the other side.

'Hold the frigging door.'

Mouse resumed duty, cursing under his breath. James tearfully took his place on the stool.

'I have a new name for you, Mick.'

'Feck off, priest, what name?'

'Mick the Door-Mouse, dormouse, do ya get it?' he tossed a beer mat at Mouse.

Sean knocked on the door, and Mouse let if fall inwards, before steering it against the wall. Pencil behind one ear, measuring tape in hand and a boiler suit all over, Sean could have passed for a DIY television show presenter. All that was missing was a modicum of skill.

'Pull yourself a free pint, Jamie boy. It's a grand solid oak door. Nagle reckons it came from the Reverend Mother's study.'

While James went around front to fill a pint, Sean set to fixing the door in place. By some miracle, the hinge placements needed little adjustment, and soon she was swinging freely. Sorting out the lock could wait.

He walked backwards to James, folded his arms and stared lovingly at the ten Euro door. 'What do you think, James?'

'It's a fine solid piece of wood. Who do you think walked into it?'

Puzzled at this remark, Sean reached into a pocket for his rarely used glasses and looked at the door again. 'I see what you mean. A good sanding and a lick of varnish will get rid of the stain. Won't it, Mouse?'

'A pint and a packet of fags would have it gleaming like a new tractor, two pints, like a Rolls Royce.'

Sean glared at Mouse.

'You, you little wanker, broke the other door. I'll pay the farming rates, but she better shine like a gentleman's family silver. Now go down to the hardware store and get sand paper. I have a tin of varnish in the shed out the back.'

He tossed a two Euro coin into the air and shook his head as Mouse grabbed it and loped off out through the front lounge.

'A brain surgeon would give a refund if he'd to operate on Mouse,' said Sean.

James smiled, 'Don't be too harsh. That could be me or you. He's had a hard life. Few of his problems are of his own making and it's as much our duty to mind him, as it's to have some harmless fun. The drink might have dulled his senses, but a strong intellect now dormant, hides behind the drunken mask. Someday, with God's help, I will see it awoken. Do you know anything about the John Divilly radio show?'

Sean stripped off the boiler suit, sat on a stool and scratched his knee before answering, 'It's mighty craic. Every eejit in the country rings up and moans at John. Only last week, a clown from Limerick was complaining that the rain was damper now than when he was a lad. Sometimes the discussions get hot and heavy, and that's the best fun of all. If there was one dying wish for busybodies and moaners, it would be to get to talk to John. Why do you ask? You're not thinking of ringing him, are you?'

James stood, downed his pint and tipped an imaginary hat at Sean. 'I am, probably tomorrow. See ya later, Woody. By the way, you need to clean out the pipes. That pint tasted worse than me mother's buttermilk.'

Sean returned his gaze to the door and shivered. His eyes traced the outline of the stain, its arms, legs and body forming the shape of a crucifix

Chapter 38.

'Good afternoon, everyone and welcome, welcome, welcome to the John Divilly show. Settle back, reach for your phone and tell us your interesting story. Tales of woe, fun or serious matters that affect your nation, your parish your home – ring John, the phone lines are open.

Yes, Mary, Mary from Cork. You have a problem with your husband and his Alsatian. Come on, Mary, tell us your story. Go on, Mary.'

James listened intently as the daily entertainment began. Story after story, people ringing John and giving their tuppence worth. Arguments began, were quashed when they got out of hand, and endless were the callers. An opportunity to join a conversation was needed and it came perfectly packaged. Anne from Donegal was going ballistic with her local priest. He refused to carry out the marriage ceremony because she stubbornly refused to do the compulsory pre-marital course. The do-goods backed the priest, the rest the girl, and soon the conversation moved onto every festering issue with the Catholic Church.

He sat on the edge of his settee. Phone in hand with the radio stations number entered, he held a finger over the button to dial. When the delicate subject of celibacy entered the discussions, cue James, he pressed the ring John button. He waited, and waited, scratched his nose, stood and paced around the room. *Patience James,* but patience failed him. As a last resort, *Lord, get that bollox to answer the phone. Amen.*

'Yes, caller, you wish to talk to John. What's your name, where are you from and what do you want to discuss?'

'Father James Brennan, from Castlebridge. I want to discuss celibacy, transvestite priests and gay priests.'

'Hold the line, Father.'

For an age, the hold music buzzed in his ear. He listened as John talked to an old lady who was having an apoplexy over the attack on her church.

'Thank you, Josie. That was very interesting. Mind yourself. Who's next? Father Brennan, are you there?'

'Hello John, this is Father Brennan,' he said and heard himself talking faintly on the radio.'

'Have you the radio on? Turn it off. Turn it off before I go deaf. Is it off?'

'Yes.'

'Celibacy. Transvestite. Gay Priests, go on, Father James, tell John.'

'John, the Catholic Priests of this country have become the scapegoats for every tattling gossiper. Only last week, rumours ran the length and breadth of my parish and beyond. It started that I had fathered a child, then that I was a transvestite, engaged in sex with animals, and that I participated in gay orgies. There were other untruths, but those were the main ones.'

'That's terrible, are the rumours true? Tell John, go on Father, is there any truth in them?'

James imagined a mirror in front. He stood, still holding the phone, raised his head proud and grinned as he let the tension build.

'Are ya there, Father Brennan? Is any of the gossip true?'

'No, John. Not true.'

'So, let's put these rumours to bed. Are you gay?'

'No, I don't think I am. I enjoy the company of men and women.'

'Are you bisexual?

James gave the mirror the thumbs up. 'I don't know, I have never thought about it. Are you bisexual, John?'

'No, this is about you, not me,' stuttered John, not used to being asked questions back.

'It's about us all, John. Me, you and the fireman, the nurse, the carpenter, it concerns everyone. Today a newspaper maliciously reported on the accusations made against me. Tomorrow it could be you, John. They even said someone was writing an erotic book about me.'

'Shocking Father, so let me start again. Are you gay?'

'No, and if I were, I would openly admit that I was.'

'Have you fathered a child?'

'No, I'm celibate and will remain so, as long as God graces me. At my age, what would be the point in trying to father a child?'

'Good man, Father, now we are getting somewhere. Are you a transvestite?'

'Yes,' he winked at the mirror and silence oozed from John as shock hit home.

'Oh. Would you like to tell us about this unusual behaviour? The phone lines are hopping.'

'I wear a frock to Mass and like wearing it. I suppose I'm a transvestite.'

'Father, you had us going there. Is there a book being written about you?'

'That's the only true bit.' The imaginary mirror reflected a priest grinning from ear to ear.

'So there is a book. Is there sex in it?'

'John, there are few books without sex in it. I would not like to say on an afternoon Radio show when children could be listening. If I wanted to talk about the book, I could only do so on a late evening chat show on television. Sorry, John, I'm sure a broadcaster of your talent and experience understands this. You would not wish for people to be complaining about your show.'

'Of course, we can't talk about it here. Thank you, Father Brennan, please hold the line. Time for an advertisement break, and when we come back I'd like some comments on the disgraceful treatment of this lovely priest.'

The on-hold tune did not seem quite as annoying as earlier. He waited, glee stretching from one ear to the other.

'Father, Bernard Mahon here. I'm the show's producer and I may be able to help you get your book published.'

Glee turned to shock, caught with his pants around his ankles, he needed time to think. 'Book published?'

'Yes, James. You came on here to publicise your opus.'

'Err! Okay, if you say so. How did you know?'

Bernard laughed before responding. 'I could say intuition, but I cannot lie to a priest. Fly fishing and a pint afterwards, are my preferred sins. I was told in confidence and will keep it that way.'

'Jesus, you know Otter?'

'If you say I know some wildlife, then I must. Look, I have to go. I will make a few calls and see if I can set something up. Your secret is safe with me. Don't deny the bullshit rumours too strongly for now. I'll be in touch. Have you an email address?'

'fatherjpb@gmail.com. Fair play to you Bernard, I'll tie you up a box of the finest flies you've ever seen.'

He winked at the mirror, took out his six-gun and fired, then blew away the smoke from the top of the barrel. *James, the Oscar is inevitable. I think a few hours on the river have been earned. Trout are harder to fool than humans. God, in his wisdom, made it so.*

Chapter 39.

The new second-hand door rattled on its hinges. James halted inside and stared at the stranger parked on *his* stool. Wild, greased hair, sculpted the top of his head, falling in dyed, multi-coloured strands down the back of his neck. Crouched over two bowls of porridge, he scooped helpings with a tablespoon. In the few seconds James stood there with his mouth open, the first bowl was shoved to one side and the second emptied. The man stood, stretched his braces, belched louder than should be humanly possible, and hollered. 'Young Lavelle, more gruel.' Slumping back on the stool, he banged the spoon on the counter, sending globules of porridge flying in every direction. For no apparent reason, he burst out laughing.

James edged his way to the other end of the counter, keeping a safe distance from the weirdo. 'Good morning. I'm Father Brennan.'

The stool nearly hit the far wall when the stranger leapt to his feet. Wielding the spoon as a weapon, he moved away from James. Beneath bushy eyebrows, his flickering eyelids only half-closed over his bulbous eyes. 'You're from the CIA. You can't fool me,' he said, edging toward the door.

'I'm a priest,' said James, proffering his hand, realising the man was far older than his nimble movements suggested, and clearly afraid, if not entirely mad.

'Vatican spy.' He wrenched the door open, half-closed one eye, and flung the spoon at James.

James sidestepped. With a clang, the missile crashed into the counter, missing him by inches. As though his life were in the gravest danger, the man flung himself through the doorway.

Mother of God. That fella is crazier than Mouse. James shoved the bowls out of his way. He grabbed a cloth from behind the counter and wiped away the mess. Just as he lit a cigarette, Sean arrived carrying two steaming bowls of porridge.

'Where is Papa Joe?' said Sean, looking more perplexed than usual.

'If you mean the lunatic who sat on my stool, he vamoosed. Who and what is he? He seemed to think I was a spy'

Sean tipped the porridge in the bin. 'Papa Joe McGargles is a friend of my late father, a master brewer from Kilcock, and possibly the most paranoid man you'll ever encounter. I hope you didn't upset him.'

'A brewery in Kilcock?'

'According to Papa Joe, in 1776 there were six breweries and distilleries there.'

'Ya learn something new every day. Pull me a pint. According to Papa Brennan, Papa Joe stunk like the liniment Pups rubs on his hounds.'

'That's Papa Joe's aftershave. I best clean up the mess,' Sean pulled a pint and set it in front of James. 'I'm going to get McGargles' stout on tap.'

'Are you crazy ...? Yes, I suppose you are. In that case, I'll take my custom elsewhere. I've suffered the taste coming from your filthy pipes for too long.'

'I'll clean them this week. Satisfied?' said Sean, looking peeved at the aspersions being cast. He reached for the can of air freshener, glanced at Brennan and smirked. 'Papa Joe's aftershave and your fag smoke are a lethal combination.'

By the time Sean had fumigated the pub, James had another cigarette lit. 'God knows what liniment infused shite you'd have me drink. If I were Jesus, I'd go up to the cemetery and raise your father from the dead so he could kick some sense into you.'

'You are dirtier than a two year old and spoilt by Maggie. Any chance the cigarette butts can go in the ashtray instead of on the floor? Lift your legs,' said Sean as he swept up.

James grunted. His humour was foul and his agitation soured the calmness of a lovely sunny Sunday morning.

Sean stopped and leaned on the brush. 'What's up, padre? You look as though murder is on your mind. Did you get out the wrong side of the bed?'

'It's Max China,' he snarled.

Sean swept under the Father's stool and made sure he knocked the head of the brush against James's leg.

'Sorry, Father, this brush has a mind of its own. Max China, that distinguished author, what about him?'

'Although a regular enough Mass goer, he's not been to confessions in years. I fear for him. He writes on very dark subjects and I worry for his soul.'

Sean shovelled the dirt into a dustpan, tipped it into a bin outside and returned to normal service behind the counter. 'Get him to send you an E-Confession.'

'Jesus, Mary and Joseph, that's a mighty idea. There is a genius somewhere in that skull of yours.'

'There is, but I choose to keep it under control. Barmen are supposed to be dumb. What put him on your priest's radar?'

James scratched his beard and pondered over whether he should answer given the current queries on his sexuality.

'His sister has started coming to Mass with him. If I wasn't celibate I wouldn't mind having a date with her.'

Sean burst out laughing.

'What's so funny?'

'If you married her, we could call her Sister Brennan. What in hells name is that racket in the lounge?'

Liam and Jimmy had burst in the front door, arguing incessantly and arriving to the backroom, they continued much to James's amusement. Both were wearing their waders and water oozed from their boots onto the recently cleaned floor.

'Good evening, lads. Dressed for dinner in your Sunday best, I see. What is all the fuss?' asked James, with a calmness that belied his intent to stir even further their petty argument.

'He is a lying, cheating bollox,' said Liam as he poked his finger into Jimmy's chest.

Hmm, Liam, the patron saint of composure has yielded to darkness. Make fun when the chance comes. He looked from one to the other.

'Sure we know that. What did he do now that has you so riled?'

'We had a bet as to who could catch the biggest trout. He measured mine, seventeen inches and his was twenty four inches. Not a chance it was bigger, somehow he cheated and I refuse to pay.'

'You both witnessed the trout being measured?'

'We did, he was looking over my shoulder and now has reneged on his bet. The little toe rag refuses to hand over the tenner. What do you think of that?' said Jimmy. A subtle wink directed towards James wasn't noticed by Liam.

Aha, the talents of an engineer, clever, very clever. James grinned at the ingenuity and salivated at a rare opportunity.

'Disgraceful. In the past, a duel at dawn sorted arguments. Thank God we live in more enlightened times. Do you both agree to my adjudication?'

'Yes,' said Jimmy.

'Fine, but he still cheated.'

James looked at the growing puddles on the floor. 'What size feet have ye?'

'Nine. What the fuck has my shoe size got to do with anything?' said a now even more irate Liam.

'Eleven and a half,' said Jimmy, 'and I'm proud of them, so don't make any skiing jokes.'

149

James stood and manoeuvred himself between the two gladiators. 'Take off your boots and we will measure them. Your tape measure please, Jimmy.'

He placed the tape along the sole of Jimmy's boot. 'Thirteen and a bit inches, agreed?'

They both nodded.

Now it was the turn of Liam's boot. Liam was incredulous when James announced the measurement. 'Twenty-five and a half. Agreed?'

Liam stepped back and sat on a stool. Completely bewildered, for it was obvious that Jimmy's boot was far longer than his. 'How?' was as much as he could say.

Tears slipped from James's eyes and flowed freely. Sean leaned over the counter and tried to wipe them away with a tea towel.

'Jimmy, will I tell them or will you?' asked James.

'You do, Father.'

'Liam, many years ago, when you were a young lad, a great change took place, and it caused much confusion. Things that were, were no more. Something that was five was no longer five. Do you follow me?'

'No.'

'Okay! Liam, I'll be blunt. We changed to metric and only gobshites like you still work in inches.'

When it finally registered with Liam, he hopped off his stool and swung a punch at Jimmy. Luckily, he slipped on the damp floor and ended on the flat of his back. Jimmy stepped over him, took a twenty Euro note from his shirt pocket and dropped it on Liam's chest. 'Here's a tenner for the bet and a tenner for the entertainment. Now get up to the counter and get me a drink.'

Sean filled the drinks, took the money, and as he handed over the change, 'Lads, I still don't get it. Which trout was bigger?'

Blank stares and silence ruled, until James stepped in and changed the conversation to allow Sean to save face. 'There have been some developments since we last met. Liam, Jimmy, you probably heard some rumours.'

Jimmy looked at Liam, then at Sean. A grin was suppressed as he turned to James, 'We did Casanova, or is it Rasputin Brennan? Liam does not agree, but my fortune teller tells me that you started the rumours and scandal, to the benefit of the book. That's what drove the gossip. If there is one thing I have learned since you orchestrated The Con, it's that there is always method to your madness. Well?'

'You don't know the half of it. He was raving a few days ago and said he was going to ring the John Divilly show,' said Sean.

All eyes settled on the priest. He lit his lighter a few times, sipped his pint and then lit a cigarette. 'Yes, I started the gossip, bad publicity is better than no publicity, or so they say. I rang the radio station on Friday. Choosing my words carefully, I denied everything except that a book was imminent. The producer knows Otter, and knew about the book. That was a stroke of luck that may see me on Late Night Show.'

'Only celebrities and criminal politicians get on that, you're neither,' interjected Liam.

'That's not true, Liam.'

'It bloody well is. I watch it every Friday night. It's the wife's idea of being romantic. A bottle of wine and we watch that shite.'

'That's unreal, baby making after watching celebs on the Late Night Show. Any offspring would be born talking shite and crying for a line of cocaine. Liam, what about priests, they are on regularly enough,' a confident Jimmy scored a point.

'And authors, bloody hell, lads, that means he sort of qualifies,' Sean clapped at his own contribution.

'If it happens, it happens, and we need to be prepared. Last Monday an article was published about me in The Midland Chronicle, written by one Gus O'Loughlin. He came to Castlebridge, got the low down from Mouse and God knows who else. I have no problem with that, indeed I welcomed it. The gossip reached Rome and the desk of O'Loughlin's brother, Xavier.

'Jesus, I might know him. Didn't I get married in Rome, blessed by the Pope and a dozen cardinals?' Sean beamed, remembering that momentous occasion.

'Jimmy, if I get a slot on the TV, I'll need Xavier in the audience. I have some business with him, don't ask, it's personal and will also help our cause. As far as Google is concerned, all guests are given some tickets for their friends. I want you to arrange two tickets for Gus. You'll tell him that you read his article and you heard that the pervert priest will be on the show. Confirm that I'm gay, a transvestite, womanising, whoring sexaholic and any other despicable thing other than child abuse. Xavier will not be able to resist.'

'Liam, I need you to set up a new Facebook page. 'Friends of Father Brennan',' he stared at Liam, 'Liam, earth calling Liam.'

Liam stared at the new door. 'Sean, where did the door come from?'

'The Convent, and it cost me ten Euros.'

'Give me a large one, Sean. Reverend Mother Concepta's door, I thought it had been destroyed years ago,' Liam reached back, grabbed the glass and downed the whiskey.

All eyes turned to the door. Jimmy hadn't noticed it before now. When he spotted the ingrained shape normally associated with crucifixion, he walked over and examined it. 'Solid Oak, but not Irish, and it's definitely handmade. It has an unusual grain. I have never seen a grain like that before.' He returned to his seat and posed a question to Liam, 'Why are you scared of a lump of wood, you big sissy?'

'Don't mock me, Jimmy, and don't anyone interrupt me. Pour me another whiskey, Sean.

'In 1899, a devout young girl named Mary Jordan became a postulant at the convent. Four months before she her final vows, a young man arrived and offered his services as a gardener. He was turned down. Day after day, he knocked on the front gate, until finally Mother Concepta relented. Finding favour with all the nuns, gardening and doing odd jobs, Mary fell under his spell.'

Liam paused and gathered his breath. Enthralled, the others sipped their drinks in silence.

'Mary succumbed to temptation. No longer chaste, in her torment she told the Reverend Mother and begged for forgiveness. In her fondness for the girl and accepting that her remorse was genuine, Concepta decided that the child would be sent for adoption when it was born. Mary would then be allowed to take her vows. It was a rash decision, against the rules of her order, a bad judgement call that she would come to regret. Will I continue?'

'Go on with the old wife's tale and hurry up,' Jimmy looked at his watch.

'Sssh, Jimmy, let him finish,' growled Sean as he sunk a very large brandy.

Lowering his voice, almost to a whisper, Liam continued the story. 'The male child was born on the 6th of June 1900, the new millennium, and for an unknown reason remained at the convent and not handed up for adoption. Instead, Mary was sent home in disgrace and had no idea what had become of her child.

On the 6th of June 1906, the 6th day of the 6th month of the 6th year of the century, the child walked into the Reverend Mothers study. Around his neck hung an upside-down crucifix and his red eyes glowed in the candlelight. She screamed in horror as he stood on his hands and moved towards her. His six inch tongue hurled obscenities, blaspheming, cursing Our Lord as hand over hand he closed in on the distraught Reverend Mother. Thinking she was doomed, she closed her eyes to the vile creature and said the Lord's Prayer. The Holy Spirit guided her hand to the bottle of holy water on the desk. She twisted the lid and fervently prayed as she splashed the water in every direction.

It's said, the shriek as its foul flesh burned was heard in Dublin. Agony gripped the beast and it flew into the door and was never seen again.'

Sean's false teeth clattered and he could not take his eyes off the door. 'Holy shit, you're taking the piss, Liam.'

'May the ground open and cast me into the bowels of hell. I know it to be true. So help me God, Mary Jordan was my great, great grandmother.'

'Feck off,' said Jimmy, 'What book have you been reading? You have the shite scared out of Sean.'

'I had to tell ye.'

'Why?' asked James.

'How else would Sean know that the door is hung upside-down?' replied Liam.

Jimmy clapped, James grinned and Sean nearly wet himself, such was his relief. He leaned heavily on the counter, his face almost restored to its normal rosy colour. 'You had us going, Liam. My heart nearly burst with fear.'

James stared at them in disbelief at their ignorance. 'Liam, your memory is as short as my temper. I'm sick of educating gobshites. The Devil is in the detail and not in that door. The convent was established in 1903.'

'Good story all the same. You're a dark horse, Liam,' said Jimmy.

They nodded in agreement, finished their drinks and bid Sean goodnight. Sean cleaned up, locked the bar, and as he turned off the lights in the back room, fear once again gripped him. He turned tail and raced up the stairs taking three steps at a time. As he closed the bedroom door he muttered, 'That cursed door has to go.'

Chapter 40.

Eoghan Kavangh enjoyed the reputation of being the finest salesman at H&H. A purveyor of whiskeys and imported beers, his success was a direct result of his simple philosophy; Spend time with your customers. He relaxed in the back room of Lavelle's pretending to savour a mug of Sean's finest instant coffee.

'Sean, it's hard times we now find ourselves living through. The bar trade suffers more than most, as people stampede towards the drink at home model. It's difficult to keep the taps flowing. You must be struggling?'

Sean, in a pensive humour, nodded in agreement. 'Eoghan, you know better than any. You see your own sales dropping every month. Look at the front lounge, two punters and not twenty Euros between them. I'll be lucky if I see another ten customers before I pull down the shutters.'

Eoghan clenched his fist and banged the counter, startling Sean. 'You have to get up of your arse, Sean. Find a way to attract them in the door. Sorry to be so blunt and were we not good friends, I would hesitate to speak cruelly. The cosy Irish village pubs are disappearing, and if you're not careful, you'll become yet another sad economic statistic.'

Sean wrung his hands, took on a defensive posture and then his shoulders sagged into submission. 'Truth be known, I have been eating into my savings for several years. I know you're right. Celtic tiger, my arse, the country is fucked.'

'It is. But that does not mean we should all lie down and die. I'm afraid to say it's every man for himself. If you want a lifeboat, then build a bloody ark. Don't expect to be thrown a lifejacket if you start to sink.'

'I'll talk to Marites and see if we can come up with fresh ideas.'

Eoghan looked at his watch and took a final sip of his coffee. 'Do that, Sean, and do it starting now. I'm out of here before that priest comes in for his pint. Speaking of Brennan, take a leaf out of his book, and make it happen, no matter the consequences.'

Sean, with a heavy heart, looked around his near empty pub for inspiration. His eyes settled on the cursed door and he stared intently at the crucified figure. Inspiration nearly knocked him over, but was it truly divine? Malevolent illumination seemed a distinct possibility if there was a modicum of truth in Liam's tale. His eyes sparkled. Strange though it may be, on two hinges hung the solution to all his problems. *Anything Brennan can do, Lavelle can do it better.* If he thought that once, he thought it fifty times. It became etched onto his mind and optimism coursed through his veins.

Sworn to secrecy, by evening Liam had assisted him in his daring ploy to save his pub from extinction.

That night, Lavelle's for the first time in years closed early, and Sean enjoyed a romantic night with his patient wife. As he snuggled up against Marites, listening to her rhythmic breathing, he felt at ease with the world and his last thought before drifting into slumber. *The devil is in the door. Father, the devil is in the door.*

Chapter 41.

Buoyed by recent decisions taken, Sean bounced around his pub with a feather duster in hand. Spiders accustomed to being lords over their manor, scuttled and wove their way to safety as their webs fell. Wearing a pink apron and waving his wand, he paused when the front door swung open, and James strode in.

'Hail, my godly priest. Hath thou a thirst that quenched within my hostelry shall be? Thou art late this morn and perhaps thy temperance leaves thee forlorn?'

Without pausing, James walked towards the back bar and shouted, 'Good morning Mrs,' as he rounded the corner.

Sean, with agility borne on a near twenty hours rush of adrenalin and optimism, raced through the gap and stood as Brennan arrived. 'Thy stool, this very morn, dirt and grime dispatched. Sit, Sir, ale and whiskey I shall pour.'

'Thank you, Sean, and may I borrow your pen?'

Sean took a pen from behind the till and held it up just out of James's reach. 'Never a borrower or lender be. Yet fair fellow, your custom means much to me. Take offered pen and when thy writing spent, return, or to hell be sent.'

James grabbed the pen and began scribbling on a beer mat. Sean, his cheesy grin unnoticed, began to fill a pint. 'Sir, why my beer mat doth thou with given quill attack, and render fit for no purpose other than my bin?'

'Shut thy gob, Sean. Before I came in here, I passed by Mick Casey's son's car. Old Mick, perched on the passenger seat, shouted after me, 'HIJKLMNO, 5 letters.' His howling laughter followed me all the way in the door. He challenges me with a clue to a crossword and judging by his gaiety, he does not expect me to solve it. Now leave me in peace.'

Still no comment regarding his new found poetic turn of phrase, Sean, undeterred, topped up the pint and skilfully etched a signature on the head. He placed it on the counter, filled a whiskey and set it alongside the pint of stout. 'Pray tell, hath thy, thy daily decision made? In yonder glass shall I water pour, for the quickened spirits diluted be easier to endure.'

Yelping like a rabid dog, James, hopped up from the stool. He leaned over the counter, grabbed Sean, and planted a kiss on his head, 'Thick maybe, and yet thy genius at unexpected times bursts forth, back anon. Water, H2O!' He raced outside, almost knocking over a painter carrying a ladder, and shouted, 'Mick, without it our trout could not swim.' He returned to his seat of power, lifted his pint and stared at the head.

'Sean, I pose a few questions. Why is a pentagram chiselled onto the head of my pint? Why is there a painter outside? Why are you talking as if you had swallowed Hamlet? And finally, why are you so bloody happy?'

'Re-branding.'

'What?'

'My pub. Our new logo is on your pint. The painter is about to change the signage out front from Lavelle's to The Devil's Door. That's why I'm so cheerful. A new beginning! Well, what do you think?'

James stifled a grin, took a creamy mouthful and licked his lips, 'Grand, as long as my pint tastes as good as this one. Did you break the plastic cover on the Guinness tap when you cleaned the pipes? I suppose that wooden thing is in keeping with the door.'

'I did and it is.'

James sank his pint. 'Like mothers milk, pull me another. Why are you misquoting and bastardising Hamlet?'

Sean reached for a clean glass. 'It's to go with the name. It will add to the intrigue. Busloads of feckin tourists will come in the front door. By the time they leave, my till will be tired from ringing. I took to reading after we started our quest to get published, and Hamlet was the only book in the house. Was I lucky or what?'

'How in God's name are you going to get the tourists to come to this out of the way village?'

'With smarts, Father, with smarts.'

Puzzled, James tiredly spoke, 'And with whose smarts, dear Sean?'

'With yours!'

'Oh, enlighten me. This, thy priest puzzled be.'

Sean lifted the remote control and pointed it at the TV. 'Look and weep, look and weep, Father know-it-all.'

Turning towards the television, fully expecting to see the ranking of their book, instead confusion set in. 'Ebay?'

'Yes, Ebay, put on your goggles and read the advert.'

'Feck off, I can see clearer than you.' He read the advert and for once was speechless.

'The Devil's Door. Buy now price €1,000,000'

'Providence, it's all in the providence, Father. Thanks to Liam's tale, that door holds as much providence as the Shroud of Turin. I would not expect a man of the cloth to agree with such an outrageous suggestion. Like I give a shite what you think.'

'How will its providence reach the ears of the populace?'

Sean pointed to his head as though intelligence oozed from every pore. 'Because there is a buy now price of one million yoyos. Liam's tale is written into the description. That will stir a storm of interest. I'm going to make contact with the reporter that was talking to Mouse, and feed him the story.'

In disbelief and unexpected admiration, James nodded. 'This will benefit the book. I'll add this to my plans.'

'Whoa, Neddy, back up and back off. This is my baby. If I want advice, I'll be sure to ask for it. My learned friend, you know me well enough to know when I'm serious.'

Distracted from their conversation, James and Sean exchanged glances as the door of the ladies toilet was almost torn from its hinges.

'Is that another tourist, Sean? Are these the clientele that will come streaming into The Devil's Door? You provide great service to travellers when nature calls. She is a noisy one.'

Sean grunted, toilet paper cost money and his profits were disappearing down the loo. 'Are you taking the piss, Father?'

'Not I, Sean. But unless my ears are waxed to deceive, the tourist is.'

The tourist, grateful, tentatively stuck her head around the corner, 'Thanks, I nearly burst my bladder,' and turned to leave.

Glint in one eye, mischief in both, James replied, 'Where are you going?'

'I have to get back on the bus.' 'That's what they all say. Madam, forget the feckin bus. Have a drink with us. We don't bite and don't entertain intellectual conversation, but the craic we have in this God forsaken room would burst an empty bladder.'

The stool grated on the floor as James pulled it away from the counter. Panic written all over, she faced a dilemma that was worth consideration and she stared at the two grinning faces. Back to boredom in the bus, or remain here and have a giggle. She chose the latter. After collecting her bags from the coach, she returned and sat on the offered stool.

'As you say, feck the bus. Water please. My name is Sebnem.'

'Water?' they said in unison, appalled at such a choice in tipple.

She looked at them, one to the other and broke out into an enormous grin. 'I was only joking. Dilute it with a large whiskey.'

James offered his hand, 'James Brennan, I'm pleased you joined us, and even more pleased to see that the stool fits as though you were a regular.'

'No, James, I rarely frequent such places. I'm a student of life and utterly bored from visiting the normal haunts of tourists.'

'Aha, so the study of local wildlife is what tempted you to sit amongst us. A good enough reason perhaps. Where is your own nest?'

She flashed a smile at Sean before turning towards James, 'My studies tend towards more unusual life-forms. The sight of a priest whose collar peeped over the collar of a jumper while he sat in a pub struck me as odd. That he'd a pint in one hand, a cigarette in the other and the eyes of a devil led me to believe that my education could be advanced. Father James? Or are you?'

'Indeed I'm not. In this room I'm James, my altar and pious ego I leave outside.'

'He has to,' interjected Sean as he shook her hand. 'His ego would not fit in that door, The Devil's Door.'

Her eyes drifted from James to the door, back and forth. She seemed to be deep in thought. 'I can see he tried, but the door stopped both his ego and his body. Ego is in my experience only a mask. No more real than the impression on that door.' As an afterthought, she asked, 'The Devil's Door?'

Sean pounced on the opening, and she graciously listened to his sales pitch. Sebnem laughed at his temerity and blessed herself, seemingly trying to ward off the evil within its timbers.

'Great story, only an Irishman could dream up such a yarn.'

James groaned, 'Sebnem, if you give him any more rope, he would have us both hanging from the rafters, or turned to dust from waiting for his story to end. You believe ego to be no more real than false modesty, a cloak?'

Her eyes narrowed, mirth replaced by a knowing smile, as the offer of debate followed tom foolery. 'James, do the clothes of a pauper comfort your body or your mind? Are they confirmation of your faith or a denial of your religion?'

Dare I answer? Respect in union with fear tempered his response.

'Part of me wishes the bus had parked elsewhere, or that your bladder had been stronger than my desire for good company. My attire neither denies nor confirms. My faith is in God and in humanity. Vices, I have many, my clothes few, and the oddity that you perceive is exactly that. In my egotistical opinion, and one which I hold resolute, if man were to mirror perfection, then God would have created us so, and I would have no job. Others of finer cloth would have it otherwise. There are reasons for everything and many are beyond our understanding. Were we all peas in the proverbial pod, life would be as boring as water in a whiskey glass. I have in part chosen how to travel my road, you yours. If fate deems it so, they may cross and our souls embrace or repel. Yours saw beyond my tattered jumper. Does anything else matter?'

She nodded, understanding the nuances of his answer, 'So you pay homage to life itself?'

His teeth grated, horrified by the question, 'Absolutely not, I pay homage to only our Creator. Life, I embrace in all its fickleness, in all its forms. You also embrace life on a daily basis at your places of work. Is that why you think deeply on such matters? Do you strive to understand the essence of that which you study? You understand how it works, but yet you seek the why.'

She straightened, seemingly grappling to understand his response. 'James, you're a priest. I know in general terms which buttons I may push to delve into the soul of the man under the crucifix. How can you presume anything about me or my work?'

'Botany is the study of life. Would you agree with that statement?'

A long silence betrayed her shock.

'I guess that's correct.'

'That's your profession. Your hobby is interaction with and study of higher life forms. This is your lucky day,' James smirked as he sank his whiskey, 'Another please, Sean, and one for my green fingered friend.'

'James, our souls may have embraced, but how did you know I was a botanist?'

Sean leaned a little closer. Drying a glass so hard that it must surely crack under the pressure, he reiterated her question. 'Come on, Father. How did you know?'

'We shook hands. Is that not so?'

'Yes.'

'Your hands are quite rough for a female, yet your skin is not dried from toiling over a sink. Your complexion suggests an outdoor life and residue from the dirt that you have tried to remove from your finger nails confirms that you work with soil.'

'But why did you consider me a Botanist, why not a gardener?'

'Oh, my dear, that was the easy bit. A quick educated mind and Botanists Monthly Journal peeping up from an open handbag narrowed the possibilities somewhat, wouldn't you agree?'

'I would, you sneaky priest.'

'Excellent, most people eventually agree with me. That's why I have a large ego and work hard at keeping it fed. And this is my final lesson. When I invited you to join us, I suggested that in this unholiest of places, intellectual conversation is not permitted. As much as I enjoyed our brief encounter, it's but a diversion from much simpler fun. No more philosophy, unless it's fuelled by the delights that Sean places in our tumblers. Agreed?'

She laughed and shook with uncontrollable mirth, before finally agreeing to the ground rules. 'I agree, but is there really a God?'

'Feck off and drink your whiskey. A fresh one grows lonely sitting on the counter.'

Three days later, Sebnem said goodbye to Sean and James. Standing at the front door holding her bags, she was ready to take a very expensive taxi ride to the airport.

'That was the most fun I have had in years, Sean. I will tell everyone what I know about 'The Devil's Door'. And I will be back. You can count on it.'

James gingerly sipped a glass of water. 'That was some woman. Three days and three nights, a right batter of drink and only a short break for Mass each day. She must have drunk a barrel of whiskey.'

'She told me to say that you looked very cute, especially when you curled up like a foetus on the ground.'

'How, Sean, how did she drink me under the table?'

'That's easy, Father, I gave her the tourist's bottle, nine parts water, one part whiskey. That will be four hundred and thirty Euros. Three hundred to pay for drink, a hundred and thirty for three nights stool and breakfast. And, Father, Marites said that Mass for the last few mornings was rather amusing, and that you're a disgrace.'

'Sean, tell your lovely wife that she is correct. My bed beckons and snores already tickle my throat. Goodnight, Sean.'

'Good morning, Father.'

Chapter 42.

10 AM August 4th

Dressed in his Sunday best, Sean sat at the counter sipping coffee. He enjoyed the peace and quiet offered by Sunday mornings, and usually went for a walk along the river. Occasionally, he even fished for a few hours. This morning though, he awaited the arrival of a very important guest. He hoped they could get their business done before Mass ended and the pub opened. Having already ripped a bar mat into tiny pieces, he now twiddled with a cuff on the sleeve of his blazer. In his heightened state of excitement, he continued to glance at the ancient and reliable clock that hung on the wall over the fireplace. Gus was expected to arrive at ten o'clock, it was now five past the hour. Sean leapt off his stool when he heard the knock on the front door.

Gus shook hands and walked in. He was followed by a second man. 'Sean, this is my brother, Xavier. He is a bit of an expert on doors.'

Sean beamed, having two reporters to tell his tale to, elevated his feeling of self-importance. He ushered them into the back room and went behind the counter. 'Gus, Xavier, welcome to The Devil's Door. Can I tempt you with an out of hours drink?'

Gus flipped a beer mat, 'Sean, it's a little early, but a small tipple will not do any harm. I'll have a whiskey. My trusted assistant has an expensive taste and will only drink Jameson Reserve, but twelve-year-old will do if you don't have Reserve.'

Sean reached for the Jameson, scratched his bald spot and wondered what planet Gus was from. Twelve-year-old Jemmies were mere pennies more expensive than normal Jameson. He glanced at Xavier as he filled the glasses. Tall, silver haired, his deep blue eyes had a shifty look. He'd the appearance of a man more used to issuing orders than receiving them. Sean's instinct warned him that this was a man not to be trusted. *Assistant my arse, he must be Gus's editor. Be careful what you say to him.*

When he set the whiskeys on the counter and awaited their approval, he watched Xavier, noting every nuance, every movement.

Xavier raised his glass to his lips and inhaled deeply, savouring the familiar aroma, testing its pedigree, before taking a measured sip. A lot can be learned about a man by the way he drinks his whiskey.

Gus on the other hand, took a deep swallow, grimaced, as the whiskey slid down his throat, and with a satisfied lick of his lips set the glass back on the counter. 'Jesus, that's a fine whiskey, no mistake, but it's beyond my wallet to enjoy it regularly. Xavier has no mortgage or squealing children to feed, lucky bastard. So, Sean, tell us about this door.'

Sean cleared his throat and began his pitch, starting with Mouse kicking in the old door, getting the second-hand one from the convent and learning of its legend. All through the tale, Gus's grin grew wider and wider, and at the end, he came very close to having tears flowing down his face.

'That's the best yarn I have heard in years. Though I doubt the truth of it, I'd be delighted to publish the tale and the sooner the better.'

Sean refilled the whiskey glasses, took a USB data key from the till and handed it to Gus. 'One finger at a time, I typed it up on the computer and saved it to that yoke.'

'Xavier, he is trying to do me out of a job. I'm supposed to be the writer.'

Xavier almost smiled, at least his lips twitched before he nodded, and then he addressed Sean. 'That's quite a story. May I examine the door, please?'

'Good man. A bit of a carpenter, are you? The door is there, examine it all you want. It's the genuine article and more valuable than the Shroud of Turin,' Sean cheerfully pointed at the door.

Unexpectedly, Xavier's eyes narrowed. He glared at Sean, and then gave the coldest smile that Sean had ever witnessed. Sean shivered, and could not ignore a growing feeling that the road to fame for his establishment was about to take a turn for the worst.

Xavier strode over to the door, took a magnifying glass from his pocket and examined both sides. Then he took out a measuring tape, pencil and a piece of paper. He noted the dimensions and then took at least a dozen pictures of both sides. It was when he examined the hinges that his expression changed to a grin. He peered through the magnifying glass, focussing on the area just below the top hinge. Then he took a second piece of paper from his pocket, placed it against an area under the hinge, and rubbed it with his pencil. He stared at the results, stuffed everything back in his pockets and returned to his seat.

'Well?' asked Gus.

Xavier took a sip of whiskey and laughed heartily. 'Sean, your story, I'm afraid, is a little far-fetched. It's a unique piece of wood,

Quercus Frainetto, Hungarian or Italian Oak in common language. The markings are quite distinct, as is its age. This door was made in 1947 and not by the devil in your local convent. I'm certain of that fact. It's however, as doors go, quite valuable. The illusion of a human form on it makes it quite attractive, but it's not a satanic relic.

The ground could have opened up and swallowed Sean. His knees sagged and he'd to hold onto the edge of the counter. Gus and Xavier engaged in some idle chat, while Sean came to terms with the fact that fame and fortune were not coming his way.

'It's a shame, Sean. That was a great story and I would have published it. If my boss found out that the story can be so easily discredited, I would be fired.' said Gus.

Sean nodded, 'No harm done, lads, it was a shot in the dark, and all for a bit of fun. Will you have one for the road?'

'I will,' said Gus.

'We won't,' said Xavier, as he gave Gus a dirty look.

'It looks like we won't. Thanks anyway.' Gus protested as Xavier grabbed his arm, and pulled him off the stool.

'He is too fond of the drink. Right, Gussie, we have wasted enough of Sean's time.'

10:45 AM August 4th

Still holding Gus's arm, Xavier dragged his younger brother towards their car. Gus protested loudly, cursed, and tried to escape the vice-like grip that held him. When they reached the car, Xavier grasped Gus by the shoulders. 'That door is more dangerous than you could imagine. Do not, I repeat, don't write anything about it, don't tell anyone about it, and don't even dream about it. If you do, so help me God, brother or not, I will see you buried in an unmarked grave. Now, drive me to the airport, as fast as this excuse for a car can go.'

All the way to the airport, Gus's protestations fell on deaf ears. Xavier texted Cardinal Ronaldeski in Rome. 'Convene Circulum Fidei for when I arrive this evening. May God empower us! Xavier'

11:07 AM August 4th

'Sean, where are you hiding?' shouted James. He was about to reach over and pull his own pint, when Sean arrived. 'What kind of pub is this? A man could die of thirst while waiting for the staff. Bad management, can I speak to the boss?'

Sean filled a pint and remained silent.

'What's wrong, Sean? You look like a ghost.'

Sean clutched the Guinness tap and groaned. 'James, I'm fucked, the pub is fucked. The door was made in 1947, and I cannot carry through with the scam that would see this bar survive the recession.'

'How do you know that? I didn't know carbon dating was one of your skills.'

'It's not, whatever that is. Gus, the reporter, and his friend, called an hour ago. The friend, a wood expert, checked the door and said it was made in 1947. Hungarian or Italian Oak, he said. He found the date under the hinge.'

'Is that so? That's a pity, Sean. Look, I'll do everything I can to help you, and by honest means, we will keep the beer flowing. Do you accept my offer?'

'Of course I do, James. Aren't you my best and only friend?'

'And you mine, Sean. What a sad pair of old fools we are. One of us is half bald and the other, as grey as an old donkey. They will put us down someday.'

'You're right. Now that you mention it, you should've a word with your barber. That carpenter must pay a fortune for his hairstyle. He has a silver mane, as shiny as a new coin. Jesus, he gave me the willies when he smiled.'

James's glass exploded when it hit the stone floor. 'Xavier!' The broken glass crunched beneath his boots, as he raced to the door. 'Which hinge, Sean, which bloody hinge?'

'Under the top hinge, that's where he placed the paper and ran a pencil over it.'

'Did he show you the markings?'

'No, James. Why?'

'Get me a pencil and paper, and don't dilly-dally, ya dithering gobshite.'

James could just about see some marks with the aid of his glasses. Additional light from his phone did not help much. He grabbed the pencil and paper from Sean when he arrived with them.

'Large one, Sean,' he said, when he stood at the counter and stared at the design on the paper. God help us, Sean, that door may well be real.' He downed the whiskey, 'I'll be in touch,' and raced home to his iPad, and the guiles of the internet.

13:00 PM August 4th

His eyes were weary from looking at the thousands of religious images that Google displayed. *Shite, this is like looking for a single pebble in a quarry. One man in Ireland may solve this puzzle, and*

165

merciful Jesus has left him alive long enough to do so. Professor Arnold Clarke.

He raced back to the pub, took a few pictures of the door and drove to Dublin.

14:47 PM August 4th

Professor Clarke had lived in the same rooms overlooking the library square in Trinity College Dublin. For fifty nine years he devoted himself to research into world religions, Catholicism in particular. He chose Trinity, as it offered a more liberal approach than the Catholic universities, and its access to rare books was without parallel. It was quite extraordinary, that at eighty-six years of age, his mind was still formidable. Though his body had weakened, he managed to reach the libraries almost every day. When ill, or feeling weak, books, some invaluable, were brought to him at his request.

James removed a disarray of papers from an old wooden stool and sat. 'Arnie, somewhere in your research you must have found the answer to immortality, would you care to share it? How are you, my friend?'

'Father Jimmy, you have the beard of Padre Pio, the body of Adonis and a wit that's uniquely un-priestly. I'm quite well. I mind myself. The sands of time run short and much unfinished work remains. You're not here to discuss my arthritis. Your presence here now, as before, intrigues this scholar. What do you seek? Wisdom? Money? Everlasting life at the end of your days, is that not adequate reward for your earthly duties?'

'If God chooses to reward me, then that would come as a shock to many. Hell, I fear, awaits my soul.'

'Nonsense, hell is not large enough to accommodate both you and Satan. Where would you fish? No, the almighty has a magical river and a very special whiskey, reserved for the kindest man I know. Now, what is on your mind?'

James handed over the scrap of paper. 'Do you recognise this crest?'

Arnold reached for a magnifying glass and gazed at the image for several minutes, before handing it back. 'James, you're one from a handful of people for whom I would answer that question. Your eyes are inquisitive, yet show no sign of fear, and that tells me that you have no knowledge of what I may reveal. Let me pose a question, its answer will determine whether I can assist you further. From what sort of artefact did this mark come?'

'A door,' James edged forward on his stool.

'Would it be an oak door? Describe it to me, as much detail as you have.'

James took out his phone, pressed a few buttons and showed the pictures to Arnold.

Arnold could not hide his delight. His fragile hands grabbed James's wrist. 'The door of Emilo Pucci, seven hundred and, let me see, yes, seven hundred and eleven years old, maybe more. In 1302, Emilio, a winemaker from Northern Italy was possessed by a demon of extraordinary power. Over many months, through Emilio's hands many priests were slain. The Vatican sent its best exorcists, but all failed, many died, others succumbed to madness.

'You are joking,' said James.

'There is no mirth in any of this. In the autumn of 1303, they played their last card and sent Father Lorenzo de'Medici. He was in his fifties and very ill. To help him, they allowed a novice nun to accompany him. It's said, for six days and nights, Father Lorenzo chanted the rites of exorcism. Emilio sat in a chair, drinking wine, sneering at the priest and making foul remarks towards the nun. Towards midnight on the sixth day, the demon spat, 'Enough, Priest. I tire from your chanting. Now you die.'

'Oh my God.' James lit a cigarette.

'Emilio flew from the chair, but before he reached Father Lorenzo, the nun in blind panic, thinking it was holy water, splashed the demon from a decanter that sat on the table beside her. Emilio's impression is on your door.'

'Holy shit! It's true, God save us, Arnold. What did the nun throw at the demon?'

'Alcohol, James, home-distilled alcohol, or Poitin as it's called on this island. Few know that's how St. Patrick rid Ireland of snakes and other demons. The Vatican has kept that one secret for a long time.' Arnold chuckled. 'No one ever believed me, thinking me a fool for making up silly stories. As God is my witness, what I tell you is true.'

'This is crazy. A demon, exorcized by Poitin, leaps into a door, and his door ends up in the Convent in Castlebridge, thousands of miles from Rome?'

Arnold sat back and folded his arms. 'That's what makes this such a remarkable story. Father Lorenzo and the young nun returned to Rome, taking the door with them. The Circulum Fidei was convened. They stamped the door with the mark that's on the paper. A decision had to be taken as to where it could safely be stored.'

James interrupted, 'The Circulum Fidei? That name, though I understand the meaning, I don't know what it is.'

Arnold nodded, 'Few know of its existence. The Vatican does not do a press release every time a demon is exorcised or located. Even the name is innocuous. The Circulum Fidei consists of six cardinals

167

and one priest. The selected Cardinals are lifelong members, the priest remains at the discretion of the Cardinals. Their function is cataloguing demons and disposal of any item through which a demon escaped following an exorcism. You see, James, though it's unlikely that the item is significant, the Church cannot take a risk. Every single door, window, table, urn and many other items, have been dispersed to the four corners of the earth.'

'Really? That is incredible,' said James.

'Your door, for a reason only known within the vaults beneath St. Peters, received special treatment. Father Lorenzo and the nun embarked on a journey that saw them travel across Europe, from convent to convent. In each, they stayed three months and then moved on to the next. Their last known location was Normandy. Father Lorenzo and the nun left the convent there in 1309, and that was the last entry in the archives of Circulum Fidei.'

'Lovers, they became lovers?'

Arnold laughed, 'Ah, you're sharp. Yes, it's likely they became lovers, an ancient priest and a nubile young nun. You should try it, James. I suspect their intentions were honourable, and that their lineage would continue with the task of moving the door from place to place. That it ended up in Castlebridge, suggests that there was still lead in old Lorenzo's pencil when they consummated their nuptials.'

'Enough problems are on my doorstep, and I don't like nuns. I have a hunch that I may know the Circulum Fidei priest. Answer me this, Arnold. Is he a silver-haired Irish Jesuit?'

'James, why many consider you a buffoon, alcoholic country priest, is obvious. They misjudge you at their peril. Don't underestimate him either, James. His position is one of the most powerful in Rome, and enjoys the freedom to do what he sees fit. To protect the church is what drives him and his office. Do you still partake in the demon drink?'

James grinned, 'Good joke, Arnie, demon drink and demon Poitin, to out the demons.' He decided to tell Arnold about Sean, his attempt to sell the door on Ebay, and finally he outlined the visit earlier by Xavier.

Arnold, with great pain evident on his face, stood and walked to the window and stared out onto the square. He was deep in thought. It was many minutes before he returned to his chair.

'James, take a bottle of the strongest Poitin you can find. Better safe than sorry, though it probably does not matter, spray the door with it. My research, if it's correct, leads me to believe that the same demon, though less powerful, has been through many doors in the intervening years. Most likely, on each occasion its powers increase. My advice would be to keep it in Castlebridge under your protection. Let Sean reap the rewards from possessing a relic. The Vatican will apply pressure directly on you to obtain the door. Failing that, they may attempt a robbery. If that also is unsuccessful, they must buy it from Sean. Take down that Ebay advertisement and make them work hard to get their paws on it.'

Fear yielded to devious pleasure, and James salivated at the prospect of being an even bigger thorn in Xavier's side. 'Arnie, your considered advice will be taken. My lips are sealed as to the source of this information.'

'According to a recent newspaper report, you have been naughty, not that I believe any of it. You have the conviction, the strength and the faith to do what is right. See it done, my friend. Now give me a final hug, as it's unlikely that we shall meet again in this life. Cinis cinerem!'

Chapter 43.

11 PM August 4th
Shadows danced around the procession of religious. In single file they marched and recited an ancient Latin hymn. Their footsteps silent, as barefoot they trod on the cold stone floor of the catacombs. Each dressed in the robes of a monk, the colour of their order distinguished one from the other, a brown Franciscan, a white Carthusian and then, a black Bendictine. These in turn were followed by a Dominican in white, a brown Carmelite and last, a grayish-white Cistercian. Black as coal, Xavier the Jesuit priest brought their number to seven.

In their left hands, they held their gilded, silver handled, sulfur-lime torches, illuminating the path ahead, casting eerie shadows as flickering flames danced to the movement of its bearer. In their red-gloved right hand, each held a golden goblet, filled with holy poitin that was brewed in Ireland, blessed in Rome.

Xavier led the way through the twisting, dank tunnels that lay under St Peter's. Ahead, a pair of ruby eyes stared out of the gloom, one rat facing another. It scurried away as they approached.

Xavier brought the procession to a halt when their path was blocked by a wooden door. Each knelt in silent prayer, affirming their vows as members of Circulum Fidei. On the door, a circle of six keyholes with silver escutcheons surrounded a golden seventh. One, by one, each came forward, splashed the door with poitin and spoke the sacred words, 'Deo vitae meae.' They removed a key that was chained to their robes and inserted it in their allotted keyhole. Xavier followed suit, turned all six keys and paused as the sound of moving tumblers echoed around the ancient tunnels. Silently, he made the prayer of entry, twisted his golden key and pushed open the door to the vaults of Circulum Fidei. In turn, each retrieved their key and entered.

Once inside, Xavier flicked the light switches and they placed their torches into a slot on the wall. The others sat at the round table that occupied the centre of the room. Xavier took a bottle from a crate near the door and poured a small measure of Jameson into each goblet. 'That will warm us. Those tunnels need central heating and proper lighting.'

Demerchant, a member for thirty seven years, gulped back the whiskey and offered his goblet up for a refill. 'God bless his Eminence for appointing an Irishman, else we would die of pneumonia. Father Xavier, what devil's work has summoned us to conclave?'

Xavier raised his goblet to his lips and closed his eyes as the aroma engulfed his senses. He salivated, knowing that what he was about to reveal, would ensure that the day would come when he would wear the ring of pontiff. Although the power to seize the door was already his, vanity determined that ceremony must be followed, so that even greater power was attained.

'Brothers, I have found that which has eluded our brethren for centuries, the door of Emilo Pucci.'

Gasp after gasp, all stared at Xavier, their eyes mirroring the still flickering flames from the torches.

Xavier displayed masterful oratory skills as he recounted the events of the past few months. How he'd left no stone unturned whilst investigating the outrageous and un-priestly behaviour of Father Brennan. They listened intently as he revealed that by astute planning, he'd found the source of the darkness whose veil had fallen over Brennan and the parish of Castlebridge. Satan walks amongst us once more, and we are called to arm ourselves, in the defence of our Church and our Lord.'

Demerchant reached across the table and filled his goblet to the brim. He downed it in one go, as he did regularly. Licking his puckered lips, he spoke, looking around the shocked faces. 'Xavier, we are old men. God has chosen you for this task. Through your hands, the cross shall defeat the darkness. Can you win back the door and block the return of the demon?'

Xavier raised his hands to silence the muttering, 'It shall be done. When the door is returned to Rome, we shall convene again. Where it shall be safely hidden, and what punishment befits a priest that has defiled his vocation, these matters we shall decide.' Before any could question that he act alone, he refilled the goblets. 'May God guide our endeavours. Amen.'

Demerchant rolled his empty goblet forwards and backwards on the table and turned to Xavier, 'Why Ireland, mon ami? We all know that the door vanished. I suggest that we open the vault and read the ancient records.'

Everyone nodded, including Xavier, who had decided before he left Dublin that the records must be opened.

Opening the door that led to the inner vaults, Xavier led them down another tunnel. Its slimy, downward path was treacherous, and as it narrowed, it became barely wide enough for a man to pass. Many groaned from the rigours of gasping breath from acrid air, and the claustrophobic confines sent ripples of terror through those who feared the walls would crush them. Ignoring the many false doors that they passed, they continued, each silent except for the grunts of their exertions. At last they reached the inner vault, paused to gather breath, knelt, prayed and finally taking their keys, they opened the door.

A fan hummed within its cage at the far corner of the vault, sucking air from the vertical shaft that was driven through the bedrock overhead. On the near-side wall, a second one drove the stale air upwards towards St. Peter's Square. Xavier retrieved an aluminium case from the long lines of shelves that ran as far as the eye could see. They once again sat at a table, the twin of the first. Much to their annoyance, a cloud of dust lifted as Xavier dropped the case onto the table. A few nearest spluttered, others were quick enough to cover their faces with the sleeves of their robes, and waited for the fans to remove the offensive grime.

Xavier opened the box, removed a leather bound volume and placed it on the table. Demerchant had already taken a pair of satin gloves from a cabinet, which he passed to Xavier. All eyes stared at the ancient tome. Xavier opened it, wondering what would be revealed. The tales he read from the manuscripts chased horror, pain, and terror across many faces. Some took out their rosary beads, silently praying while they listened.

'*Enough, Priest. I tire from your chanting. Now you die.* Emilo flew from the chair, but before he reached Father Lorenzo, the nun in blind panic, thinking it was holy water, splashed the demon from a decanter that sat on the table beside her.'

'Holy poitin,' muttered Demerchant, as he licked his parched lips.

'Yes, Holy poitin,' Xavier agreed and continued. 'The demon shrieked as the sacred liquid tore it from Emilo. Before it flew into the door, it screamed a parting warning at Father Lorenzo. *Seven hundred years from now. If he who watches over is not pure, in the Emerald Isle, I return through this door.*' Xavier dropped the sheet of parchment as panic replaced confidence.

One by one, they blessed themselves as the enormity of this revelation became clear. 'Sacre bleu,' shouted Demerchant. 'The Demon has prophesised that he will return in two weeks. Father Brennan, an emissary of Satan guards the door. Xavier, you must, with all haste, retrieve the door and guard it day and night until it leaves that cursed island.'

Xavier stood, 'I cannot waste any further time here.' He replaced the records back in the aluminium case and returned it to its shelf. 'Come, let us leave.'

One man remained sitting as the others made to leave, Raul Gongalez from Mexico, a man that almost seemed slow on the uptake. The corridors of the Vatican often resonated from muffled laughter, cloaked jokes shared after the barefooted Raul had passed. 'He would be thirty seconds late for his own death.' Wisdom and humility are often happy bed-fellows. Raul rarely gave voice to wisdom, for the offering of it to deaf ears usually only led to conflict.

Xavier pleaded, 'Brother, we must leave, now!'

Raul raised his hand to his furrowed brow, stroked a loose strand of hair and smiled gently at Xavier. 'Por favor, is it certain that Father Brennan is not virtuous? What proof exists that he isn't?'

Xavier strode back towards the table and banged it with his fist with such ferocity that a new layer of dust rose heavenward. 'Have you been asleep? Have you not heard the allegations against him?'

'Father, the guiles of the devil are many. Is it not strange, all these allegations occurred a short time before the door was found?'

Xavier leaned a little closer, 'Brennan is the devil incarnate. I shall have the door and his collar before the week is out. Damn your shallow understanding! Your prevarications only delay my mission.'

Raul stared at Xavier, a curious twitch forming in the corner of his left eye. 'Of course, Xavier, you must do whatever you see fit. Many years I have studied the word of God. It's my understanding that a virtuous heart can only be gifted by God and is not attainable by human desire or labour. Do what you must do. I will pray. That which must come to pass, will. I fear it will test your faith beyond endurance.'

Before leaving, Demerchant, spying the whiskey bottle on the table, secreted it up the sleeve of his robe.

Back they marched along the tunnels, chanting their prayer of return. Only Demerchant dallied, as he paused several times to take a swig from the almost empty bottle of Jameson. They mounted the long flight of steps that would take them from the catacombs. Demerchant stumbled and fell. The bottle smashed on the floor and a single sliver of glass slashed through an artery. A pool of blood seeped through his white robe and the others could do nothing to quench the flow.

'God save us, the devil has taken Demerchant,' cried the Franciscan. This was their first casualty since the sixteenth century.

Xavier held the dying man's wrist. Feeling the pulse weaken and cease, he closed the lids over unseeing eyes. Slowly, he rose, stood resolutely over the corpse, and swore an oath that Brennan would pay for this murder.

8 AM August 5th

Xavier took one last look at Rome, before the clouds enveloped the plane that was bound for London.

10:30 AM August 5th

Gus was in a foul humour. He'd wasted an entire day ferrying Xavier around the countryside. *A complete waste of my time. I'm sick of being bullied by that nit-wit priest. Gus, do this. Gus, don't do that. All my sorry life that bastard has bossed me around.*

He'd not written a decent piece in weeks. It was only a matter of days, maybe hours, before he received the dreaded email that demanded his presence upstairs. His boss, like all good newspapermen, was ruthless. He was the nicest man in the world when story, after story, found its way to print. When the ink dried up, his fury was venomous and his firing of reporters was legendary.

Gus scoured the national broadsheets for some inspiration. When he remembered the USB key that Sean had given him, he plugged it in, and read the story. Riddled with grammar errors, poor use of vocabulary and bugger all inventiveness, it irked Gus. His fingers found their way to the keyboard.

An hour later, muck had turned to gold. Gus, holding his hands behind his head, lay back on his chair and grinned as he read his professional rendition of 'The Devil's Door.'

His reverie and good humour came crashing down when the back of his chair was kicked.

'O'Loughlin, you're a lazy, useless piece of shit. If you want to take a siesta then pack your bags and fuck off to Spain.' Mr Hennigan's jowls shook with red rage. He folded his arms and glared at Gus.

'Mr Hennigan, good morning, sir.'

'Unless you have something to fill the front page this afternoon, don't good fucking morning me.'

Gus shrivelled as he slunk down the chair, desperately reaching for an excuse. Finding none, he took the riskiest decision of his life. 'Good morning it is, Mr. Hennigan. I have your front page, a story that will demand a second edition. If not, I'll vacate this chair. If it does, would a small pay rise in recognition of my excellent work be offered?'

What else could a pig do, but grunt?

'Send it up to me and I'll decide.'

7 PM August 5th

Sean panted heavily as he burst in the front door of the presbytery. He raced past a startled James, ran into the dining room and placed

174

the newspaper face-up on the table. James casually closed the door and followed Sean.

'Father, Gus has published an article, look!'

James stared at the bold lettered headline.

'Castlebridge Priest drinks with the DEVIL'

'Sean, now that the cat is out of the proverbial bag, the hornet will out from its nest in Rome. I'm about to have some beans and burnt toast, would you like some?'

'Someone defames you in the worst way possible and you suggest beans on toast? Father, has the devil melted your brains?'

'Sean, my dearest friend. Our book will soon be finished and this journey ended. You have a new pub, its future assured by the legend that now surrounds it. What more do you want?'

Sean smiled. 'That's mighty and I'm happy. What is all that worth? Not a thing, if my friend is in trouble. This will mean a whole heap of shite coming your way. Won't it?'

James placed his hand on Sean's shoulder. 'Do you remember Hamlet?'

'Yes?'

'Ah, concerned my barman be. There are more things in heaven and earth, Sean, than are dreamt of in your philosophy. The carpenter is Gus's brother. Father Xavier O'Loughlin, a powerful member of those who rule from Rome. That door left Italy in the fourteenth century, a relic the Vatican could not destroy, but had to hide. I will not bore or scare you with the details. Sean, despite my obvious flaws, I try to be virtuous in my actions.'

'I suppose you are, Father. You have been kind to many people. Remove the fags, the booze, and your enormous ego, and you could pass as a normal priest.'

'In all things, I trust the will of God. There is a reason why this door has come into my care, and why it now sits yards from where I drink. What that reason is, I don't fully understand. A choice made by God is not for me to question.'

'I'm the baton and the hand of God conducts my every move, as strange as that may seem. The quest that takes our book towards publication is not by chance. It, and the events that will soon take place are intertwined. That's my belief.'

Sean nodded as though he understood. 'One thing puzzles me. Why did you throw poitin on the door? The feckin varnish is ruined and Mouse refuses to apply another coat.'

'To keep the demon locked inside. Every single day, that door will receive such a blessing. I don't believe it's necessary, but at this stage I will not risk tempting fate.'

James laughed at the expression on Sean's face. 'Ring the lads, meeting to-morrow morning at eleven o'clock in 'The Devil's Door', our quest is near the finishing post.'

'A waste of good poitin is my opinion. See you in the morning, Father. By the way, the book is up to fifty-five in the charts.'

Chapter 44.

11 AM August 5th

'Rain, rain and more rain means no fishing, no gardening and no peace. My wife has taken up residence in the paint shop. I suspect that before the week is out, a tin and a brush will be thrust into my hands. A pint please, Sean' said Liam as he draped his sodden jacket over the back of his stool.

'Have you ever considered playing darts, Liam?'

'What? The River Inn is the only public-house in town with a dartboard. I value my life too much to frequent such a hell-hole.'

'I was thinking of putting one on that wall behind you.'

'Over my dead body!' shouted James as he rounded the corner from the lounge area. 'It's a mindless game for fat bellied, beer swilling layabouts. Good morning, a damp one that's only fit for a high stool and semi-intellectual conversation.'

'Exactly, Father, beer swilling is what fills the till.'

Liam looked around the room, 'Are you expecting someone else that will necessitate you to reduce the quality of conversation on their behalf?'

'Yes! Jimmy.'

Raucous laughter greeted Jimmy as he entered.

'Jimmy, we were commenting on the fact that you're the only one amongst us with a university education. You should've a higher stool than the rest of us.' said Liam.

'That should be easy for a bloody engineer. He can weld on another inch to each leg. A pint, Dr Jim?' said Sean.

'Yes, a McGargles'

James stared at Jimmy. 'What? Did you say McGargles?'

Jimmy pointed to the wooden tap cover on the counter. 'Yep, lovely isn't it?'

'Lavelle, I'll feckin kill you.'

Sean, Liam and Jimmy burst out laughing. In unison, they delivered a direct hit. 'Father MaGargles, you've been conned.'

'Feck off.'

'A packet of pistachio nuts,' said Jimmy, lifting his glass.

'This is not the Ritz. Peanuts, salted or dry-roasted?'

'Salted. Why the call to arms? Are we about to overthrow our useless government?'

James coughed, lit a cigarette and waited until Sean had finished his tasks. 'Liam, there is no easy way to tell you. The tale concerning that door is not very far off the mark. I'm curious, where did you hear about the legend?'

'My grandmother must have told me the story a hundred times. Now that you ask, I do recall her saying that it had been a tradition in her family to pass on the legend. As a child, I once eavesdropped on a conversation between her and my mother. Her family tree and some other documents had been passed down from one generation to another. They were destroyed in a fire in the late eighteen hundreds. I also recall that her parents were the first from our family to settle in this locality. Maybe I come from a long line of travellers and storytellers.'

Sean laughed, 'A Gypsy! If I cross your palm with gold, will you tell my fortune?'

'Lads, if Sean places a gold coin in my or anybody's palm, it will be the Eighth Wonder of the Modern World.'

Sean retreated and occupied himself with drying glasses.

After the mirth faded, James continued. When he came to describing the exorcism, all muttering, sipping of pints and general pub behaviour ceased.

'Lads, those markings on the door are as real as the birthmark on Sean's arse.'

Jimmy swivelled on his stool, looked at the door and then returned his gaze to James. 'You're joking?'

Liam sunk his pint and called for a large brandy. This sudden need for strong liquor surprised the others. James grimaced when the brandy disappeared and Liam called for another.

'Easy! Liam. Why the sudden impulse to get pissed so fast that Sean cannot pour quick enough?'

Liam gazed into the empty glass and answered, as he raised his head and stared at the door. 'My Grandmothers maiden name is,' he paused, faced James and stuttered, 'Lorenzo.'

'That makes everything a little clearer. You should be proud of your lineage. Lorenzo and the nun spent many years lugging that door around the convents of Europe. They probably married, spawning generation after generation, in whose care the door rested. Those documents that were lost in the fire, it's likely they explained the origins of the door and your family's obligation to guard it. Liam, you're closer to God than you may believe.'

Liam gazed into space. He needed time to come to terms with these startling revelations. Like Jimmy, he wasn't a religious man and paid scant attention to any tales of this kind.

'Father Xavier O'Loughlin, a power-hungry, over-zealous Vatican official, is aware of the door, thanks to his brother Gus. Amongst his many roles, heads a select group, founded nearly eight hundred years ago. Their holy task is the cataloguing, and the destruction or safe keeping of such items. Jimmy, you seem puzzled?'

'If the demon disappeared through the nearest door, why pay such reverence to what is only a door?' said Jimmy, a smug grin on his face.

'Fear that the demon may return through the way in which it left, that's why.'

'I don't get it at all. Men of faith allowing fear to rule their actions. That's a daft concept.'

'Gus is the reporter from the Midland Chronicle that penned the articles about your disgraced priest,' said James.

Jimmy raised his glass, 'Good man, Gus. So we are handing over the door to Xavier and next week this pub will be Lavelle's again. Problem solved, James.'

James Brennan growled and stomped his foot on the floor. 'No! That cannot happen. I know that you probably think demons are the stuff of fantasy novels and horror films. This is real, and you, my friends, are charged to help me protect that door. It could be a matter of life or death, my death.'

'Your death?' said Jimmy.

'Yes, my death and possibly many other priests as well, were the demon to return. Can I count on your support?'

Liam quickly responded, valour, like cream rising to the top, he pledged to honour his family duty. Sean reluctantly nodded.

'Make no mistake, Xavier is a maverick and dangerous,' said James.

'Maverick! He is not alone, is he, Father?' said Jimmy.

The cut from the dagger of truth went deep, stopped James dead in his tracks and he looked at his friends. His eyes pleaded for some indication that this label was untrue, seeing none, he spoke quietly.

'Perhaps I'm as you say. Let me relate to you, a story most sad, but totally true, so help me God.

'Three years ago, one of the most saintly priests ever to serve God and man, died a horrible death. He was murdered, though the law of the land could not see it as such. Father Bernard Ryan had served the poor of inner-city Dublin all his life. His clothes were more tattered than mine. By day he ran a soup kitchen, by night he trod the streets caring for the homeless. Ill health did not lessen his resolve, or his workload. At the height of the clerical abuse storm, a false allegation was made against him. The state and the Vatican investigated and the allegation was withdrawn.

'For an unknown reason, Xavier O'Loughlin could not let it go. Week after week, he tormented Father Ryan, interrogating, demanding a confession. A humble, simple man, Ryan pleaded his innocence to uncaring ears. His health deteriorated further and his mind became a maelstrom of confusion. This led to him taking his own life.'

Jimmy winced, 'Are you certain of his innocence? Many priests denied their wrongdoings.'

'Yes, I'm certain. He was a cancer survivor. The life-saving operation removed the appendages of abuse.'

Sean stood on the tips of his toes and leaned over the counter. 'Murdering bastard, we are behind you all the way.'

'Good! Gentlemen of the Con, we have much work to do. A security firm will be here within the hour. Cameras will be installed and hooked up to the TV and viewable via the Internet. Sean, until this is over, except for Mass and urgent business I will be your guest. During my absence, Liam and Jimmy will take my place. Xavier, I suspect, is already on the way. His ego will demand that he alone secures the door, and that makes him unpredictable. I will be in touch. Keep your phones charged and about you at all times. Now before I go, let us pray.'

Though astonished at this request, fear demanded that the others bowed their heads reverently.

'Lord, you led Moses and the Israelites out of bondage. Look down on your servant. As long as he takes refuge in this hostelry, make sure he does not die from food poisoning. Amen.'

Before Sean could react, he downed his pint, hopped off his stool and raced out through the lounge.

'Feckin priest,' screamed Sean, as the front door shut.

* * *

'My wardrobe,' announced James as he placed a small bag on the counter.

Sean barely noticed his arrival as he was busy playing with his latest toy. He pressed the remote control for the new security cameras.

'Look, Father, Mouse is outside counting the few coins he has left.'

James looked up at the television. The screen was split into four panels, each showing the output from the cameras. The first, in high definition, displayed a view of the street outside. The other three covered the alleyway, the back yard and the small kitchenette inside the backdoor. Sean zoomed in on Mouse, and as he counted, so did they.

'Two Euros and eighty-seven cents, not enough for a pint,' said Sean.

Enthralled, they watched as Mouse stalked anyone passing by, seeing the curses leave his mouth as each victim hurried away. Shylock Whelan the solicitor, was unaware of the spit that landed behind him, as he scurried across the street.

As comedic as it looked, James merely grunted and placed twenty Euros on the counter beside Sean. 'Excellent! Now our pub is a fortress. Fill me a pint and drag Mouse in off the road, and give him the change.'

'Go up to Marites and bring that smelly bag with you. She has a fine meal prepared. Here's your pint,' said Sean.

Marites stood in front of the cooker, and nodded coldly when he ambled into Lavelle's kitchen.

'Sorry, Marites, for intruding, hopefully my stay will be a short one.'

'So do I. Be seated.'

He dropped his bag beside the door and sat at the oval table. Marites placed a plate on the worktop, took a steak from the oven, piled some onions on top and spooned mash potato alongside. She glared, as she banged the plate down in front of him. 'Eat!'

'Thank you, Marites, it looks delicious.'

'Eat!'

He sliced through the tender steak, gathered some onions with his fork and stared at Marites as he took a mouthful.

'Delicious!'

'Eat!' she commanded once again.

The fork clanged as it fell onto the plate and the knife clattered onto the table. He folded his arms, and sat straight up in defiance. 'Not another mouthful will pass my lips until you explain why, for two years, you have avoided me? Sit!'

Hands on hips, she stood her ground. Fury grew in her eyes, and a more hateful look than he'd ever experienced, made him shudder.

'Please sit. If I have offended you, which I clearly have, I'm truly sorry.'

Reluctantly, she sat, but her posture remained defensive and her eyes did not soften. Lifting his cutlery, he devoured the meal in watchful silence.

'Excuse my poor manners. Rituals must be observed.' He wiped his lips with the sleeve of his jumper and a final lick sealed the deal. In the full knowledge that she abhorred smoking, he took a cigarette from his pack and lit it.

She did not flinch, or turn her head away as the putrid smoke clouded the small room. He tipped ash onto a plate, she did not react. When more ash fell onto the floor, her eyes followed its fall and immediately swung back to him. An impasse, they stubbornly faced each other across the table. He stood, pushed his chair to one side and attempted an Irish dance. 'Diddle iddle, diddle iddle, diddley iddle day,' he whistled as he glided back and forth.

'What do you think? Am I good enough for a part in Riverdance?'

Her gaze did not waver.

Old arthritic knees soon wobbled. He collapsed back onto the chair and lit another cigarette to sedate his gasping lungs. *Jesus, why does she hate me?* He steepled his hands and rested his grizzled chin on top. Resorting to a weapon that must surely work, he sang a bastardised rendition of a Beatles hit.

'She says she hates you. That can't be bad. Yes, she hates you. You should be sad. She said you hurt...'

Tears running down her cheeks, she screamed at him to stop. He reached over and tried to hold her hand. She savagely drew it away and began to sob.

'I don't hate you. I'm scared of you, scared of any Irish priest!'

Relieved that it wasn't personal, he gently asked, 'Why Marites, why such fear in one so beautiful?'

Her eyes softened and she wiped away the tears. Only then, did the deep hurt within reveal itself. 'Because one of you tried to rape me when I was sixteen,' she whimpered.

Shocked, his heart almost broke for this poor girl. *Lord, give me strength and wisdom.* 'Oh, Marites, I'm so sorry. Please, though I cannot even guess how painful this must be, please tell me what happened?'

Her sorrowful story gushed from lips that for too long had kept the memory locked deep within. 'He pushed me onto the kitchen table. I screamed and screamed, but still no one came. With one hand on my neck, he furiously reached down and lifted my skirt. With no more tears to shed, no screams left, I silenced and prayed that God would stop the beast. My head banged hard on the table as he ripped my underwear away. I could feel his foul breath on my neck, and knew that I had to make one last effort to fight him off. Fear pushed my hands across the table, seeking anything that I could use. In a daze, I felt my fingers grasp a bread knife. Clenching my teeth, I swivelled and slashed his left arm with it. Blood, his awful blood, gushed onto me and he ran, leaving me bereft of any dignity or self-worth.'

James brushed away his tears of shame, reached for her hand and held it gently. 'What was this filthy creature's name? Was he punished, brought to justice?'

She shook her head and sobbed again, 'No, my father whipped me and warned that he would disown me, if I ever uttered such lies again.'

'Can I say a prayer of healing and forgiveness? You must forgive yourself, Marites.'

He knelt and begged God to heal her broken heart, and tortured mind. And silently, *God, let me find the bastard priest that defiled this girl and broke his solemn vows. Amen!*

'Leave me here alone,' she said, after she hugged him and sat, staring into space.

'Does Sean know about this?'

'No,' she sobbed, 'He will not be told, not ever.'

'Peace be with you, my child,' he lifted his pint and went back downstairs.

The identity of the priest troubled him. *It couldn't be, could it? Of course it bloody could. God, why choose me as the instrument of your retribution? Any chance you could send me an email in future and outline your plans?*

Late though the hour, he rang an old colleague in Dublin and asked a single question. 'Was Xavier O'Loughlin ever a priest in the Philippines?' Two hours later he received confirmation of his suspicion.

Chapter 45.

Just after midnight, Sean locked up, handed James a strong coffee, and set up a camper bed on the floor of the back room.

'Will I tuck you in, James?'

'Yes! Goldilocks and the Three Bears, will you read it to me?'

Sean glanced at the television to check the images from the four cameras. Satisfied that everything was secure, he blew James a kiss goodnight and went to enjoy the comfort of his own bed.

People that do shift work are well aware that trying to stay awake the first night is torture. James had a plan drawn up, a schedule that he would rigorously follow, guaranteed to keep him awake until Sean rose at eight AM.

Pen in hand, steam rose from the strong cup of coffee that sat on the counter, and a crossword puzzle was perused. It did not take long to solve the easier ones. Thankfully, a few tested his mettle, and by one-thirty AM, he admitted defeat, unable to solve two final clues. Considering that his concentration was divided between the puzzle and the images from the cameras, he was pleased.

He scoffed a sandwich Marites had prepared earlier, filled another cup of coffee and set to dealing with the backlog of e-confessions. Most of them were mind-numbingly boring, and had he stuck to the task of replying to them all, he would surely have fallen asleep. His tired eyes ached and he found it harder to stifle the yawns and resist the urge to close his eyes for a moment of respite.

By three AM, the cloud of cigarette smoke was suffocating, he wobbled on the stool, and the images on the television screen were a blur. He contemplated going out back for some fresh air, instead he opened a back window, inhaled deeply and left it open until the stench of stale smoke dissipated. Revitalised, he made the error of sitting on the bed, attempting to read a book. In minutes, the book fell onto the floor, its thud barely registering against the din of his snores.

'Useless, bollox, don't give up the day job,' shouted Sean, as he let water drip from the jug he was holding, onto James's cheek.

He twisted and turned, tried to bury his head under the blanket, but at the sudden realisation that he wasn't at home, he leapt to his feet. When it registered that the door was still there, he groaned, 'Feck, I can't let that happen again. Fill the kettle, Sean. I need to freshen up. May I use your shower? Jesus! Mass is in an hour. Liam and Jimmy should be here soon, they'd better arrive or else I will castrate the pair of them.'

'That would be cut the balls off the pair of bolloxes. Ouch! Black coffee is coming your way. You need take a siesta after Mass. That should tune that old body-clock of yours to the way of a vampire. No harm done this time. The door is still hanging on its hinges.'

Another coffee followed the first, and a brandy found its way into a third cup.

Mass was an event that was best forgotten. Ready to read from the gospel, he yawned, forgot his lines and apologised to the tiny congregation. 'Forgive me. I had a toothache last night.'

A Dublin registered transporter van was parked directly across from Lavelle's, its engine running. The darkened windows concealed any occupants, and at James's return after saying Mass, it edged out onto the road and drove away towards the garage.

'Lads, if I'm not mistaken, the rat from Rome has arrived. A new van was parked outside. It moved away when I walked down the lane. I suspect it's a hire van, and that Xavier is the driver.'

Jimmy and Liam abandoned their game of cards, and all eyes focussed on their surveillance screen. When a lorry stopped outside, to let Agnes 'The Banshee' Murphy, cross the road, Jimmy shouted, 'Sean, pan in on camera one. Ha ha, she has dropped her shopping bag.'

Sean reached for the remote, and zoomed the camera in on the groceries that were scattered on the road. 'Feck me pink, look at the naggin of gin lying between the bread and the packet of sausages. I thought that bitch was a teetotaller.'

'Maybe it's for medicinal purposes,' said Liam.

'My arse, she is a two faced wagon that looks down her nose at every eejit that enjoys a pint.'

'The windscreen, focus on the bottom left,' roared Jimmy. 'Stop!'

James put on his glasses and peered at the screen. 'What are we looking at?'

Jimmy rubbed his hands together. 'That clown McGrath owes me a tenner from a bet made on a round of golf. The miserable git can't putt and won't pay his dues. Look at the colour of the motor-tax disc, two months out of date. The bastard will cough up now, if not, I will report him.' Jimmy sent a text message, 'McGrath, big brother is watching you. Your tax is out. Pay your bets or else!!!' They observed McGrath lift his phone, read the text and throw the phone back onto the passenger seat.

Sean set the camera to zoom onto the passenger-side tyre. 'For feck sake, that front tyre is balder than my arse.'

Howling laughter erupted when Jimmy sent a second text. McGrath hopped out of the lorry, found a path through the groceries on the road and examined the tyre. He looked around and scratched his head. He grabbed the shopping bag from Agnes and stuffed the groceries into it. The look of shock on her face and the movement of his lips, left little doubt that his vocabulary contained the words, *fuck off*. He returned to his seat, slammed the door shut and started the engine.

Jimmy, with the nimblest of fingers, typed up another text. 'Are you insured?'

McGrath opened the door, stood out on the step, craned his neck and searched for Jimmy. Perplexed, he raised his arm, and gave a double fingered salute. When he beeped his horn before driving off, it gave Agnes such a fright that the contents of her bag ended up on the footpath.

As the laughter died away, James pointed to the view of the lane. 'Look! Here comes rat-face.'

In silence, they stared at the screen, seeing the van move at a snail's pace along the lane. It paused at the side-gate, the driver's window rolled down a few inches and a flash of light lit the interior of the van. It then moved out onto the main road and away.

'That's the proof. The bastard took a photo of the gate,' said James.

'C'mon, Liam, it's time for the tough to get going. We will drag him from the van and give him a good kicking. That will be the end of the matter. Then I can concentrate on more important issues, such as golf or fishing,' ordered Jimmy.

'No! No violence, don't lay a finger on him. God will offer up his sorry arse on a platter when the time is right,' said James.

Sean groaned, 'Here come Mouse and Gerry. I better open the bar. Another day in the annals of this great pub is about to be written. A barman's lot is monotonous, but never predictable. Is it, Father?'

'Not when I'm here.'

Liam and Jimmy left by the back gate, as Sean opened for business.

* * *

James yawned, made his way to his bed upstairs and soon fell into a broken sleep. His dreams left him twisting and turning. Violent scenes, played over and over again. He grappled with Xavier and had horrible visions of a demon, its red eyes glowing, as it emerged from a door.

At four o'clock, he awoke to the sound of his phone ringing, an unknown number. He hopped out of bed and paced around the room.

When the conversation ended, he scrambled into his clothes and raced downstairs.

'Sean, where the fuck are you?'

Sean emerged from the ladies toilet, bucket in one hand and a mop in the other. 'What's the matter, Padre?'

'I love it when a plan comes together. Give me a cigar, a large brandy and have one yourself.'

Sean did as ordered, came out front and sat on a stool facing James. 'Well?'

'When the earth casts its shadow, and the moon hides behind our planet, a lunar eclipse occurs. Darkness falls over the master of the tides. Light ultimately prevails, it always does. Do you follow me?'

'No, not a fucking clue. What are you on about? Is there an eclipse due?'

'Sean, the long eclipse is at an end. On Friday evening, I emerge into the light, the light of a television studio to be precise. Three days from now, your Padre is making an appearance on The Late Night Show.'

'Are you serious?'

James lit the cigar and took a long drag, exhaled and watched the circular plume spiral towards the rafters. He settled his gaze on Sean and nodded. 'I'm due on the last slot, just after two other Irish saints, Sir Bob Geldof and Bono.'

Sean gasped, drank his brandy, and reaching over the counter for the bottle, refilled both glasses as he blurted, 'Father, I have a little secret, kept to myself for years.'

'For fecks sake, do I really want to know about your dirty little secrets?'

'Not dirty, I always hoped that someone on television would wave and say, 'Hello to Sean Lavelle from Castlebridge.' That's the nearest I could ever get to being famous. Will you, Father?'

'I will, Sean, ya gobshite!'

Little out of the ordinary occurred during the next few days. The daily routine of surveillance noted that Xavier was never far away. They assumed his frequent driving up and down the road coincided with the movements of his bladder. It seemed he was oblivious to their awareness of his presence. They watched him, as he, in turn, kept a vigilant eye on the pub.

Late Friday evening, James received a curious email.

'Padre Brennan. My heart tells me that you're aware of the existence of Circulum Fidei. I am part of this circle. The rumours that have reached Rome, concerning certain distasteful sins, please, are they true? My heart wishes that they are not. Are you a virtuous man beneath your cloak? Please, please reply with haste. Yours in Christ. Padre Raul. '

Hmm, most intriguing. Could I have an unknown ally, another servant of God compelled to my assistance? Or is it a guile orchestrated by Xavier? There is only one way to find out.

He typed up a response.

'Padre Raul. I'm a sinner. Though the rumours are not true, they are of my making. Righteousness is not a light that has ever shone on me, nor will it ever. I'm a child of God, prone to childish behaviour that decries my position. All that I do is guided by my maker and I fear nothing in this world, or the next. Are you a virtuous priest or the son of the rat that prowls my doorstep? I trust God, and He, me. Father J.P. Brennan.'

The expectancy of a return email from Raul and preparation for the television show occupied his thoughts. He begged his phone to display a reply from Raul, but none came. Hope of having a religious ally deserted him, so he focused on the task ahead.

In his darkest hour, the night before the show, he rang his only true confidant, Emily Jane. Her parting words rekindled his enthusiasm.

'Jamie boy, if any amateur actor can do it, you can. Now fuck off and practise with your mirror'.

Chapter 46.

Thank you, Ronan, for inviting me onto your show. It's an honour to appear alongside such illustrious Irish saints. Good evening Bob, good evening Bono.

He winked at the mirror, confident that he was mentally prepared for his appearance on the 'Late Night Show'. His attire had been chosen with care. His baggiest and oldest jeans, sat beneath his most tattered grey jumper. The clerical collar, the only vestment of priesthood, peeped out above the neck of the sweater. *James, your audience awaits you.*

'Sean, please pour a gin for your celebrity priest,' said James, as he paced around the backroom in the pub. He glanced at his watch several times, muttered under his breath and scratched his dishevelled beard.

'Here, Father, a large one, on the house,' said Sean.

'What do you think? Am I suitably dressed for a television appearance?'

'Father, you could pass as an impoverished, Jewish pig farmer. The audience will do a whip around for your benefit. Feck, even Mouse would take pity on you.'

'Where the hell are Liam and Jimmy?'

'Upstairs with Marites, they are having their last supper. I'll call them down so you can give them the last rites.'

James walked over to the 'Devil's Door', said a short prayer, and returned to the counter, as the others arrived. 'Mind that door in my absence. Marites, I'm leaving you in charge.'

Marites smiled, 'God bless, Father. No swearing, no farting and don't start a row.'

'Would I?' he replied.

'Tell that punk Geldof that I Love Mondays and order Bono to remove his shades,' said Jimmy.

One by one, they shook his hand and wished him good luck.

He downed the gin and strode out of the pub. After glancing at Xavier's van, he spat on the ground and then set off on his journey to stardom.

Rain splattered against the windshield and dusk cast eerie shadows on the horizon. As he drove along the motorway, his mind was in turmoil from worrying about the door, apprehensive that he would make a fool of himself and wondering whether he was equipped for the task ahead. Despite his unequivocal belief in the Almighty, fear of failure still preyed on his mind. *What if I say the wrong thing, react in an inappropriate manner?*

A few kilometres from the television studios, the petrol light flashed on the dashboard. Though he admonished himself for being so careless, it gave him an excuse to pull over at a garage and take a short walk. 'Damn,' he shouted, as the petrol splashed from the rim of the full tank over his jeans. He paid for the fuel, parked the car to one side, and took a short stroll around the forecourt to settle his nerves. A vibration from his phone announced the arrival of an e-mail.

'URGENT: The demon prophesied that at midnight tonight, he would return, unless he who guarded the door had a virtuous heart. I believe that you're that man, chosen by God. I pray that I'm right. Godspeed! Raul.'

James raced back to his car, hammered the steering wheel with both fists and considered this mother and father of dilemmas. Ahead lay the television studio, offering fame and a possible publishing contract. In Castlebridge, his friends guarded the door. He glanced at his watch, read the text again and cursed. *God, your sense of timing is a pain in the arse.*

He slammed the car into gear, let the clutch slip and the tyres squealed. Letting the Almighty know that he was less than pleased seemed a little childish, but in letting off steam his temper calmed.

Every set of traffic lights turned red as he approached and each received a tirade of abusive cursing. When he reached the motorway, a glance at his watch confirmed that getting to Castlebridge before midnight would be a close call. Clio responded with a groan and a backfire as he floored the accelerator. Gradually she responded, sixty, sixty-five, and at eighty she'd reached her limit. His teeth clattered in tune with the rusty exhaust that rattled on its couplings. Black smoke billowed in his wake.

At fifteen minutes to midnight, he reached the off-ramp for Castlebridge. Leaning out the window, he strained to see if there were any cars coming. Seeing none, he drove onto the over-pass without braking, bounced of the barrier on the far side, and somehow regained control. *Holy shit! That was close!* At eight minutes to twelve, he rolled up the main street and drove past Lavelle's.

The van was parked outside the side-gate. Xavier, not insight, was likely to be inside the pub, hell bent on removing the door. He parked his car, took the wheel brace from the boot and walked to Lavelle's. Coupling his hands, wheel brace under an arm, he peered through the grimy window into the lounge. Inside, he could see Sean slouched over the taps and he feared the worst.

The front door was locked, but luckily, since taking up residence in Lavelle's, he'd a key. His fingers trembled as he placed the key in the keyhole, twisted it slowly, and grimaced when the tumblers clicked home. He paused before turning the handle, and pushed the door open with his left hand, wheel brace raised in his right. *Grrrgh!* The door creaked as he opened it. Seeing no danger inside, he entered.

At the sound of the door opening, Sean looked up and rapidly swung his eyes to his left and back, leaving no doubt that all wasn't well. James tippy toed to the counter. Sean was handcuffed to one of the beer taps.

'Are you okay? Is he in the back room?' whispered James.

Sean nodded, 'He has a gun!'

'Fuck! I hadn't expected that he would be armed.'

Sean grinned, 'Don't worry, it's a plastic replica.'

'Are you sure?'

'Yes. I could see 'Made in China' engraved on it, when he stuck it in my nose.'

James smiled, but seeing a half-finished pint sat on the counter, his stomach churned. 'Mouse, where is he?'

'He scarpered when the madman burst in, and is likely to be cowering in the backyard.'

James reached across the counter and grabbed a bottle of whiskey. Now fully armed, he crept around the corner. The lights were off in the back room, yet there was a strange, flickering glow. The sound of the Latin chant was unmistakable. He tensed, ready to deal with whatever came at him, and inched his way into the backroom.

Jimmy and Liam stood in front of the counter, both handcuffed to the rail that ran along its edge. They did not notice his arrival. On the floor, cross-legged, Xavier sat within a circle of candles. In his right hand he held his gold watch. Dressed entirely in black, his silver mane sparkled in the candlelight. He concentrated on the door and regularly glanced at his watch.

Jimmy gasped when James whispered in his ear, 'The Cavalry is here. Sheriff James Brennan, Sssh!'

Jimmy nudged Liam. James grabbed a pint from the counter, sat on the free stool and forced a mouthful of flat Guinness down his throat. All three watched on in amazement, as though treated to a live performance of a wizard.

At a minute to twelve, Xavier stiffened and ceased reciting. At midnight, his sudden exhalation was followed by a guttural shout, 'Fuck, I don't understand.' He jumped to his feet, kissed the silver cross that hung around his neck and spat at the door.

191

'That was a fine theatrical display. What do you fail to understand?' shouted Brennan.

Xavier turned, his steely eyes peering through the darkness, he hissed, 'Brennan, I curse you and the God that sent you. I have failed.'

James stood and clapped. 'Failed? Success was never yours to achieve. Midnight is not upon us yet. Did you perhaps set your watch by the church clock? It's three minutes fast, set so on purpose, to urge punctuality at Mass.'

Elated by this news, Xavier resumed his position. James sat back on his stool and smiled, 'Lads, he is treating us to an encore.'

At thirty seconds to go, he began to count down. 'Thirty, twenty-nine...'

A bead of sweat broke out on Liam's face. He stooped down to the handcuffs, and tried to bless himself.

'Twenty-five, twenty-four.....'

Xavier quivered, crisscrossing his hands, muttering incoherently and oblivious of the grinning priest behind him.

At fifteen seconds to go, the handle on the door twisted as though in slow motion and the door opened, an inch at a time. Xavier roared, 'Come, my Lord.' He leapt to his feet, knocked over several candles and screamed, 'The end of days has come.'

Liam and Jimmy nearly pulled the rail off the counter in their efforts to escape, and James had to restrain them.

Mouse's head appeared around the edge of the door, his face breaking into a toothless grin when he spotted James, 'Fuck, is that Ninja priest gone?'

Xavier turned and spat at James, launched an attack, but was easily brushed aside. His head smashed against the counter when he lost balance. Blood oozed from the corner of his mouth. He rubbed it away with the back of his hand, snarled and raced out front.

James bounded after Xavier, but shouted back before he reached the front door, 'Mouse, come in out of the cold. I owe you a gallon of beer and a year's supply of fags.'

Rounding the corner, Brennan raced down the lane, waving the wheel brace, 'Come back, you bloody coward!'

Xavier was climbing into the van when Brennan caught up with him. James dived, seized Xavier's leg and dragged him onto the ground. Xavier screamed and lashed out with his feet as Brennan stood and raised his weapon.

'Quiet! I will send you to the fires of hell where you belong.'

Xavier cowered, a grin gradually formed and he hissed 'Mother-fucking asshole, you, your church, will crumble beneath my reign. Darkness will descend and you'll beg for your fucking life.'

James gasped when he noticed that Xavier's cross bore the figure of the crucified Christ, hung upside-down.

192

Feck, he is deranged.

James lined up his boot with Xavier's groin and kicked as hard as he could. 'That's from Marites, a Filipino girl that you attempted to rape.' A second into his stomach, 'and that's from me.' The last kick, aimed at his temple, almost rendered Xavier unconscious. 'That's from the man you murdered, Father Ryan.'

Keeping the brace in his left hand, he reached down, grabbed the collar of Xavier's shirt and dragged the semi-conscious priest back into the pub and shoved him into the corner of the backroom.

Thankfully, the keys to the handcuffs were on the floor. With a careful eye on the writhing snake, he freed Liam and Jimmy. They in turn removed the handcuffs from Sean.

When he told them that Xavier was possessed, they fled to the front bar and sought refuge in a bottle of brandy. Another kick to Xavier's groin sent him into shock, allowing ample time to truss him up like a turkey using the three sets of handcuffs.

It took an age to get the distraught Bishop to calm down. Frustrated from listening to the blithering idiot, Brennan screamed at the phone, 'Shut your fat face and listen. Ring the Archbishop and arrange for an exorcist to take this rat from my pub.'

* * *

Incoherent rambling still spewed from Xavier's lips and his eyes rolled around their sockets. Father Higgins, an exorcist, still in his dressing gown, shook James's hand, and then they followed those carrying Xavier to the waiting car.

Shaken by the unexpected turn of events, James sat on the curb and watched the car move away. Then he emailed Raul, winked at the heavens and returned inside for a drinking session that lasted until sunrise.

Chapter 47.

'Benvenuti a Roma,' said a pleasant lady at customs, sliding his passport across the desk.

From Fiumicino airport to St. Peter's Square, the journey left James a little nauseous, though the exhilaration at being in Rome was overwhelming. Pleasant warm autumn air funnelled in through the open window of the taxi. He gasped for a cigarette, ached for a drink and his ears still hurt. When the taxi halted close to St.Peter's Square, he grinned at the realisation that, after all these years, he would finally meet senior management. Raul's summons to Rome was initially met with hostility, but vanity soon quashed his stubbornness, and he acquiesced. After all, a papal blessing is a badge of honour that he could wave at his detractors.

As the taxi pulled away, he heaved his rucksack onto his back, lit a cigarette and walked towards the piazza. He marvelled at the magnificence, the wonderful travertine paving stretching as far as the Basilica. Guarding its entrance on each side, the colonnades, were four columns deep. In the centre, the Egyptian obelisk that overlooked the piazza was larger than he expected. Sean's lavish descriptions fell well short of describing the beauty of this religious, historical site.

By the time he reached the steps leading up to the Basilica, his knees wobbled. He sat, observing the tourists take pictures, groups of nuns in lines, toing and froing across the piazza, and everywhere, men of the cloth defined the sanctity of this holiest of places. He raised his mischievous eyes to the heavens, *All this, whilst half the world starves. Little has changed since the time of Nero. God, have you no shame?*

'Father Brennan, I presume? You're welcome to the seat of the fisherman. Wisely, you left your rod at home.'

He struggled to his feet, grinned and shook hands with Raul. 'I hear it never rains in Rome. Maybe I will do a rain dance before I leave and send all the dust into the famous Tiber. Thank you for inviting me, an unexpected delight.'

'Come, James, the will of God is not always a pleasure, so enjoy your time in the limelight. Somehow, I do believe the foundations will shake before you leave.'

'I doubt that, Raul. I have caused enough excitement these past months. I'm a humble tourist, no more than that. Your command of English is excellent.'

'Thank you. I spent nine years in England before coming to Rome.'

Raul led James on a tour of the Basilica, casually remarking that the genius of Michelangelo paled into significance compared to the deeds of James, the angel priest of Castlebridge.

Brennan stopped dead in his tracks and faced Raul, angered jowls displaying his obvious annoyance at such a comparison.

'Raul, you're a kind man. Don't place shoes on my feet, robes on my body or raise me beyond that which I am. I carry out the will of God as best I know. I was born a sinner, live a sinful life and will die a sinner. God alone will be my judge. In Him, and Him alone, I have faith. All else is nonsense, whims of man.'

Raul grinned and embraced a startled James.

'We are few but not alone. Xavier is in a monastery far from here. The demon was expelled and Xavier's tortured mind is at the mercy of God. The Circulum Fidei is now leaderless. I ask of you a favour.'

James after having listened intently, nodded that he would help.

Each was dressed in the robes of a monk, the colour of their Order distinguishing one from the other. A brown Franciscan, a white Carthusian and then a black Benedictine. These in turn were followed by a Dominican in white, a brown Carmelite and last, a grayish-white Cistercian. Following their leader, in single file, they marched along a tunnel beneath Rome.

After several hundred paces, their leader stopped and placed his goblet on the cobblestone floor. He reached into his pocket, took out a cigarette and lit it from flames of his torch. After a quick pull on the cigarette, he retrieved his goblet and continued. Those in his wake chanted, their dulcet tones occasionally interrupted by coughing when the lingering cigarette smoke overcame them.

Finally, they reached the end and the door to the vaults. Raul whispered in James's ear. Brennan smirked, turned and addressed the gathering as they kneeled.

'Stand, place your key in the lock, remove your hoodies and place them in a heap on the ground.'

'Hoodies?' one asked.

'Jesus, what planet are ye from. Remove your hooded robes.'

Shocked, they stood, one looking to the other for understanding. This wasn't following the sacred rituals.

'Now!' he growled.

Stone faced, they stood their ground.

'I assume you question my authority. Let me make myself clear, so that there is no misunderstanding. Disobey my order and each of you'll find yourself standing naked, sharing a cell with Xavier.'

Each, like sheep, they stepped forward, gave him a dirty look and did as bid. The last, Father Vincenzi blushed, his eyes begging James not to force him to remove his robe.

'Are you naked, perhaps wearing women's underwear?' demanded Brennan.

'No, that's not the problemo.'

'Off with the robe.'

Vincenzi, red-faced, drew the robe over his head, bowed in shame and added his to the mound.

At first, James was puzzled. The ignominy that he'd caused, slowly dawned on him, and he guffawed.

'My apologies, Vincenzi. I also like AC Milano, is that the away jersey?'

'Yes, Father, we play Roma this evening.'

The others mostly smiled, one or two still seethed.

He took his own golden key, inserted it in the central escutcheon, twisted the silver keys and then turned to his brethren. 'In God we trust, not black magic, voodoo or other such medieval nonsense. We don't need to continually remind him that we are faithful.'

He twisted his key and said the magic words, 'Open Sesame.' After opening the door, he laughed and then spoke, 'See, that wasn't so difficult, quite amazing that a key should open a lock. Lighten up, lads. Gods work should entail a little craic and that means fun. Now, either drink or toss the poitin on those hoodies.'

Maybe they wondered whether the wrong priest was in psychiatric care, but perhaps fearful of the consequences, they complied and entered the vault.

James stood on the threshold, tossed a lit match on the mound and declared, 'Brothers, God does not expect us to wear archaic clothing or follow rituals that were dreamed up during times of great ignorance. You're each a servant of God, answerable only to him. If you want to belong to a group of nutcases, then do as Vincenzi, support a football team, join a book club or even take up golf.'

Raul gestured for James to sit at the table. 'Father, you're indeed strange, but we welcome change and know that we have been weighed down by tradition.'

James gazed from one face to the next, noting expressions of doubt.

'I apologise if I have seemed to bully. Your work is vital. The cataloguing of demons is necessary, but housing the artefacts and playing out rituals is utter nonsense. Does anyone still disagree?'

One or two, at first, argued the point, but soon all nodded in agreement. He seized the moment, enforcing the ideas and finished with a single statement. 'Brethren, fear has no place for those who place their faith in the Almighty. Are we agreed?'

In unison, they responded, 'YES!'

Jesus, they are like the kids from the hurling team.

He turned to Raul, winked and lit a cigarette.

'We have defeated a demon. Where I come from, it would be a just cause for celebration. Tonight, we are going to a football match, drink ourselves silly and enjoy our rewards.'

Raul interrupted, 'Father, it's not possible, tonight you have an audience with the Pontiff.

Holy shit! I forgot about that minor matter.

'Raul, have you not understood a single word? Tell the Pope to feck off, I mean, send him my apologies. My brothers and I have to deal with a demon this very night.'

'What demon?' gasped Raul.

'The bloody demon drink, Raul. Tequila will do as starters.'

* * *

Nursing very bad hangovers, James and Raul sipped espressos in a quiet corner of the departure lounge at the airport.

'Raul, my request, can it be achieved?'

His voice hoarse from shouting at the football match, Raul whispered, 'It seems our maker has already made that decision. Si! Mi amigo; it will be done. James Brennan, someday, you'll be Pope.'

'Feck off. Don't be a daft hombre.'

* * *

Raul stared out onto the concourse, as the jet powered up the runway. 'God bless, and stay safe until your time to lead us comes.'

Chapter 48.

Sean leaned towards the bed-side locker, silenced the alarm clock and settled back onto his pillow. Battling the desire to succumb to the solace offered by sleep, he rubbed his tired eyes and yawned. Marites stirred, nestled against his chest and fell back asleep. Sometimes, he wished they could just lie there, and ignore the demands of life and business. Today, for a few hours, the river would be his mistress. The last day of the trout season would be spent in the company of his friends. He kissed a tuft of her hair, slipped out of bed and stretched.

Marites groaned, woke suddenly and bounded towards the bathroom. He listened to her moans, as she retched. For several weeks, she'd been unwell. Despite his daily request, she refused to go to the doctor. He was almost finished dressing when Marites returned and lay on the bed.

'My love, promise me you'll go to the doctor. All that chocolate you eat every morning, it's unnatural. You must have diabetes, worms, or something worse,' he said, as he fumbled with his shoe laces.

'I'm fine, Sean. Stop fretting. Now off with you, enjoy some fishing with Brennan and the lads.'

'I'm not going anywhere. Unless you swear that you'll visit the doctor today, I'm staying right here,' Sean leaned over and kissed her, folded his arms and stood at the door.

'Okay, okay. Brennan will go berserk if you keep him waiting,' she nodded and curled up under the duvet.

It had been a hectic few weeks. Thanks to James's scheming, 'The Devil's Door' now enjoyed regular footfall, and the till rang with a frequency that eased the pressure on Sean's savings. Jimmy, Liam and James were heading west with some other club members that afternoon. A weekend of salmon fishing, drinking and general misbehaviour was enticing, but he could not leave Marites on her own for the weekend. A few hours this morning would have to do.

Liam and Jimmy's cars were parked alongside James's and they were preparing their fishing tackle. Of James, there was no sign.

'Morning, lads, where is St. James?'

Jimmy made a remark to Liam, at which they both sniggered.

'The bollox is probably netting a large trout and will claim he caught it fairly. What's the craic, Sean?' said Jimmy.

'No craic. I've a hole in me waders, but feck it, the season is over. I'll buy a new pair next year,' said Sean as he took his fishing gear from the car.

Liam watched Sean struggle into his waders, winked at Jimmy and casually posed a question. 'Sean, have you put on weight? I could have sworn those waders fitted you perfectly when you bought them ten years ago. Jesus, there must be a patch for every year you've had them.'

Sean grunted, slotted his left leg home and pulled the braces over his shoulders. 'Feck off, ya red-neck. These are custom-fitted, comfortable and...'

'Holier than Brennan,' shouted Jimmy as he clapped Sean's back.

It was a half mile hike to the graveyard pool. They strolled along, not in any particular rush, a little melancholic, as the winter was about to close its door on their hobby.

'Lads, I wish I could go on the salmon fishing trip. Marites isn't keeping well, so I best stay put.'

Liam leaned towards Sean and punched him lightly on the shoulder, 'I warned you that married life was a pain in the arse. Sex is great; the rest is a nuisance.'

'Leave the poor sod alone, Liam. What's ailing the unfortunate woman?'

Tears welled up in Sean's eyes. 'For... for the past few weeks she has been sick every morning. By lunchtime, she is as contrary as Mouse when he cannot afford a drink. She has the till emptied and the larder full of chocolate bars.'

Liam looked at Jimmy. They stopped walking and burst out laughing. 'Brennan is right. Sean, you're one dumb gobshite!' said Liam.

Sean, as usual, was lost, and red cheeks could not hide the fact that he was ready to explode.

'I wonder who the father might be. Any idea, Liam?' asked Jimmy.

'Not a clue. Maybe it's a miraculous conception. Clean out the stable, Sean.' replied Liam.

Jimmy stifled a laugh. 'There's a turkey in the oven,'

After a lengthy silence, and tired from looking at the dumb exasperated look on Sean's face, Jimmy delivered the coup de grace, 'Sean, welcome to parenthood.'

Sean was still blabbing like a village idiot when they reached the graveyard. At the bottom of the pool stood James, his rod held high and bent in two.

Brennan hollered, 'I've caught a monster. Give me a hand!'

'What did I say? His ego and his arse need a good kicking. I bet the trout is already dead,' snarled Jimmy.

Liam and Sean raced downstream. Sean lifted James's net from the bank and waded out.

'Where the hell were ye? I've been playing this trout for twenty minutes. The bastard has taken me up and down the pool twice. It's stuck to the bottom, and I can't shift it.'

'Try some side strain,' offered Sean.

'Side strain, my arse. If I put any more pressure on the rod, it will snap in two. Liam, you grab the line and pull! Sean, be ready with the net!'

Liam waded out, pulled his sleeve down over his hand and took hold of the nylon. He twisted it around his hand, until he felt it tighten. With even tension on the line, he inched backwards, feeling the trout slowly yield.

'It's moving and it's heavy.'

As he neared the shore, something broke the surface. James screamed, 'Net it, net it, Sean'.

Sean lunged forward with the net and bagged their quarry. Shouts of encouragement rang in his ears as he dragged it ashore.

Mouths agape, they stared at the black plastic rubbish bag.

'Fair play, Father, cleaning out the river is work fit for a priest,' jibed Jimmy.

'Open it, Sean. Let's see what's inside,' demanded James.

'Feck off. It's probably a dead dog or cat. Open it yourself. You caught it, you open it.'

James grabbed Sean by the ear, 'Are you a man or a wimp? Open the bloody bag!' He lit a cigarette and smiled, as Sean sought the necessary courage.

Sean's trembling hands took his scissors from his jacket, and cut through the plastic.

'Another three bags, no dead cats, thank God,' said Sean, releasing his breath.

'Open them,' said James, blowing away the cloud of smoke.

Sean lifted the three bags and threw them on the ground. He reached down, sliced through the plastic and gasped as he lifted out a book. 'Holy fucking Nora!' *Father McGargles.*

Liam and Jimmy grabbed the remaining bags, and all three stared at James.

'Did ye ever doubt me, lads?'

Hysterical could not even begin to describe Sean's jabbering while he leafed through the pages. 'I'll put a stack of them alongside the McGargles taps in the pub. Can ye see them weird writers clambering for a pint and a read. Alas, poor Father McGargles, we knew him well.'

Jimmy, an avid reader, gasped when he read the publisher's name. 'James, this is a scam. Printed by 'The Nacitav Press', no way the Vatican printed this.'

'No, Jimmy, this is not a swindle. They printed twenty thousand copies, free of charge. By the end of the month, every bookshop and the best pubs in the country will have them for sale. All the profit is going to a good charity.'

'Why would they do that for a disgraced priest? Don't dare tell us that the devil is in the detail.' asked Liam.

'In Rome, there is one that knows the truth, and he's ordered the publication. No, Liam, the divil is in the door, the book will be in the shops, and this time tomorrow you'll be standing in a river far from here.'

Liam flicked through the book. 'Which charity?'

'One which cares for those who have been abused by priests.'

Liam held up the book, looked at the others and laughed, 'Who could have foreseen, that from his single confession of jealousy, a book would be born?'

Chapter 49.

James stood at the door of the minibus. As each angler boarded, he handed them a tee-shirt and a four-pack of McGargles.

'What do you think of the tee-shirts?' he asked Liam.

Liam took a step back. 'Black suits you, Father McGargles.'

James grunted. 'Stop calling me that. Never mind the colour. The logo?'

"Shereen Anglers. The Wild Bunch Tour 2013." 'I think we might be mistaken for a hen party.'

'The back, Liam?' said James as he turned around.

Liam read the bold, red writing on James's back. 'Cigarette Free Zone.'

'There is nothing worse than a reformed addict. May God help us, Father, should you ever decide to give up the booze.'

James threw a half smoked cigar on the ground, and squashed it with his foot.

'Right, lads, let's be going! There are salmon and trout to be caught.'

That's another story, a story for another day.
Amen!

Printed in Great Britain
by Amazon